The Wicked Governess

Blackhaven Brides
Book 6

MARY LANCASTER

Books from Dragonblade Publishing

Knights of Honor Series by Alexa Aston
Word of Honor
Marked By Honor
Code of Honor
Journey to Honor
Heart of Honor
Bold in Honor

Legends of Love Series by Avril Borthiry
The Wishing Well
Isolated Hearts
Sentinel

The Lost Lords Series by Chasity Bowlin
The Lost Lord of Castle Black
The Vanishing of Lord Vale
The Missing Marquess of Althorn

By Elizabeth Ellen Carter
Captive of the Corsairs, *Heart of the Corsairs Series*
Revenge of the Corsairs, *Heart of the Corsairs Series*
Dark Heart

Knight Everlasting Series by Cassidy Cayman
Endearing
Enchanted
Evermore

Table of Contents

Chapter One

CAROLINE GREY HURRIED into the empty schoolroom. After the excitement of yesterday's wedding, she had allowed her pupils a day of rest and expected no interruptions.

Sinking into the chair normally occupied by Lady Maria, the eldest of her three charges, she tore open her mother's letter. But if she had hoped to chase away her unaccountable blue devils with cheerful news from her family, she was doomed to disappointment.

The cottage was cold, apparently, and coals expensive. The roof had sprung a leak, and no one would fix it for less than an extortionate fee. In the circumstances, it was no wonder that Eliza had taken herself off to Edinburgh for a fortnight to visit a friend. Poor Peter had developed the worst cold of his short life, and the doctor's fee needed to be paid from the few pennies left. Her mother claimed none of that mattered to her, only it broke her heart when Peter cried for Caroline. In short, could she please send another few shillings.

Caroline closed her eyes. She would lay money on her sister Eliza having left *because* of Peter's cold. She could never deal with illness. It irritated Caroline but hardly surprised her. She could even forgive the fact that Eliza's trip had no doubt led to the money shortage, and that there would therefore be no new winter boots for Caroline this year either. After all, the old ones could be repaired *again*. What brought the helpless tears to her eyes was Peter's illness and not being there when he cried for her. Churned with anxiety and longing, she laid her head on her arm and wept.

"Miss Grey? Where are my sisters?"

With a gasp of dismay, she sprang to her feet, hastily dashing her sleeve across her face as she spun to see her employer in the doorway. *He should not even be here!*

Lord Braithwaite had left the castle for London first thing that morning and taken his mother with him.

"My lord!" she exclaimed. "I did not expect... Has something happened?"

"Wretched coach broke a wheel not half an hour from here. We had to walk most of the way back until we could borrow another conveyance." He peered at her. "Miss Grey, are you quite well?"

"Oh yes, perfectly," she assured him, with another surreptitious swipe at her eyes. "I'm afraid I allowed the girls a morning away from lessons. After yesterday, they were too excited to settle, and I'm afraid they have probably gone to visit Lady Serena, I mean Lady Tamar, though—"

"Miss Grey," he interrupted, frowning as he walked across to her. "What has upset you?"

Inevitably, his kindness produced another flood of tears which she tried in vain to swallow back down.

"Oh, it is nothing," she whispered. "Merely, my little nephew is ill, and I feel helpless, but I'm sure it is not serious, so truly, this is silliness." Drawing a shuddering breath, she again wiped her eyes.

The earl, who was normally aloof if civil, presented her with a handkerchief and a sympathetic smile.

"We all worry about distant family," he assured her, and gave her shoulder a kindly pat.

"Miss Grey," uttered a quite different voice from the doorway, icy with barely suppressed fury.

Caroline jerked away from the earl in what must surely have looked a guilty manner.

Lady Braithwaite, the mother of the earl and of Caroline's pupils, swept into the room and deliberately closed the door.

"What is the meaning of this?" she demanded.

His lordship cast his eyes to the ceiling. "Of what mother?" he asked impatiently. "Miss Grey has been upset by news from home."

"And that necessitates you sending your sisters away and cuddling her with the door closed?" her ladyship snapped.

"Oh for the love of... Mother, the door was *not* closed!"

"Then how come I had to push it open?" she retorted.

"The window is open." Caroline gestured toward the open casement. "The draught must have blown the door. Forgive my weakness, my lady, my lord. If you will excuse me, I—"

"Society is *unforgiving*, Miss Grey," the countess interrupted. "And where my daughters are concerned, I do not allow myself the luxury of ignoring appearances. Whatever the truth of your grief—or your designs upon my son—you are dismissed."

Caroline's mouth fell open. Her ears sang with shock. She barely noticed Lady Braithwaite's regal exit, merely stared after her, speechless.

"Braithwaite!" the countess snapped.

The earl swore beneath his breath. "Excuse me," he said grimly to Caroline. "Wait here."

As he strode after his mother, Caroline doubted she was capable of doing anything *but* staying where she was. Slowly, she sank back into Lady Maria's chair, wondering how on earth this could have happened.

From nowhere, from nothing, she was without a home, a post, a future. Without a reference, she had little hope of a respectable position in another household. She would have to spend the last of her money journeying to her mother, and then who would pay Peter's doctor...?

This is not fair!

But she'd known for a long time that life was rarely fair. Not to the powerless.

Oh, but she would miss those bright, lively girls she'd grown to love.

She swallowed. *I will not cry again. I will not.*

She wasn't sure how much time passed before she was summoned by a maid to the earl's study. Straightening her shoulders, she lifted her chin and determined to keep her dignity for the final interview.

"Don't close the door, for God's sake," the earl said as she entered his study.

She was relieved that the countess wasn't present. There would be less temptation to give in to fury.

"I'm so sorry for this, but the devil's in it that I can't change her mind right now."

Of course, he couldn't. She was surprised, almost touched, that he had apparently tried. But the countess, already smarting from being overruled on Lady Serena's marriage to the impoverished Marquis of Tamar, would not give in a second time in a month.

"I have obtained you a stay of execution until tomorrow morning," he said, with an apologetic twist of his lips. "Which at least gives me time to warn Benedict of your arrival."

"Benedict?" she repeated, bewildered.

"Mr. Benedict at Haven Hall."

Haven Hall… A flash of memory distracted her—a tall, grim figure striding from the trees, an ugly scar, livid and jagged, across a swarthy, frowning face.

"I spoke to him the other day," Lord Braithwaite explained, "and he is in need of a governess."

"Why?" Caroline blurted.

"He has a daughter, and I'm sure he'll accept my recommendation."

"But I'm not sure I can," Caroline said in panic. "Haven Hall, sir!"

The earl waved that aside. "Rumor and nonsense. He's just a little eccentric, but a perfect gentleman and extremely well educated. Besides, it shouldn't be for long."

She regarded him unhappily. "You expect me to lose that position, too?"

"Well, yes, in so far as I expect you to come back here."

She blinked at him. "I beg your pardon?"

He gave a lopsided smile. "Contrary to today's evidence, my

mother is neither an unkind nor an unjust woman. She is merely subject to temper and impulse—as well as being most stern about the proprieties. You must know she was angry with Serena when she sent her up here last month, only then, nothing would do but that we had to rush up here after her because she acknowledged her mistake. In a week or so, she will acknowledge her mistake toward you, too, and I hope you will come back to us."

Caroline seemed to be spending a lot of today with her mouth open. She closed it.

"My sisters will miss you, Miss Grey," he said uncomfortably. "They love you, and they certainly seem to learn a great deal more from you than their previous governesses. My understanding is that you also were happy in the position."

"I was."

"Then with your permission, I will merely loan you to Benedict and his daughter and reclaim you for my sisters in a week or so. By which time, hopefully, Benedict will have found a permanent governess for his own daughter."

"I never even knew he had a daughter!"

Braithwaite shrugged. "I doubt anyone knew. He brought his own servants with him to the hall. I gather neither he nor they associate with anyone in Blackhaven, so no one really knows anything about him at all."

And yet you will send me there like a lamb to the slaughter.

"However, he has recently employed a cook who is a Blackhaven woman," Braithwaite continued cheerfully. "She used to work in our kitchen and is an excellent person. You may trust her implicitly."

"Oh, good."

He cast her a sidelong glance, as though suspecting her—quite rightly—of sarcasm. But he let it go. "As I say, I'm sorry for this, Miss Grey, but I hope we may make it right in the end."

She met his gaze. "Then I wonder if I might ask a favor? I need to send something to my mother."

"I shall frank it for you."

As contented as she could be, in the circumstances, she left him to pack her meagre bag.

LORD BRAITHWAITE HAD told her to order the gig when she was ready to leave, but having gazed upon the sleeping faces of his sisters for what could be the last time, she found she needed to walk off her anger.

She had neither asked for nor wanted the earl's sympathy, and his mother must surely be an imbecile to imagine any impropriety in such an innocent moment. She seemed to regard Caroline suddenly as some kind of designing hussy, a siren in a drab grey gown and damaged boots, quite set upon getting her claws into Lady Braithwaite's precious son. So now she was to be parted from the pupils she'd grown so fond of, disrupting their lives and her own.

It was a long walk to Haven Hall, but not the first time she'd taken the path. Then, she had just been walking in the autumn sunshine, unaware of where her feet had taken her until later. The hall itself had only been glimpsed between the trees, its tenant unidentified, even after he'd confronted her.

Her stomach tightened in memory of that encounter. She must have looked somewhat foolish and timid to him. But in truth, there had been reason for her nervousness. Strangers in the neighborhood had recently attacked Lady Serena and were hiding smuggled goods in the castle cellar—goods rather more dangerous than the illicit French brandy so familiar in Blackhaven. So, when she'd heard the unmistakable sounds of someone in the wood, seemingly paralleling her own path, she had been understandably alarmed.

Especially when she'd walked back the way she'd come, and still the crackling of twigs and swishing of branches had followed her. At last, the sound of breath panting louder than hers had compelled her to face the danger head on. After all, she'd doubted she could outrun it.

"Show yourself!" she'd commanded, halting and glaring into the trees. A huge, grey wolfhound had loped out of the undergrowth, wagging its tail. She'd never seen anything quite so large look so unthreatening. But her relief had been short-lived, for hard on the heels of the dog had come a large, scarred man, so casually dressed that she couldn't tell his class or occupation. Swarthy and unshaven, wearing a battered wide-brimmed hat, he could have been a gentleman, or a farm laborer, or even a poacher. Or, with that scar, Lady Serena's villainous attacker.

"What do you want?" she'd demanded, as the dark eyes regarded her with annoyance.

His black eyebrows flew up. "A rabbit for dinner. What do you want?"

Although his voice had been rough, at least his accent had been that of an educated man.

"Peace to walk undisturbed," she'd retorted, although her ill-nature had been immediately diluted by the wolfhound pushing its great head under her hand. Without meaning to, she'd stroked the dog and even smiled at it.

And when she'd raised her gaze to its owner, he was staring at her with grim, secretive, unblinking eyes. A thrill of fear had twisted through her. At least, she'd supposed it to be fear.

However, apart from the dominating scar running right across one side of his face, he was not an ill-looking man. Perhaps in his mid or late thirties, he was tall and straight, his features harsh but even, his hard, grey eyes compelling, and his lips fine. She'd wondered if he ever smiled. Certainly, he hadn't at her. Instead, his gaze had flickered over her like a lash and returned to her face. He hadn't looked impressed. She'd wanted to step back from him, to run, but something, whether fright or mere refusal to give in, had kept her rooted to the same spot, her hand still on the dog's great head.

"Peace," the stranger had repeated with a twist of his lips. "Here? I suggest you look elsewhere. Good afternoon." And he'd whistled for the dog and strode back into the trees. His gait seemed more uneven than the rough ground warranted, as though he were lame—or drunk.

The wolfhound, with a farewell lick at her mended gloves, had trotted off after him.

For some reason she couldn't fathom, the brief encounter had troubled Caroline, even after Lord Tamar had guessed the identity of her scarred man as the tenant of Haven Hall. Mr. Benedict, according to Lord Braithwaite. Mr. Javan Benedict, whose daughter was called Rosa. There was no Mrs. Benedict, the earl had said.

That was all she knew of him for sure. But as she walked, she couldn't help remembering all the rumors about him, for after her brush with him, she'd made a point of listening to the servants' gossip and even asking the odd question in Blackhaven.

According to some, he had murdered his wife. Others said he kept her locked up in one of the rooms at the hall. Others said she had given him the scar on his face, or that her lover had caused it during a duel. Someone else had told her he stole children, a rumor which could, Caroline supposed, have come from the sudden discovery of the daughter who lived with him.

Then, on top of all those personal rumors, some said Haven Hall was haunted by the tragedy of its owners, the Gardyn family, and that its tenants were all either scared away or driven insane by the ghosts. Terrifying noises and unearthly visions in the vicinity of the hall had been reported for years.

Caroline discounted rumors. And yet, whether or not the man she'd encountered close to the hall had indeed been Javan Benedict, she could not help being alarmed by the prospect of the coming meeting. Lord Braithwaite had told her Mr. Benedict expected her and that, subject to an interview, she would be engaged for a trial period. This did not comfort Caroline. She didn't want to be farmed out to strangers and strange children while she waited for Lady Braithwaite to forgive her for something she hadn't done. She wanted to be teaching Maria and Alice and Helen...and enjoying the occasional company of the newly married Lady Serena who had become something approaching a friend over recent weeks.

But that was not an option. She could go home with no reference. Or she could go to Haven Hall and try to earn one. She would not even think of the countess's forgiveness. She began to wonder, in fact, if *she* might not forgive Lady Braithwaite.

By the time she reached the overgrown drive, her meagre carpet bag of possessions felt as if it weighed a ton. Worse, the rain had come on half an hour before, and the wind had blown her bonnet off her head, playing havoc with her hair. If she had to come here, she would have preferred not to turn up on the doorstep looking like a drowned rat or some waif from the poor house.

The hall was even less comforting than the grounds. In the rain, covered with dark ivy and framed by filthy grey clouds, it looked even grimmer than its tenant. If Caroline had been fanciful—which she hoped she was not—she would have shivered with foreboding. Her current trembling was due merely to the cold and damp. Truly.

She trudged up the broken, weed-strewn path to the front door and lifted the knocker. Covering her uncertainty, she knocked rather too loudly for civility, but having done it, she couldn't take it back. She stepped away and waited.

It seemed to take a long time before the door opened with a painful creak of hinges. An ill-dressed, dark-visaged manservant regarded her.

"Caroline Grey," she said as briskly as she could with water running down her face. "Mr. Benedict is expecting me."

The manservant didn't trouble to hide his grin of amusement at her appearance. But at least he stood aside to admit her. She took a deep breath and crossed the threshold.

"One moment, Miss," said the servant, after he'd swung the door closed behind her. He crossed the wide, wood-paneled hall to what seemed a very distant door. Despite his unconventional dress for a butler, he had a straight, vaguely military bearing.

Clearly, she wasn't meant to follow him, so she used the time to squeeze what moisture she could out of her hair, cram some loose pins back in place, and drag her bonnet from her neck back onto her head.

That way, she could pretend she was not staying, that there was still some alternative to this situation.

At least the inside of the house looked less dilapidated than the outside, although the wall panels and the table beside her could have done with a dusting.

The manservant didn't vanish for long. He reappeared outside the distant door only moments later and beckoned to her. Feeling as though she took her life in her hands, she walked toward him. She tilted her chin for courage and sailed past him into the room.

It appeared to be a dining room, the table set for luncheon. A girl of perhaps nine or ten years old sat there gazing at Caroline, an angry lady of perhaps forty winters at her side. A gentleman, presumably Mr., Benedict, had his back to the door, standing about halfway between Caroline and the table.

As Caroline halted just inside the door, the angry lady sprang to her feet, snatching up a whole cake from the table. She hurled it with force and fury, straight at Mr. Benedict.

Caroline gasped, for the woman's aim was true, and she was sure the cake, plate and all, must hit him. But he simply ducked, and the plate flew over his head, shattering against the wall only inches from where Caroline stood.

Cake dripped down the wall and landed among the rest of the crumbs and broken china on the floor.

In the silence, Caroline turned her bemused attention to the scarred face she recognized. His gaze lashed her. Then he turned his back and walked to the table, his stride uneven as she remembered from their first meeting.

"Marjorie," he said quietly.

The lady glared at him in defiance, her chest heaving. And then, muttering, she stalked around the table until she stood beside him. Together, they walked directly toward Caroline, who stepped smartly aside—away from the cake.

The lady, misery rather than fury staring out from her face, didn't so much as glance at her. She seemed to be held together by a very fine thread.

Mr. Benedict deigned to flick another glance in Caroline's direction. "I'll be with you directly. Please sit down. Eat, if you wish."

At least he didn't comment on her disheveled appearance. Perhaps he was hindered by the cake dripping down his wall.

Chapter Two

FIGHTING A STRANGE sense of unreality, Caroline crossed the room to the table. The child stared at her curiously.

"You must be Rosa," Caroline observed. "I'm Miss Grey."

The girl nodded but said nothing. She was a pretty child, with thick, black hair and large, brown eyes.

Caroline hesitated. She had had nothing to eat all day and was ravenous after her long walk. "May I join you?"

Again, the girl nodded.

Very conscious of her rain-soaked cloak, Caroline sat on the edge of a chair, and taking an unused plate, helped herself to cold meat, cheese, pickles, and bread and butter.

"How old are you, Rosa?" she asked pleasantly, between mouthfuls.

The girl didn't answer. Perhaps she didn't hear, so concentrated did she appear to be on Caroline's face. Caroline let it pass, and since her companion was not inclined to talk, she merely ate and hoped the child would get used to her. After that, she could teach her good manners.

The girl picked up the bread on her own plate and began to nibble.

When she heard the approaching footsteps that heralded Mr. Benedict's return, Caroline hastily swallowed the food in her mouth and rose in time to see him limp into the room.

"Miss...Grey, is it?" he said, unexpectedly offering his hand.

"Yes." Her hand seemed to vanish inside his large fingers. They felt rough in texture and strong, though his grip was brief and firm rather than harsh. His eyes betrayed no recognition that they'd met before.

"Javan Benedict. This is Rosa."

"So I gather."

Gesturing for Caroline to be seated, Mr. Benedict casually ruffled his daughter's dark head as he passed and sat beside her.

He frowned at Caroline. "Take off your wet things, Miss Grey. Did the Braithwaites not provide you with a suitable conveyance?"

"I chose not to take up the offer. It wasn't raining when I set off." With difficulty, she untied the wet ribbons of her bonnet, then stood to remove her heavy cloak. Unexpectedly, Rosa took them from her, and with a quick smile at her father, ran to the door.

"Make sure they're dried off," he called after her.

"Thank you," Caroline murmured. Stupidly, without the cloak and bonnet, she felt defenseless, vulnerable.

The man who sat opposite her and controlled her future might have been better dressed and groomed than on that first encounter, but he still seemed alarmingly harsh. And large, in a way that had less to do with his height than the force of his sheer presence. His hard, grey eyes pierced hers, searching. She wondered if he were recalling her insolence only a few weeks ago.

"What did you fall out about?" he asked abruptly, taking her by surprise once more. "You and Lady Braithwaite."

She blinked. "I'm not sure that's your concern, sir."

"*I* am sure it is. If you are to care for my daughter, I need to know why you were dismissed."

"Perhaps I chose to leave," she snapped back.

"Did you?"

She dragged her gaze free of the sudden mockery in his. "No." She took a deep breath. "Lady Braithwaite misunderstood a...passage between his lordship and myself and imagined I was insolent enough to...*set my cap* at him."

"Were you?" he drawled.

She stared at him indignantly. "I am not *foolish* enough!" she retorted. "My living depends on my spotless reputation."

"This is an odd place to come to keep your reputation—er—spotless."

"Beggars," she pointed out, "cannot be choosers."

It was hardly the most conciliatory response she could have made. Mr. Benedict however, appeared more amused than annoyed. "Is that what you are? A beggar?"

She tilted her chin. "I need a paying position."

He sat back, thrusting his hand into his pocket. "Was it a difficult position? With the Braithwaite girls?"

"No. It was a good position and I was happy there."

His eyes searched hers again. "Were you?" he said deliberately.

"I believe I said so."

Again, instead of being offended by her haughtiness, he appeared to be entertained. Certainly, his lips twitched.

"This will *not* be an easy position," he observed.

Involuntarily, her gaze strayed to the shattered plate still on the floor by the door.

His breath caught. "*That*, however, is a rare drama, for which I apologize. Teaching Rosa would be your main challenge."

"I am used to teaching girls of all ages."

His gaze held hers. "You may have noticed Rosa has…special demands."

"All children do," she returned.

"Most of them, however, speak."

Caroline's eyes widened. "She does not speak? She is mute?"

"For the last two years."

"Then she was not born mute? She is not deaf, is she?"

"No, she hears and understands everything. The doctors believe she *can* speak. She simply chooses not to."

"Do you know why?"

"A nervous disorder, they tell me. What will you do if you don't take up this post?"

It was an odd way to phrase it. Was he allowing her a pretense of choice? Or reminding her that she had none? He was the one who currently held her fate in his hands. His gaze, direct and penetrating, disconcerted her.

"I shall look for another position," she said calmly.

"From where?" he asked at once.

She stared back at him. "From wherever I choose. Please don't feel obliged to give me this position, sir. I am not destitute and I do have friends."

"I am pleased for you," he returned. "Though I've no idea why you should consider me so benevolent. I'm merely trying to work out if Braithwaite has done me a favor or dumped an annoyance upon me."

Since his words left her speechless, the sudden return of Rosa was a relief. She ran into the room at high speed, the wolfhound Caroline remembered close on her heels. They both ran around the table until it was impossible to tell who was chasing whom. And then the dog leapt on the girl, bringing her down so suddenly that Caroline was alarmed, afraid she'd misjudged the dog's good nature on their last encounter.

Since Mr. Benedict didn't move, Caroline half rose from her chair to intervene. The dog had pinned the child to the floor and was enthusiastically licking her face while she hugged him and tried to push him off at once. Her whole face was alight with silent laughter.

Over the animal's head, Rosa's merry eyes met Caroline's, and she couldn't help smiling back. It was clearly an old and well-established game. She relaxed back into her chair and glanced at Benedict, who's attention was all focused on her. His thoughts were entirely masked. Whatever the test had been, she suspected she'd failed. She wondered if he'd lend her a conveyance of some kind to Carlisle, from where she could buy a seat on the mail coach to Edinburgh...

He muttered something below his breath. It sounded like, "I'm going to regret this." Then his gaze shifted to Rosa. "Show Miss Grey to her chamber, Rosa."

Without meaning to, Caroline smiled—partly with relief and partly because in spite of herself, the child intrigued her. "Thank you."

He rose abruptly. "Don't thank me yet. You and Rosa may see if you suit." And with that, he simply walked out of the room.

ROSA PROVED TO be even more of an enigma than she'd imagined. Although in many ways she seemed younger than her ten years, she was clearly quick-witted and intelligent, always understanding Caroline's murmured jokes and occasionally sardonic asides. And while she didn't speak, her face was very expressive, and she supplemented that with her own sign language and with writing things down.

She wrote quickly and clearly and could calculate quite complicated sums. Not that Caroline confined her to lessons that first afternoon. But they took tea together in the school room, and Caroline used the opportunity to discover a little of what her charge could and couldn't do in the way of formal learning. For the rest of the afternoon, Rosa showed her around the house—which was not huge, but which contained a rather beautiful drawing room, a large library, and a study. The study's closed door was not breached, and Rosa gave her to understand that Mr. Benedict was working in there.

"What work does he do?" Caroline asked casually.

Rosa made a ring with her finger and forefinger and raised it to her eye before making hasty writing motions with one hand on the other. From which Caroline guessed she meant he studied things under a glass and wrote about them. She didn't feel much wiser.

When the rain went off, Rosa took her hand and tugged her to the side door, where several coats and cloaks—including her own—hung on hooks.

"You wish to go for a walk?" Caroline guessed. Personally, she had had enough of walking for one day, but she was loathe to disappoint her new pupil. "Do you have stout boots to wear? The ground will be very muddy."

But Rosa was already climbing into a sturdy pair of walking boots.

As Caroline reached for her cloak and bonnet, the wolfhound careened around the corner and lolloped toward them, barking.

"Should we take him?" Caroline asked doubtfully.

"I'm afraid he will insist upon it," replied a dry male voice.

Caroline spun around to face Mr. Benedict, who strolled up to them wearing an open overcoat and a battered wide-brimmed hat. Without surprise, Rosa ran to seize his hand. The afternoon walk, clearly, was a regular occurrence. Caroline wondered if her presence was required or wanted.

"Heel, Tiny," Mr. Benedict commanded.

"Tiny?" Caroline repeated breathlessly as the dog scampered to obey.

"Well, he was once," Mr. Benedict said and opened the door, bowing her out with only a hint of irony.

Laughter bubbled up in her throat as she followed Rosa outside. "Tiny" bounded ahead, Rosa racing after him into the wild undergrowth encroaching over the paths. A few moments later, they bolted out again. Seizing her father and Caroline by the hands, Rosa tugged until they accompanied her back the way she'd come.

To Caroline's surprise, the stern-looking Mr. Benedict seemed neither surprised nor annoyed to be dragged through untamed grass and thorns. Rosa crouched down and pulled back a tangle of wild rose branches to reveal a single small flower. She turned up her face and smiled at her father and then at Caroline.

"Well, that's quite a discovery," Mr. Benedict said warmly. "How is it surviving in there without any sun?"

Rosa grinned and jumped up to run on in search of the dog.

"So," Mr. Benedict said as they fought their way back to the path. "How peaceful do you find the environs of Haven Hall?"

It was the first indication he'd given that he remembered her, and she couldn't help flushing with embarrassment.

"Acceptably so," she replied as calmly as she could. Forcing herself, she met his sardonic gaze. "We have met before today. I didn't think you remembered."

"I'm sure it doesn't count since no one introduced us."

"If I was rude, I apologize," she blurted. "I didn't realize it was your land, and you gave me a fright."

"Oh, it's not my land. I only rent the house. For what it's worth, I don't recall your rudeness, and would be unlikely to dismiss you for it if I did. How do you find your pupil?"

Caroline blinked at the change of subject. "I find her very bright and thoughtful and knowledgeable for one so young. Clearly, she has been well taught."

"Now and again," Mr. Benedict said with a faint curl of his lips. "What of you, Miss Grey? How did you receive your learning?"

"From my own governess," she replied honestly. "Until I was twelve years old and pursued my own studies."

"Why?"

"I was lamentably bookish."

"How fortunate, but as you very well know, I was prying. What happened when you were twelve years old?"

"My father died, leaving us...if not quite destitute, then at least in genteel poverty," she replied frankly. "A governess was no longer an affordable expense."

"And now you governess for others. What of the rest of your family?"

"My mother lives quietly in the Scottish Borders with my widowed sister and nephew."

"And you are their sole support?"

"Not sole, but my earnings are necessary, yes."

"Then I hope Braithwaite paid you better than most governesses."

"He did," she replied calmly.

Rosa, who'd been rushing ahead, ran back with sheer exuberance to skip along beside them, examining interestingly colored leaves she'd swept up on the way. She showed her favorites to her father and to Caroline. Again, Caroline was surprised by how much attention the saturnine Mr. Benedict gave to her childish interests. Whatever the reasons behind Rosa's refusal to speak, they didn't appear to include parental neglect.

Since the daylight was fading, their walk was not long, and they all piled back into the house with Tiny, who shook mud all over them and then wagged his tail.

"I'll see you at dinner," Mr. Benedict said in his abrupt way, giving his daughter's hair a careless ruffle as he strode away.

"Mr. Benedict," Caroline called, hurrying after him as she untied the ribbons of her bonnet. He paused, glancing back at her. "Rosa dines with you?" she asked.

He nodded curtly.

"Where should I dine?" she asked. It was a thorny problem in many households, where the governess was neither servant nor guest. In the Braithwaites' establishments, she had always eaten with her pupils, whether that was in the schoolroom or the formal dining room, but every family had its own preferences.

"With Rosa," he said in surprise. "And me."

For some reason, her stomach tightened. It wasn't displeasure or even fear, for he intrigued her, and she wanted to know more about him as well as Rosa. He didn't wait for her acceptance, merely limped off into the bowels of the house.

SINCE SHE MADE Rosa put on a clean dress for dinner—a demand that appeared to surprise Rosa but which she obeyed—Caroline changed her own mud-splashed, workaday garment for her Sunday gown, the only other she possessed. This was a slightly newer but equally drab brown dress. It wasn't precisely evening wear, but she doubted Mr. Benedict was a stickler for etiquette. She did wonder about the lady who'd thrown the cake at him. But when she and Rosa entered the dining room, the table was set only for three.

Rosa obviously noticed, for when her father arrived, she went and looked at him in silent question.

"Marjorie isn't dining with us tonight," he said briskly. "You may go and see her after dinner."

Although the food was surprisingly good—thanks no doubt to the cook who had once worked at Braithwaite Castle—it was rather an odd meal. Since Rosa didn't speak, and Mr. Benedict appeared to be silent by nature, Caroline didn't feel she should be the one to break the silence. Rosa did smile at her encouragingly a couple of times, so she smiled back and continued eating her soup.

The soup was eventually removed and a dish of chicken brought in. As she helped herself to vegetables, Caroline was aware of Rosa nudging her father and staring at him significantly.

He picked up his knife and fork. "My daughter wishes me to make conversation, so that you don't desert us for some more civilized family. Ouch," he added with amusement as Rosa clearly kicked him under the table.

"I'm happy to converse on any subject you wish," Caroline replied, refusing to be put out. "Although, I have never been in favor of simply filling silence with noise if one has nothing to say."

"You see?" Mr. Benedict said to Rosa. "Miss Grey is clearly a lady of superior understanding. On the other hand, Rosa and I are both curious, so I hope you won't consider it mere noise when I ask you about your life."

She met his gaze. "Sadly, I have nothing to say. My life has been largely too dull for conversation."

"But you give us hope in the word *largely*. When has your life *not* been dull?"

"I did not say it was dull to me," she retorted. "But it would most certainly be so to you and Rosa."

"I think you must allow Rosa and me to judge for ourselves. I know you have a sister. Do you have other siblings?"

"No."

"Where did you grow up?"

"In a country vicarage in Yorkshire."

His eyebrows flew up. "You are a vicar's daughter?"

She inclined her head. "The fact does not usually elicit so

much…astonishment."

"I am adjusting my preconceived ideas," he said obscurely. He chased his food around his plate for a little bit. Then, just as she shot him a surreptitious glance, he looked up. "So, were you good children, as a vicar's should be? Or naughty like Rosa?"

Rosa grinned at both her father and Caroline. Caroline couldn't help smiling back.

"I'm sure we were both," she replied lightly. "Perhaps it's my mother you should consult on the subject."

"Perhaps I will."

Her gaze flew back to his, and he set down his fork. "Interesting. You don't like that idea at all."

"I have never had an employer interview my mother before," she retorted.

"It would be outrageous, wouldn't it? You must learn to tell when I'm jesting."

Caroline pronged her chicken with unnecessary force. "Must I?"

"For your own peace of mind. What of your sister? Is she a governess, too?"

"No. She has a child."

"And no means of support but you?"

Caroline flushed. "Sir, my sister is not your concern."

"But she is yours. I find that does concern me."

"Why?"

His glass froze in midair. A short bark of laughter escaped him before he raised the wine the rest of the way to his lips and drank. "Good question," he allowed, setting the glass down again and pushing once more at his food. "You're not afraid of me, are you, Miss Grey?"

"I don't know," she replied honestly. She swallowed. "I apologize for my rudeness."

"Oh, don't spoil it," he mocked. "You weren't rude. And if you were, I am impervious to such things. Eat up."

It was advice he would have been better taking than giving. Caroline's plate was almost cleared, Rosa's all but polished, while Mr. Benedict's remained nearly untouched. She recalled his soup plate had been removed still half full and he seemed disinclined to eat more than the couple of forkfuls he'd already taken of the chicken.

She raised her eyes to his face. "Are you quite well, sir?"

"Quite." His fingers curled around the stem of his glass, his expression unchanging.

It was Rosa who looked suddenly anxious, her large, scared eyes fixed on her father's face. Caroline's question had inspired that fear.

"Rosa, did you not get any dinner?" Caroline tried a teasing note. "There's hardly any left for you now."

Rosa gave a distracted smile, while Caroline ladled the last of the chicken on to her plate. "Eat up," she said cheerfully. "Will there be pastry now?"

That attracted a more enthusiastic nod.

"What kind?" Caroline asked.

While Rosa tried to sign the answers, Caroline was aware of Mr. Benedict's gaze on her, but she refused to look to see if it was with disapproval or otherwise. However, by the time the servant brought the pastries, Mr. Benedict's plate was not quite so full. As if he'd made an effort, at least to stop his daughter worrying—or to prevent the governess from blurting unhelpful remarks.

Rosa set about her pastry with enthusiasm, and indeed it was delicious. The fact that her father took none did not appear to upset her. Presumably, he rarely did. Instead, he picked at some cheese and, having finished the wine, poured himself a glass of port.

Rosa swallowed the last of her pastry. Catching her father's gaze, she pointed upward in a hopeful manner.

"Go and see Marjorie, then," he said. "I'll be up in a little to make sure you go to bed."

Rosa bounced to her feet and held out her hand invitingly to Caroline, who laid down her napkin.

"No, Marjorie would prefer you alone," Mr. Benedict said. "Besides, I wish to talk to Miss Grey."

Rosa wrinkled her nose but shrugged apologetically to Caroline and ran out of the room.

"Is the lady ill?" Caroline asked. "Is there something I might do for her?"

"No, she will come about with a little peace. Don't we all?"

"I didn't mean to upset Rosa by drawing attention to your lack of appetite," she said quickly. "I was thoughtless."

"Or too thoughtful? Interesting point. My wife died a year ago. Rosa...watches me quite carefully to be sure I don't follow her to the grave."

It made sense, although it filled Caroline with a hundred other questions. She opted for, "*Are* you ill, sir? It would make my position simpler if I knew."

"But your position isn't simple. I told you that."

If it was an attempt to intimidate her to silence, she resisted, holding his gaze as she waited for her answer. After a moment, he let out another short laugh and reached for his glass. "I am convalescing, Miss Grey. Will that suffice? But talking of your position, I need to know your intentions."

"My intentions?" she repeated blankly. After all, her intentions hadn't appeared to matter to anyone since yesterday morning. She had been blown around by other people's until she'd landed here.

"Rosa needs a governess. I hoped she would grow used to the idea of having you here. But it appears she's taken a liking to you. I refuse to have her feelings hurt if you go running back to Braithwaite."

A flush of anger rose up from her toes. "Running back to... If I return to Braithwaite *Castle*, it will be to the ladies Maria, Alice and Helen. And only at *Lady* Braithwaite's invitation. Whatever you imagine my relationship with the earl to be, you are wrong!"

His lips curved. "Truly? Then you are his mistress?"

She gasped, jumping to her feet. "I beg your pardon?"

He rose with her, albeit languidly, which brought him a shade too close. But Caroline was far too indignant to back away.

His gaze mocked her relentlessly. "I imagined your relationship to be entirely innocent," he drawled. "I wouldn't otherwise have employed you. I'm not much of a moral stickler myself, but even I draw the line at employing a neighbor's bit of muslin to teach my daughter. You're very touchy on the subject. Perhaps you harbor a *tendre* for the earl? He is very handsome."

"Then perhaps *you* should be his *bit of muslin!*" she said furiously.

To her surprise, he threw back his head and laughed. "What a picture! Wouldn't that set the tongues of Blackhaven wagging with a vengeance? Oh, sit down, Miss Grey," he added, throwing himself back into his chair. "I impugn neither your honor nor his. Nor do I actually care whether either of you gives a jot for the other. What concerns me is your returning there and leaving Rosa once she has grown to rely upon you."

Grudgingly, Caroline resumed her own seat. "Lord Braithwaite spoke of a week or so," she admitted. "By then, he believes his mother's temper will have calmed and her good sense be restored." She drew a deep breath. "I believe his lordship to be a just man, offended by his mother's *in*justice to me. Besides, he believes me to be a good influence on his younger sister. While I...I value my well-paid position and I am fond of the girls. I am ashamed to say neither of us gave much thought to you or Rosa in these plans."

She met his gaze with conscious bravery. "If you think it better for Rosa, I will leave tomorrow. I can give you the address of a good agency to find another governess."

There was a hint of curiosity in his hard eyes. "You would, too, wouldn't you? Where would you go?"

"I should be grateful for a conveyance to Carlisle. From there I can travel home to my mother's house north of the border. Lady Braithwaite may reach me there as easily as here."

"Not quite so easily," he observed. He raised his glass and finished his port. He shrugged with a hint of impatience. "Rosa knows you are on loan. If her affections are too engaged, well, she will have to grow used to disappointment like the rest of us." Pushing back his chair, he rose to his feet. "Stay if you wish."

Baffled, she watched him limp across the room and out the door.

Chapter Three

DESPITE DESPERATE TIREDNESS, Caroline found it hard to fall asleep that night. Her allotted bedchamber on the west side of the main first floor passage, lay next to the schoolroom, to which there was also a connecting door. A third door connected her to Rosa's chamber. It felt like a room consisting *only* of doors. Even with them all closed, it resembled a corridor more than a bedchamber. She supposed she would get used to it in time. She was not sure, however, that she would ever get used to her temporary employer.

Javan Benedict filled her thoughts as his presence tended to fill a room. Since he didn't appear to find her replies insolent, she had no objection to sharpening her wits on his mockery. Or whatever it was. She didn't pretend to understand him, and he was clearly not in the best of health. One thing was clear, though—he did care deeply for his daughter.

The door between Caroline's and Rosa's bedchambers had been left slightly ajar from the child first showing her to her room. So, before she sat down by the candlelight to write to her mother, she had glanced in on Rosa to say goodnight. To Caroline's surprise, Mr. Benedict was still there, sitting on the edge of the bed.

His back was to Caroline. She must have let very little light into the room, for he did not seem aware of her. His attention was all on Rosa, who lay on her side, facing him, her eyes closed, her little hand lost in her father's large one. She was either asleep or on the verge of it, but he did not move, simply sat there giving what Caroline imagined to be silent comfort.

She had crept out, closing the door as silently as she could. Then, she'd written part of a letter and was undressing for bed before she heard him leave his daughter's room and walk quietly along the passage. She wondered if he did this every night, or if Rosa had just been unsettled by Caroline's unwary words.

The child missed her late mother, of course, and was terrified of losing her father, too. Was that the cause of her silence? But no, Mr. Benedict had said his wife died last year, while Rosa hadn't spoken for two. Perhaps Mrs. Benedict had had a long illness?

And then who was the mysterious Marjorie, who threw cake at the master of the house and retired to her chamber for the rest of the day? Caroline could understand the impulse. Even on such a short acquaintance, there had been times when she would have dearly liked to throw things at him herself.

What illness was he recovering from? Why was he…the way he was? Why ask her about Braithwaite if he was already sure of her innocence? Did he approve of her or not? Did he *like* her?

While she realized the latter question was quite irrelevant, she found herself coming back to it all too often. It wasn't as if *she* actually liked Benedict himself. At least, she didn't think she did. She did like the erratic appearances of his humor. And his laughter. But he was hardly easy company. He was sardonic and mocking and occasionally rude. Prying. Arrogant.

What or who had scarred his face? And why did he limp? Why was he hiding out here in isolation from everyone else in the environs of Blackhaven?

Her mind continued to spin with questions long after she blew out the last candle and climbed into bed. Someone had taken the chill off with a warming pan, for which she was eternally grateful. Winter was in the air.

She'd only just nodded off to sleep when she was awakened by a heart-rending cry.

Caroline sprang out of bed, instinctively blundering to Rosa's bedchamber door. She opened it to discover the child peacefully asleep in the glow of a small, covered night light.

Hastily, she crept out again. Another wail caused her to feel for the flint and light a candle. In Blackhaven, they said the hall was haunted by the ghost of the Gardyn child and those cries did sound childlike…

But Caroline did not believe in ghosts. And Rosa was the only child in the house.

Throwing her threadbare wrapper over her night rail, she opened the door to the passage and walked barefoot into the corridor. Soft sobs in the distance, followed by occasional outbursts of howling, drew her warily along, her candle held in front of her like a shield.

On the other side of the staircase which divided the house, lights bobbed by an open door. A maidservant in a cap and wrapper whispered in the passage to a man with a lamp and then vanished back into the room, closing the door. The crisis, whatever it was, appeared to be over; even the soft cries had subsided.

The man turned in her direction, and her heart lurched, because it was Mr. Benedict, not a servant. In his shirt sleeves with no necktie, the last vestiges of a civilized gentleman seemed to have fallen away from him. He was simply a tall, very physical man, and for some reason, Caroline's throat went dry as he approached her.

"Why are you abroad?" he demanded, low-voiced but clearly irritated.

"I heard crying. Is someone ill?"

His gaze flickered over her. "She is better now," he muttered.

Who is better? she couldn't help wondering. *The lady who threw cake?* "Is there anything I can do?" she asked aloud.

"Yes, you can make sure Rosa wasn't disturbed."

"She wasn't. She was sound asleep."

He nodded curtly. "Come, then."

There was nothing she could do but turn and trot after him to keep up with his long if uneven stride. He didn't speak until they reached her open bedchamber door.

"You must think us all unhinged," he said softly, coming to a halt.

She could only shake her head. "I have heard unhappiness before.

Good night."

She expected him to walk on, but to her surprise, his eyes focused on her face. They seemed to glow in the lamplight while the rest of his face was cast into shadow. "Was it yours?"

A frown tugged at her brow. "I beg your pardon?"

"The unhappiness that you heard before. Was it your own?"

It had been, although she had been more careful to unleash it only where it could not be overheard.

"I don't remember," she whispered hastily. "I was speaking generally."

His lips twisted. "It seems we all have our secrets." His gaze dropped to her lips, flickered lower over her flimsily wrapped body before returning more slowly to her flushed face. The flame of the candle seemed to leap in his eyes, turning them suddenly warm and dangerous. The moment stretched, paralyzing her. She couldn't breathe.

"Go in, Miss Grey," he said softly, "before I forget I was once a gentleman."

With a gasp, she whisked herself inside and closed the door. Leaning against it, she listened to the incomprehensible thundering of her heart. She thought she heard a faint, deprecating laugh as his footsteps walked on. It seemed his bedchamber, too, was in this part of the house, close to his daughter's. And hers. She wasn't sure why that mattered to her, but it did.

SHE WOKE TO daylight and a strange, soft, scratching noise. Rosa's head poked through the bed curtains while her fingernails scratched at their fabric. She smiled.

"Good morning," Caroline croaked.

Rosa made hasty eating motions with her hands.

"Ah, breakfast!" Caroline sat up in alarm, "Have I slept too long?"

Rosa shook her head, gestured for her to hurry, and skipped back off to her own room.

There was fresh water for washing—she must have been so heavily asleep that she hadn't even heard the maid bringing it. Having attended to her ablutions, she dressed in her usual grey gown and brushed her hair by the mirror provided. As she bundled up her hair and reached for the pins, she caught her own eye in the glass and paused. She rarely looked at herself for longer than it took to ensure her neatness. Today, for some reason, she stared at her austere reflection with disfavor.

Miss Grey the governess, severe, dull, part of the schoolroom furniture.

She released the grip on her hair and shook it about her face and shoulders. She blushed to think that this was how Mr. Benedict had seen her last night—only worse, of course, for she had worn only her flimsy night gown and wrapper.

"Go in, before I forget that I was once a gentleman."

He'd seen her, not as the governess but as a woman. His eyes had been all over her... only for an instant, of course, but he'd liked what he'd seen. Heat spread through her at the memory, at the implication. Just for a moment, he'd been attracted to her. He'd *seen* her.

She touched her cheek, her lips, the corners of her eyes. Her skin was still soft. Her eyes still held the sparkle of life. Her dark blond hair shone with vitality. She was only twenty-eight years old. She should have been a young matron, the mother of Peter...

The old pain of loss cramped her stomach, but it didn't last. For it wasn't Theo's handsome face that swam into her mind. It was Javan Benedict's scarred one.

"Oh, no," she muttered and seized her hair, drawing it into a tight knot at the back of her head. She inserted the pins with unnecessary force and regarded herself somewhat ruefully.

Miss Grey the governess, she mocked, and walked through the connecting door to collect Rosa.

"So, where do we have breakfast?" she asked.

To her surprise, Rosa led her down the quiet staircase to the front hall and then away from the direction of the dining room toward the back of the house. There, they took the stairs to the kitchen, which was empty save for a very thin maid and a fat cook. Neither woman looked remotely surprised to see Rosa.

"Good morning," the cook greeted them cheerfully, pulling two chairs out from the large table in the center of the kitchen. "Sit ye down."

As they sat, the maid set a plate of fresh bread rolls in front of them with a slab of butter. The girl smiled at Rosa and, more timidly, at Caroline.

"You'll be the new governess," Cook said comfortably, returning to her frying pan.

"Caroline Grey." She reached for a roll. "They smell delicious."

"I'm Betty Smith, the cook. This here is Nan the kitchen maid. Is it true you've come from the castle? I used to work there. How is everything?"

"Well, I believe."

"Broke my heart not to be able to see Lady Serena get married. I saw her sister, Lady Frances, marry a year or so back, but I was working at the castle then. This time, for Lady Serena's, I couldn't get away. She'll have been a beautiful bride."

"Indeed she was."

"So, what brings you from there to the hall?" Mrs. Smith asked with open curiosity.

"I go where I'm told," Caroline said lightly, nodding her thanks to Nan the maid who presented her with a steaming hot cup of coffee. "I suppose his lordship felt the young ladies deserved a little time off lessons, while Mr. Benedict clearly felt Rosa should have some time *on*."

Rosa grinned around her roll.

"Do we always have breakfast in the kitchen?" Caroline asked her.

Rosa nodded.

"The others have breakfast in their chambers as a rule," Cook said, waddling over with a plate of ham and eggs. "Only Miss Rosa likes company in the morning."

The child smiled gratefully and helped herself.

"Well," Caroline said, when even Rosa appeared to be full. "Shall we have a brisk walk before we begin lessons?"

Rosa nodded with enthusiasm. Jumping to her feet, she gestured for Caroline to wait and ran off, leaping up the stairs two at a time.

Caroline swallowed the last of her coffee. "I expect she's gone to find the dog."

"And her father," Cook said.

Caroline's heart gave a little lurch at the prospect of Mr. Benedict's company. She wasn't sure if it was dismay or excitement.

"She goes to see him every morning after her breakfast," Cook went on. "I think she's afraid he'll vanish, poor dear." She glanced at Nan, who was some yards away, noisily loading pans and crockery into a bowl for washing. Lowering her voice, she added, "Not surprised, the goings-on in this house."

As the governess, Caroline was, of course, above such below-stairs gossip—although Lord Braithwaite had implied she would find a trusted ally in the cook. Taking her hesitation for encouragement, Cook said, "The child loves them, of course, but it's no wonder she doesn't speak. They're both mad."

"Who is mad?" Caroline asked, slightly bewildered.

"The master, of course," Cook said, as if Caroline was proving herself to be little better. "*And* Miss Benedict. Ha, *Miss Benedict* indeed! According to him, she's his sister, but it's my belief she's *Mrs.* Benedict, and he doesn't want anyone to know!"

Caroline frowned. "You're saying the lady who has taken to her room is his *wife?*"

"Hush, Miss, none of *them* would ever admit it." Cook jerked her head at Nan, presumably encompassing all the servants the Benedicts had brought with them. From wherever they'd been before. Cook lowered her voice further. "It's not so much that she *takes* to her room. It's that he locks her in there!"

Caroline's eyes widened.

"And before you tell me it's lies and gossip, I saw it with my own eyes. Took her hot chocolate up to her chamber myself one morning—maids had come down with something and there was only Williams and me on our feet. I couldn't get in. Then he—the master—turns up, casual as you please, and unlocks the door!"

"I can't see why that makes her his wife," Caroline observed. She shouldn't be allowing this conversation at all. She stood up.

Cook blinked at her. "He wouldn't bring his mad old sister with him, would he?" she said reasonably. "But not much he can do about a wife. I know they say in Blackhaven that he murdered her, but I don't believe that. Besides, the girl is clearly fond of her. And his people, the servants, won't talk about how the wife is supposed to have died. They don't talk about her at all. Or the sister. It isn't natural. Mix that up with how this house is haunted and—"

"You don't enjoy your work here, Mrs. Smith?" Caroline interrupted, a shade desperately. Lord Braithwaite might have imagined she and the cook could be allies, but Caroline already felt appallingly disloyal. She had to nip this gossip in the bud.

"Well, as to that—" Cook began.

Caroline hurried toward the stairs. "I'm very glad to have met you, Mrs. Smith. Thank you for the delicious breakfast. I'd better hurry and meet Miss Rosa."

She found her own way to the side door and was tying her bonnet when Rosa and Tiny came flying around the corner. Although Caroline held her breath, no uneven footsteps followed them. Only as they returned from their short walk, did she catch a glimpse of her employer, and that was when Rosa waved up at one of the windows of the house. A dark shadowy figure moved away, just as Caroline glanced up.

"Was that your father?" she asked, and the girl nodded happily. "Well, he will expect us to do some work. So, let us go and begin."

"WRITE ABOUT YOUR family and your home, so that I might know them as well as you do." Caroline generally began her first lesson with new pupils in this way. She found it a useful gauge to a child's skill with the English language as well as other areas of necessary education. Besides which, it provided her with useful clues about the new family she was working for.

In Rosa's case, she was conscious of a too-urgent desire to know more, and not just to discover if Cook could be right in her speculations. She wanted to know about Mr. Benedict for his own good. And the lady who'd thrown the cake at him. And she didn't want rumor and superstition. She wanted truth.

While Rosa wrote, Caroline continued looking at her previous work, and discovered her pupil to be good at sketching and painting. One notebook was filled with colored pictures of leaves, flowers, and descriptions, complete with Latin and common names.

"Who taught you this?" Caroline asked when Rosa brought her work over.

Rosa smiled and pointed to the essay she'd just written. In particular, she pointed to the first paragraph which she'd titled: *My Father, Javan Benedict.*

"Your father teaches you botany?" Caroline said in surprise, and when the girl nodded, Caroline smiled. "It is beautifully done. Now, let me see your new work."

Rosa released it to her but made urgent eating motions with her hand.

Caroline glanced at the watch she had pinned to her gown. "Is it time for luncheon already? You had better run and wash your hands."

While Rosa ran off to obey, Caroline glanced quickly at the essay. The second paragraph was *My Aunt, Marjorie Benedict.*

"Ha," Caroline said aloud with triumph, before the third paragraph caught her attention. *My Governess, Miss Grey. Miss Grey's services have been kindly lent to us by the Earl of Braithwaite, who lives in the castle. She is kind, clever, and pretty. Both my father and I like her because her eyes laugh, though they don't always. Sometimes I think she might be sadder than she seems, but I hope she is not unhappy to be at Haven Hall.*

Caroline shifted uncomfortably. Was it not speaking that made the child so perceptive? Rosa went on to talk about the servants, including the manservant Williams, whom she called her father's valet who came home with her father and *takes care of everything for us.*

Came home with him... a curious turn of phrase.

Nan, Mrs. Smith, and the other servants were all listed as people who looked after the family. Even Tiny had his own, disproportionately long paragraph. Well, there were more funny stories to tell about him than about anyone else.

But it was an odd household that had no housekeeper and no butler. She had never heard of a valet being in charge of the servants before.

Smiling, Caroline returned to the beginning, to the passage about Mr. Benedict. She felt strange reading this, as though she were prying. *Papa is very good and strong and protects me, even when he is convalescing. He is also very clever and always wins at jackstraws. He can make anything funny and he understands everything.*

Caroline frowned. These lines seemed to throw up more questions than they answered. *Protects me...* Why did Rosa imagine she needed protection? Was it just a child feeling safe with her father? A word he'd said, perhaps, when she was afraid of monsters under the bed—*Don't worry, nothing can harm you, I will protect you*? He had sat by her bed last night until she was asleep.

And what was it, exactly, that he understood? Why Rosa didn't speak? Or was she simply a child in awe of her omnipotent father's cleverness?

On top of all that, most people would probably have struggled with the idea of the harsh-faced, taciturn Benedict making everything *funny...*

Hastily, Caroline set the notebook aside and hurried to wash her hands for luncheon.

When she entered the dining room, Rosa and her father were already there. Mr. Benedict stood and, to her surprise, held her chair for her to sit.

"Forgive my tardiness," she apologized. "I got caught up reading Rosa's work of this morning. You are very observant and articulate, Rosa. I feel I know everyone so much better now."

Rosa beamed under the praise. Caroline felt Mr. Benedict's gaze burning into her face, but she concentrated on Rosa and her food.

"Rosa, do you play the pianoforte? Or any other musical instrument?"

Rosa's eyes widened. She shook her head vigorously.

"Is there such a thing in the house, sir?" Caroline asked, braving the harsh gaze.

"There's a pianoforte in the ante-room off the drawing room," he said with odd reluctance. "Why? Do you play?"

"Adequately enough to teach Rosa. It is a necessary accomplishment for a young lady."

His lips twisted. "Of course. It's under Holland covers and I've no idea what state it's in but make free with it by all means. Williams will help you if you need to move it."

"Thank you."

"Can you tune it as well?" he asked with false civility.

"Enough to erase the worst faults," she replied calmly. "If you have the correct tools. But there is a piano tuner in Blackhaven, a retired musician, whom Lady Braithwaite called upon."

Benedict shifted his gaze to his daughter. "Do you wish to learn?"

For some reason, Rosa hesitated, then nodded.

Mr. Benedict shrugged. "Then by all means, try it. Tell me if it needs even greater skills than you possess."

It felt like a small victory.

When she had eaten her fill, Rosa again caught her attention, spread her fingers on an imaginary keyboard, and wiggled them.

"Later," Caroline said. "First, arithmetic."

Rosa wrinkled her nose.

"Go up to the schoolroom and find for me the most difficult calculations you've completed. I will be up directly, after I've spoken to your father."

"You have work for me, too?" Benedict drawled, making Rosa grin over her shoulder before she ran off.

"Would you do it if I had?" she retorted.

He laughed. "I might. I just might."

"I shall bear it in mind," she said wryly. "For now, I merely wished to talk to you about Rosa's speech. Or lack of it."

"Oh?"

"I was wondering...has she ever slipped up and let a word fall? Does she ever laugh or cry aloud?"

His face remained impassive. "Nothing more than a guttural...growl for want of a better word, and that only when something has startled or frightened her. In the year since I have been home, I have never heard her utter a word. Why?"

"She is very articulate on paper. She reads and thinks and observes *in words*. I am at a loss as to why she won't say them. Is it grief over her mother's death or illness?"

"She'd stopped talking nearly a year before my wife died. I found her like this when I came home."

Caroline frowned, deep in thought. "And could your wife offer no insight?"

"None that she shared with me. With respect, Miss Grey, your task is to teach her. For the rest, we have doctors."

"But you said it was not a medical problem," Caroline pointed out. "And as for teaching, I would be failing in my duties if I didn't at least try to teach her to speak again."

"In the one week or two which you have allotted to us?" he retorted.

Caroline flushed. "I always work to the best of my ability. Should I have a scale of effort to match the time I spend with my pupils?"

She knew, as the words spilled out, that it was insolence. As his eyebrows flew up, she bit her lip, waiting to be dismissed—from the room at the very least. But again, he surprised her.

"I've hurt your feelings. I apologize," he said curtly. "If you can make her speak, we would both be forever in your debt. I merely doubt the possibility. However, if you are asking for my permission to try, you have it, on condition you say or do nothing to upset her or hurt her."

"I agree, of course," Caroline said at once. "Which is why I was asking for some clue as to the circumstances. I don't wish to say anything to upset her, or subject her to any hurtful influence."

"If I knew the circumstances, I would tell you. As I said, I was away at the time. Neither my wife nor the servants could elucidate."

"The servants here were with her at the time?"

He nodded. "Except for Williams. And the cook."

Of course, Williams, as his valet, would have been with him, wherever he was.

Caroline nodded thoughtfully and rose to her feet. "Thank you," she said, walking away.

Civilly, he rose with her. On impulse, realizing it must have seemed an abrupt departure, she glanced back over her shoulder. He was watching her, his eyes alight with amusement and something vaguely predatory that reminded her of last night's encounter at her bedchamber door.

Chapter Four

THE FOLLOWING EVENING, while Mr. Benedict sat with Rosa in her chamber, Caroline took a candle and went to the library. She went partly to find a new book to read, and partly to avoid the strange bated breath with which she seemed to await Mr. Benedict's departure from his daughter's room. Shut up in the library, she would not hear his uneven footsteps or imagine his hand raised to knock at her door.

She found the library, a rather dusty room with a large and ancient fireplace, in total darkness. By the light of her own candle, she discovered others and lit them from hers. She carried one with her as she prowled along the book-lined walls, examining titles and occasionally kneeling on the floor with a book to look further.

Overall, it was a motley collection, with nothing about plants that she could discover, so she doubted they were Benedict's books. It must have belonged to the house's owners, the tragic Gardyn family whose last heir had vanished as a child. Most people believed she was dead, but without proof, the estate was apparently kept in trust for her by distant family.

Caroline hated to think of dead or frightened children, so she hastily plucked a novel off the shelf to distract herself and went to the window seat to read. Neither the shutters nor the curtains had been drawn, so although it was rather chilly without a fire, she could press her back to the wall and occasionally glance up from her book to the dark, starkly beautiful scenery that surrounded the hall. All that was missing was the sea. At Braithwaite Castle, you could see the water from almost every side.

She allowed herself a moment to think of the Braithwaite girls and miss them. But since sentiment achieved nothing, she concentrated determinedly on *Pamela*.

Soft, uneven footsteps passed the library and hurried down the stairs. Mr. Benedict, no doubt, going back to his study instead of to his bedchamber. Even here, she was aware of his movements.

Drawing the shawl tighter around her, she read on. Another ten minutes and she would return to her cozy bedchamber.

Without warning, the library door banged shut.

Caroline jumped, dropping the book, which tumbled onto the floor. How had the door banged? She'd closed it when she'd come in. She rose, picked up the book, and hastened to the door. Pulling it open, she gazed onto the dark landing. A light shone under the drawing room door, and she had just taken a step toward it when she glimpsed something from the corner of her eye, something flitting silently past at the foot of the stairs.

Uneasily, she relit her candle and walked downstairs to investigate. But before she was half way down, a strange, unearthly howl filled her ears, making the hairs on her neck stand on end. It didn't sound like the same crying she'd heard emanating from Miss Benedict's room. It seemed to come from downstairs, though she supposed Miss Benedict could move around the house if she chose. Unless Betty Smith was right that Javan Benedict locked her in.

This was a truly bizarre household.

The howl came again, more distant. Her curiosity thoroughly aroused—along with a desire to make it stop in case it woke and frightened Rosa—she ran the rest of the way downstairs, following what she thought was the direction of the noise, across the entrance hall to the passage that led to the side door and the study beyond.

Rounding the corner at full tilt, she ran up against something— someone—hurtling in the opposite direction. She gasped in shock as hands seized her by the shoulders and her candle wobbled precarious- ly, it's flame flickering wildly over the face of her assailant. Javan Benedict.

Fortunately, he looked as stunned as she. "Miss Grey!" he exclaimed. "What the devil are you doing?"

"I heard something, a howling," she blurted. "I thought it came from this direction."

"And I from the other," he said ruefully. He didn't seem to be aware he still held her by the shoulders, the candle squashed dangerously between them. "The layout of this house seems to bounce sound so that you cannot locate it. Where were you?"

"I was in the library and the door banged. I came out to investigate and I thought I saw something downstairs, and then I heard the howling."

"The library door?" he repeated. "That's interesting." He released her without apology and took the candle from her before striding on down the passage back to the entrance hall.

Since she didn't know what else to do, she trotted after him. At last, as they crossed the hall, she said, low, "Why is the library interesting?"

She froze as he whipped around and thrust one finger over her lips. Although quite clearly a demand for silence—and an irritable one at that—his touch seemed to fizz through her. It only lasted a moment, though, for a knocking sound above was swiftly followed by a most horrible screeching and clanking. Like the clanking chains she'd heard tell of Blackhaven. A shudder ran through her.

Forgetting about silence, Benedict broke into a run, taking the stairs three at a time, while Caroline hurried after him. She held onto the bannister as a guide, since she could barely make out any of the bouncing light carried by her employer.

He threw open the library door, allowing some of the light from there to spill out. Relieved, Caroline ran up the last couple of steps and followed him inside. Apart from Mr. Benedict, the room was empty. He stood in the middle, slowly turning to peer into every corner.

"The library is interesting," he said without interrupting his deliberate search, "because he has never been there before. Or at least made no noise there. It has always been on the ground floor."

"He?" she pounced. "Then someone *was* here?"

"Do you believe in ghosts, Miss Grey?" he asked, blowing out her candle and setting it down on the table.

"No."

"Neither do I. Therefore, I believe it was quite distinctly a *live* someone."

"Who?" she asked bewildered.

"Someone who wants to frighten us away, I suspect, as they frightened previous tenants."

She searched his face and shivered. It was the intruder who should have been frightened. "You're not afraid," she observed.

"No, but I won't have him frightening Rosa, so I *will* put a stop to it."

"How often does this happen?" she asked.

He shrugged. "Several times within a couple of weeks when we first came. Lately, only once or twice a month. As if they lost heart because we didn't immediately run but can't quite give up what worked so well for them in the past."

"Does Rosa hear the commotion?"

"Not so far. It always happens around this time, when she is already asleep and fortunately, she sleeps deeply. Otherwise, I doubt we would still be here. He doesn't go near people, even the servants, just makes noises from a distance. His aim is to scare not to harm."

"Do you know who it is?"

He shrugged. "One of the local well-to-do farmers who wants to buy up the hall and grounds cheaply. While the estate still makes money from the rent of the hall, the trustees are less likely to sell it. At least, that's all I can think of. I'd suspect it was young boys out for a lark, except I'm fairly sure there's only one of them."

"But how does he get in?" Caroline wondered.

"Incisive as always," Benedict said with unexpected approval. "I wondered if he might have an old key, but I had all the locks changed, and still he comes in. My money now is on some kind of secret passage. Do you know what I think?"

She frowned, her breath catching with the possibility. "That the passage opens here in the library! No one uses this room. He came in earlier and tried to leave by the same means, only *I* was here and he rushed out in shock, letting the door bang behind him!" She frowned. "But the howling came *after* the door banged."

"Maybe this wasn't a howling night," he said flippantly. "Sometimes, he just moves things around. We find boots in the dining room, a fruit bowl on the hall stand, a painting on the wrong wall. I think he howled to get you out of the library so he could get in unobserved. He won't have expected you to follow him, so I do hope you gave him a fright."

"So do I! Have you reported these intrusions to the magistrate?"

"No, I couldn't abide the fuss. I'll deal with it myself."

"If you know who it is, perhaps you should call on him and make it clear you know. Frighten him."

"I tried that. I think it is Nairn's son from White Farm. But old Nairn refused to take the hint. He denied it to my face, in fact, but he knew more than he pretended."

"That was when the visitations lessened?" she asked.

He nodded, casting her a curious glance. "You're very quick witted, Miss Grey."

"Thank you."

He sank onto the window seat she had vacated only minutes before and fixed her with his direct, curious gaze. "Are *you* not frightened away by this intrusion?"

She thought about it. It might have been his presence, but she didn't feel scared at all. "No. I believe I would like *him* frightened off. He may be no physical threat to Rosa, but any stranger in her home is alarming and inexcusable. Hence my advice to inform the magistrate. Mr. Winslow is most helpful."

"He may be, but I shall have him—our intruder—next time. All I have to do is find where the passage opens."

Caroline frowned. "The clanking we heard must have been the secret door opening and closing." She went to the fireplace wall, knocking it in various places with her knuckles in search of a hollow sound. The big fireplace made a likelier noise, so, under his apparently amused scrutiny, she knocked and poked in various places, eventually crouching down to try the lower tiles and twisting the decorative roses at the bottom.

"Enough, Miss Grey," came his voice behind her, so close that it made her jump. She had been so involved in finding the passage that she hadn't seen him move. His boots were planted close beside her. His hand appeared as he bent to help her rise. "While I appreciate your enthusiasm, I fear your continuous knocking is more likely than the howling to disturb Rosa and Marjorie."

She flushed and tried to rise without his aid, but he caught her fingers and tugged her to her feet more swiftly than she was prepared for. She clutched the mantelpiece with her free hand, while he held on to her hand until she was steady.

"I apologize," she said, mortified. "I'm afraid I got stupidly carried away. You are quite right."

He stood too close. His warmth seemed to seep into her own. She could smell his distinctive scent, soap and sandalwood, and the hint of wine on his breath. Though it took conscious bravery to meet and hold his gaze, he did not appear to be angry. In fact, there was a hint of humor in those hard, grey eyes.

"There is no need for apologies," he said mildly. "If Williams and I find it tomorrow, you will be the first to know. Though we had best keep it from Rosa, at least until we've caught the miscreant and blocked up the passage."

"She is bound to hear you knocking from the schoolroom," Caroline pointed out.

"Then we'll pretend to be checking for woodworm."

"And if you don't find the passage?"

"Williams or I will sit in here every evening until our intruder returns. One way or another, we will find it."

His eyes weren't really hard at all, she decided, just veiled, secretive. In fact, reflecting the glow of the candles on the mantel shelf, they were warm, intense and rather beautiful. The shadows emphasized the strong lines and hollows of his face, and she had the sudden, insane urge to touch the ridged scar on his cheek.

Somehow, she managed to nod. She didn't seem able to breathe freely enough to speak. His lips curved into a faint smile, drawing her gaze, and her wayward thoughts. How would they feel against hers? How did such a man as Javan Benedict kiss?

Shocked by her own speculation, she almost snatched her hand free and slipped past him.

"Yes, please do let me know what you find," she managed to say as she walked to the door. "I shall be most intrigued. Goodnight, Mr. Benedict."

She wasn't sure he answered, but she did feel the heat of his gaze burning into the back of her neck as she fled.

Chapter Five

IT WAS SOME days before Serena, the new Marchioness of Tamar, noticed the absence of her sisters' governess. For one thing, she was absorbed in the wonder of her marriage and the joy of being with her new husband. For another, no one troubled to mention it to her. She only discovered it when Tamar set up his easel in their bedchamber one morning, and she used the opportunity offered by his preoccupation to go in search of her sisters.

Her sisters had visited her new apartments several times since the wedding, and she and Tamar had dined with the family after her mother and brother's failed departure for London. But Miss Grey's absence had, stupidly, not occurred to her until she walked into the schoolroom and found it empty. When calling for her sisters elicited no response, she wandered down to the drawing room. In the long gallery, she encountered her brother, striding off to his study, no doubt, since the steward was at his heels.

"Gervaise, where are the girls?" Serena asked. "Are they out somewhere in the rain with Miss Grey?"

Braithwaite paused. "Ah. Go on to the study," he instructed his steward. "I'll join you directly. Serena..." Drawing her further away from the drawing room, where, no doubt, their mother lurked, he said low, "I've been meaning to talk to you about Miss Grey. She had a letter from home that upset her."

"She's gone home?" Serena said in surprise. "I wish she would have said goodbye!"

"Well, no, not home," Braithwaite said uncomfortably. "I found her alone in the schoolroom—upset, as I said—when I was looking for the girls. I stayed to offer a word of comfort, and of course, Mother walked in and immediately read the worst into an entirely innocent situation. The devil was in it that the door had blown over and she chose to believe Miss Grey had closed it deliberately and was somehow trying to trap or inveigle me into marriage."

Serena's jaw dropped. "*Miss Grey?*"

"Well, exactly. I won't say I haven't noticed her because I have. But I would no more act upon it than…than…well, I just wouldn't! Besides, she is so proper and efficient that I have no idea where mother got the stupid notion. She could easily have passed it off, but she chose to dismiss Miss Grey on the spot."

"She what?" Serena said furiously. "And for such a reason? Has she any idea how that will affect Miss Grey's future?"

"None, until she stops and thinks about it. Which she will, eventually, as you know. And she will be sorry in the end, so I sent Miss Grey up to Haven Hall for a week or two while Mother cools off."

"*Haven Hall?*" Serena repeated in accents of horror. "How could you, Gervaise? What on earth is there for her in that place?"

"A pupil," Braithwaite said impatiently. "Benedict has a daughter. Benedict being the tenant himself, whom I ran into when I was riding last week."

"What is he like?" Serena asked, distracted in spite of herself. "Miss Grey encountered him while walking one day and found him strange and grumpy."

Her brother shrugged. "Well, I wouldn't say he was friendly, but he was not boorish."

"How did you find out he had a daughter?"

"She was with him," Braithwaite said in surprise. "Didn't I tell you that? Pretty child but shy. A year or so younger than Helen, perhaps."

"And was he kind to the child?" Serena asked anxiously.

Braithwaite blinked. "Well, he did not beat her in front of me! But she looked perfectly content to be with him, if that's what you mean. Listen, though, since you brought the subject up, Mother and I are making another attempt to go to London tomorrow, now that the wretched coach is finally repaired. I shall have to write when Mother relents about Miss Grey."

"You'll forget to ask her," Serena said indignantly. "Why don't I just bring Miss Grey back once you've gone? Then you may write here whenever you remember to get Mama to relent and I'll write back as though I've only just brought her."

Braithwaite scowled. "You are untruthful and Machiavellian," he said severely and strode away. It was noticeable, however, that he had not forbidden her. Not that Braithwaite's prohibition would have made the slightest difference to Serena.

CONSIDERING THE ODDITY of the household, Caroline grew used to it much more quickly than she'd expected. Although the morning after the intruder's visit, several items including umbrellas, hats, and plates had indeed been moved randomly around the ground floor, it didn't reoccur over the next week. She knew either Williams or Mr. Benedict spent time in the library each evening in the hope of catching the intruder, but without any luck. Nor did they find a way to open the passage they were convinced was there. Caroline knew, because she made a point of asking Mr. Benedict.

Neither, fortunately, was there a repeat of the heartrending cries of that first night, though Caroline confirmed a little more about their origin. One day, when she went looking for Rosa after luncheon, she found her in one of the bedchambers on the other side of the house from the schoolroom—the same chamber, she was sure, where she'd seen Mr. Benedict waiting that first night.

This time the door was open, as were the bed curtains inside. The lady who'd thrown the cake the day Caroline had arrived lay on the bed. Miss Marjorie Benedict. Rosa stretched out beside her, gently stroking her hair.

It was a private scene, and Caroline chose not to interrupt it. She withdrew silently and went to the schoolroom to wait for Rosa.

That evening, when she and Rosa entered the dining room, Miss Benedict was already there, flitting around the table as though checking the simple place settings were in order. Rosa ran to her immediately and hugged her, receiving a hug in return, after which she took her aunt's hand and all but dragged her toward Caroline.

Caroline curtsied.

"Ah, you are Miss Grey," the lady said with a surprisingly sweet smile. Close to her, Caroline could see family likeness, not only to Rosa but to Mr. Benedict. There was something around her eyes and the shape of her face. In Miss Benedict, the features were softened, but she was quite clearly related.

So much for the cook's conviction that she was his wife.

Miss Benedict offered her hand. "I have heard so much about you. Welcome to Haven Hall. I have been ill, you understand, or I would have welcomed you before and helped you find your feet here. Is everything comfortable for you?"

"Most comfortable, thank you."

At that moment, Mr. Benedict limped in. "Well met, Marjorie," he said without any surprise. "I see you've introduced yourself to Miss Grey. Shall we sit? The soup is on its way."

There was certainly more chatter at dinner than Caroline had grown used to. Miss Benedict initiated conversation on many topics, from the latest novels to possible peace with France, interspersing it all with questions about Caroline's teaching experience. It was kindly done, as though the lady were satisfying herself as to the new governess's suitability without appearing to be interviewing her. Caroline knew she was right when she intercepted Mr. Benedict's sardonic glance.

He said little on any subject, merely smiled sourly when Bonaparte and the French were mentioned. Clearly, he had opinions he chose not to share. Intrigued, Caroline opened her mouth to ask him, but his sister had changed topics suddenly.

"And do you find our Rosa a good pupil?"

Caroline turned to her civilly. "Indeed I do."

"Is her learning advanced for her age?" Miss Benedict inquired.

"In some areas, yes," Caroline replied.

"Just in some?" Miss Benedict seemed inclined to take umbrage at this.

"For her years, she is excellent at reading and writing, arithmetic, geography, and the sciences," Caroline replied. "It is only in the ladylike accomplishments that she has little training so far. But she is quick, and the matter is easily remedied." Caroline caught her pupil's gaze with mock severity. "If she works hard."

Rosa gave her a mischievous smile.

"Ladylike accomplishments," Miss Benedict repeated in triumph. "Well, there you are. Javan does not have many of those."

Caroline's gaze flew to Benedict's. "*You* have been teaching, Rosa?"

His lips twisted into a wry smile. "Is it so hard to believe I have been educated, too?"

"Of course not," Caroline said hurriedly. "Then it's from you she developed her interest in botany?"

"It's a hobby of mine," Mr. Benedict allowed.

"Hobby," his sister disparaged. "He is most learned, is even writing a book on the subject."

"But even I know music and watercolors are more important to a young lady's education than botany," Mr. Benedict said. "Hence, the necessity of a governess."

An idea arrived in Caroline's head. "If you wish her to be a cut above the ordinary in painting, I believe I could arrange a few lessons with Lord Tamar, who is Lord Braithwaite's brother-in-law and a most accomplished artist—"

"No, that won't be necessary," Mr. Benedict interrupted. "*You* are tasked with teaching my daughter."

Caroline flushed. "Of course," she said stiffly. "I beg your pardon."

She was spared further embarrassment by the entry of the servants to clear the plates and serve the pudding.

Abruptly, Mr. Benedict said, "How do you find the piano?"

It might have been an olive branch, or a way of showing her he was not angered by her presumption. Or he might just have thought of it.

"A little out of tune," she replied. "But not enough to hurt the ears. Otherwise, it works perfectly. We have had only a couple of lessons so far, but I believe Rosa is enjoying it."

Rosa nodded enthusiastically, and Miss Benedict began to plan her niece's first recital.

WHEN ROSA WAS in bed, Caroline read to her for a little, before handing the book over. They agreed Rosa should read by herself until her father came to say goodnight. Caroline was just crossing to the door which connected to her own chamber, when the passage door opened and Mr. Benedict came in. He paused at sight of her, as though surprised.

"Good night, sir," she said civilly.

Unexpectedly, he changed direction, and opened her bedchamber door. "Good night, Miss Grey."

There was something unspeakably intimate about walking past him into her bedchamber. It wasn't just that he controlled the door, or that crossing the threshold brought her so close to him that she could smell the warm spice of his skin and the wine and coffee on his breath. She made the mistake of glancing up at him to prove she was not intimidated. His hard, grey eyes glowed in the candle light, flaming with a heat that seemed to scorch her. Her stomach plunged as she recognized the look for what it was. Lust.

Go in before I forget I was once a gentleman.

By the time he closed the door softly behind her, his heat seemed to have spread to her own trembling body. She released her breath in a rush, trying to laugh at herself or him, wondering which of them she truly feared.

WITH THE KNOWLEDGE of his presence on the other side of the door, Caroline's foolish heart beat too quickly to allow her to settle to anything. Which was ridiculous, since this happened every evening. This time, was just *more*.

But she would not think of that. In desperation, she lit another candle and took out her sewing box. She'd retrieved two pairs of Rosa's stockings which needed mending, and now, suddenly, seemed the best time to do it.

While she worked, the occasional murmur from the other chamber died away. She heard a faint rustle, his uneven footfall as he crossed the room. She held her breath, waiting for what, she couldn't imagine, although she'd lowered her work into her lap and all her concentration focused on the connecting door. She even imagined a hesitation in his step...before it continued and Rosa's door to the passage opened and softly closed, and his footsteps faded on into the distance.

She released her breath in a rush of relief. At least, she called it relief, though the feeling was made up of so many more conflicting emotions, including a bizarre disappointment, and a wish that things were different. That *she* was different.

Taking herself to task, she forced her brain and body to calm by concentrating once more on her mending. It wasn't easy in the dim light, especially as the rising wind now rattled the window panes and made the candles flicker, but she didn't make a bad job of it. After that, she began to patch together some old material she'd horded over the years to make a lining for her old boots. It might provide some protection from the rain until she could get to the cobbler in Blackhaven.

She had to stop in the end because her eyes were too tired to see properly. The rain battered against her window in a sudden squall. Caroline put another shawl around her shoulders to protect against the fierce draughts and huddled a little closer to the fire while she finished her letter home.

She had been waiting to hear from her mother that she had received the money she'd sent via Lord Braithwaite, hoping to hear good news of Peter's health before she sent her own letter. She could only suppose the silence meant the emergency was over, but anxiety nagged at her. She finished her letter with an urgent appeal for her mother—or Eliza—to write back at once, even if only a few words to tell her Peter was recovering.

Finally, she thought she might be tired enough to sleep. It was late. Even the servants had retired and the house would have been quiet save for the storm raging outside. On impulse, she walked to the window and drew back the curtain and the shutter. The night sky was filthy, thick, scudding clouds obscuring the moon and stars. The rain had let up, in a temporary kind of way but the wind, lashing and bending the trees, was, if anything, even fiercer.

Caroline began to close the shutter again, when something below caught her eye. A dark, male figure moving from the house through the untamed garden toward the encroaching woods. Their intruder? Had he been into the house again? So far as she knew, neither Mr. Benedict nor Williams had found the entrance to the suspected secret passage, despite a thorough "examination for woodworm". But there was nothing furtive about the man outside. He simply ploughed his way through the wind and rain. Why? Where on earth could he be going? Certainly, it was a wild night for a tryst.

"True love," Caroline murmured disparagingly, but still her hand lingered on the shutter, holding it open, for though she could barely make out the shape, let alone the features of the brave figure, he moved in a slow, uneven manner. With a limp.

Her breath caught, just as a flash of lightning lit the sky and the lame man below. He wore no coat or hat but walked determinedly through the storm in his shirt sleeves.

Something was wrong. It had to be. No one in their right mind would go out in this weather, even for a secret tryst, dressed like that. There had to be an emergency, and it was her instinct to help.

Thunder rumbled and cracked. Without hesitation, she snatched up a candle and ran out of the room, along the corridor and downstairs, veering along the passage that led to the side door. It stood open, the wind holding it right back against the wall. Shocked by the cold and the force of it, Caroline only just managed to spin around to protect her candle flame. Hastily, she used it to light the lantern by the coat stand. She paused only long enough to haul her cloak about her and seize up the lantern and Mr. Benedict's old great coat that hung on the stand. Then, dragging her hood up, she ran outside and pulled the door closed behind her.

Helped by the wind, which blew her along rather faster than she would normally have run, she hurtled toward the wood, in the direction she'd last seen Mr. Benedict. Several things bothered her. Why hadn't *he* taken the lantern? Why had he not even donned the greatcoat or closed the door? How could he even see where he was going?

Another flash of lightning showed the white of his shirt vanishing into the wood. Holding the lantern in front of her, she hurried after him as the thunder crashed overhead. The force of the rain was almost painful now, blasting against the side of her face when she swerved into the wood.

"Sir!" she called. "Mr. Benedict, wait!" Holding the lantern high, she paused, searching between the trees. There. Only a few yards ahead. The wind must have whipped her voice away, for he didn't appear to have heard her. At least he was following the track. She ran after him, calling again.

Still he didn't turn. Exhausted, she caught up with him and in desperation, grasped his drenched arm. "Sir, please, what is—" She got no further, for he whirled around, throwing off her detaining hand, and shoved her roughly away.

Shocked, she stumbled back against a tree, too winded to speak. But surely, he had heard her voice? Surely, he could see who she was by the light of the lantern which she'd somehow managed to hold on to?

He flew after her so ferociously that she threw up her arms in defense. He merely knocked them aside with one hand and the lantern finally fell to the ground, casting the light upward over his scarred, agonized face. He thrust one arm over her throat and drew back his other fist to strike.

Lightning burst across the sky at almost the same moment as the thunder crashed.

"Don't you dare," she said furiously, even while something inside her seemed to die at the very idea that he would hurt her.

Abruptly, his face changed. The weird light and shadow cast by the fallen lantern remained the same, but the strange, blank agony vanished, leaving him bewildered. His fist opened and fell to his side. He released her neck and instead, dragged her into his arms.

"Dear God," he whispered. "What am I doing here? What are you...?" He swallowed convulsively. Water streamed off him. His clothing was utterly soaked, leaving little barrier between them. His breath heaved. "Jesus, not this... I dream, I sleepwalk..." His lips dragged across her ear, her cheek, interspersing his words with short, desperate kisses of remorse. "Know I would never hurt you, not knowingly..."

She threw back her head, trying to tell him she wasn't hurt. "Sir, you did not—" The rest of her words were lost as his kiss landed on her upturned lips. Stunned, she didn't move.

"I wouldn't," he said unsteadily against her mouth and then his lips sank deeper as though trying to convince her, or himself. In spite of the cold and the rain and the thunder bellowing across the night, heat flamed through her body. She was aware of every hard inch of him, not just his urgent, pleading mouth.

"I'm not," she whispered against his lips. "Sir, you did not hurt me." Certainly not in the way he meant.

His lips left her trembling mouth. For an instant his forehead touched hers. "Thank God," he muttered. And then, without stepping back, he gazed around, as if really seeing where they were for the first time.

"Oh, Christ," he uttered, and choked on something very like a laugh. He bent and swept up the lantern, still miraculously alight, and as he straightened, she thrust his overcoat between them like a shield.

"I brought you this," she said, as though offering a gift on a social occasion.

Again, his breath caught, but he made no move to take it from her. She shook it out and flung it up over his shoulders, standing on tiptoe to do it. Impatiently, he thrust his arms through the sleeves. "Thank you," he muttered. "Come, let's get back to the house."

She jumped when he threw his arm around her waist, but there seemed to be nothing either loverlike or threatening about the gesture, merely a desire to hurry her. In fact, she understood there was nothing loverlike about any of his actions, even his kisses. He was merely acting from shock at waking from his dream here, in such weather, and from fear and remorse at what he'd done or might have done.

"Does this happen to you often?" she managed over the noise of the wind.

"Not now. Only occasionally. But what are *you* doing out here?"

"I saw you from my window. I thought you were running to some emergency and I wanted to help."

"Well, you did. God knows where I'd have ended up if you hadn't wakened me. I'm grateful, though I shouldn't be."

The storm seemed to be grumbling its way past, but the rain still lashed into them and the wind fought them most of the way back to the house.

"Which way did you come out?" he asked.

"By the side door. You'd left it open."

He swore beneath his breath, releasing her at last as they reached the door. Stupidly, she missed the strength of his arm, even soaked and dripping as it was. Ushering her inside, he locked the door behind them, then blew out the lantern and picked up the candle she'd left burning in its holder on the table. There wasn't much of it left.

"Come," he commanded, and she followed along the passage to the closed door that Rosa had once pointed out to her as her father's study. He threw the door wide. "Go in and wait for me there. It will be warmest."

She obeyed, drawn in spite of herself to the fire still burning merrily in the grate. Kneeling on the rug before it, she shook out her cloak and bonnet and gazed around her.

Well-lit by several lamps, the room was dominated by a large mahogany desk, covered with papers and books. Glass cabinets scattered about the room displayed live plants and dried specimens of leaves and flowers. There was also a large couch, on which she suspected he'd been sleeping before he'd walked out of the house, for a blanket seemed to have half-fallen off it.

Caroline sat right down on the rug and drew off her wet boots, then thrust her soaked stockinged feet out toward the fire. The warmth was delicious, almost sensual.

She wondered why she was waiting here, what he wanted to say. To explain, perhaps, about his sleepwalking. Perhaps it would solve a few of the mysteries surrounding him.

Chapter Six

MUCH QUICKER THAN she expected, soft footsteps sounded in the passage outside. Caroline dropped her stretched out foot to the floor and whisked her skirts down to cover it.

Mr. Benedict strode into the room, still shrugging himself into a coat for the sake, presumably, of respectability in her company. Beneath it, he wore a dry white shirt, without a necktie, and a pair of smart buckskins—probably the first garments he had found.

He limped over to the cabinet by the wall, and from the decanter there poured a measure of amber liquid into two glasses. He crossed to the fire and casually held out a glass to her.

"What is it?" she asked, accepting it.

"Brandy." His lips twisted. "Blackhaven's best, I was assured by the rogue who brought it. I assume it has never paid a penny in duty."

"I don't believe it's quite proper for me to drink brandy," she said, eyeing it doubtfully.

He threw himself into the armchair by the fire. "My dear girl, you have just been out alone in a storm at night with a man to whom you are in no way related, the same man you are now closeted with behind a door quite firmly closed. It's a little late to preach propriety to yourself. Drink up—it will warm you."

He raised his glass to her and knocked most of the content down his throat in one swift tilt.

"I could make you hot tea, if you prefer," she offered.

"I don't," he said bluntly.

She sipped the liquid, enjoying the unexpected burn on her tongue and throat.

He watched her for a moment, searching her face. "Tell me truthfully," he commanded. "Did I strike you? Did I hurt you at all?"

She shook her head. "You pushed me away when I tugged your arm to make you halt. But you did not strike me. I am not hurt."

Without warning, he reached down, placed a finger under her chin and tilted it upward, gazing at her neck. "I had my arm across your throat. Is it sore?"

She shook her head, and he released her.

Distractedly, he picked up her discarded boot from the floor and frowned over it. "I'm sorry I frightened you."

"I wouldn't have crept up on you if I'd known you were asleep." She regarded him curiously. "Were you dreaming?"

"Yes. But not about here."

"A nightmare?"

"That, certainly."

"Do you always have the same dream?"

"Variations on a theme. Why do you ask?"

"My nephew walks and cries in his sleep and does not seem to know you when you take him up and carry him back to bed. Afterward, he can't remember his dreams."

"Lucky nephew." His gaze fell away to the boot, which he began to examine, more as an excuse to avoid her gaze, she suspected.

"What do you dream of?" she asked curiously.

He turned the boot up and discovered the hole. "Escape."

That made sense. He had been getting away from the house. "Escape from where?"

"You really don't want to know." He thrust his hand inside the boot, which he cast aside with sudden displeasure. "Your boot is soaked through. The sole is so fine I could pierce it with a finger, and there is a hole in it already. You have a day off on Saturday, do you not?"

They had never discussed such things. "Do I?"

"Yes. Oblige me by going into Blackhaven and ordering a new

pair. They may send me the bill."

Caroline bridled, and his lips curved in mockery.

He reached behind him for the decanter. "I won't have you catching cold and failing to teach my daughter. I require you to have new boots." He raised the decanter to her invitingly, and when she shook her head, merely sloshed brandy into his own empty glass.

"Thank you," she said at last. "If we may count it an advance on my salary."

He sat back, regarding her. "You're very proud, Miss Grey."

"I suppose it is a sin in a mere governess."

His lips curved. "But there is nothing *mere* about you, is there, Miss Grey?"

"I don't know what you mean," she replied with dignity, suspecting him of further mockery.

He only smiled around his glass as he took another mouthful of brandy. "No, I don't suppose you do, and therein lies my salvation."

Disconcerted, she rose to her feet, forgetting that he would stand with her. But although she meant to say goodnight, her slightly desperate gaze landed beyond him to his glass cabinets, which immediately distracted her.

"What are these plants? Are they rare?"

"Yes. Various samples and cuttings I have collected on my travels."

She walked over to the nearest case. "Where have you travelled?"

He shrugged. "Southern Europe, the Ottoman Empire and beyond. India, China. Over many years."

"I would love to see such places," she said wistfully.

"Then you will."

"Perhaps," she replied, unconvinced. "Do you miss travelling? Do you find England boring now?"

There was a pause before he replied. "No. Not just yet."

"What is this flower?" she asked him.

A couple of questions seemed to be enough to unlock his enthusiasm. He told her about the plants and sometimes amusing stories about how he'd come across them. And he talked of his plans to replant some of them in England, breeding them to hardier climates. After some time, she became more intrigued by *his* interest, in the suddenly mobile expressions of his usually harsh face. Whatever lay behind his injuries or his nightmares, this was an uncomplicated enthusiasm.

"I'm boring you," he said at last. "I'm sorry. You want to go to bed."

"I should," she acknowledged. "Since I have work to do tomorrow. But I am fascinated rather than bored."

He looked skeptical as he limped back to the rug by the fire and picked up her damp cloak and hat and boots, which were gently steaming in the heat. "Saturday," he said, dropping them into her waiting arms.

She took them with an uncertain smile and inclined her head. His scar stood out lividly against the swarthy skin of his face. His nearness did strange things to her breathing, to her whole body.

"Goodnight, sir," she said breathlessly, and all but fled to the door.

"Goodnight, Miss Grey. Sleep well." His mocking voice sounded too aware as it followed her. But she suspected that on some level at least, it was himself he mocked.

JAVAN BENEDICT WAS not in good health. On top of which, he was lame. So why was it only now, after finding him sleepwalking in a storm, that she felt she'd found a vulnerability in him?

Not that it solved any of the mysteries surrounding him. Instead, last night's revelations, such as they were, only inspired more questions. Why did he dream of escape, and where he did imagine he was escaping from? Had he travelled so widely, simply for botanical purposes? Or was the botany a substitute, an interest to distract him from his troubles—which were what exactly?

A daughter who chose to be mute for reasons he either could not or would not reveal to her.

Nevertheless, there was a shared awareness between them now, a shared bond of closeness.

Teaching Rosa the following morning, she found herself longing for a glimpse of him, awaiting luncheon with much more than normal anticipation.

And yet, when luncheon came, he barely looked at her. He seemed more distracted than usual, hardly spoke and reserved his one smile for Rosa, ruffling her hair when she caught his hand to see if he was well. He finally excused himself from the room.

"Busy," Miss Benedict observed vaguely. "Always busy... And what will you two be doing this afternoon?"

"A little arithmetic and then some watercolor painting, I think. And if we finish early enough, I wondered about walking into Blackhaven. Perhaps a vehicle could be sent to bring us home again?"

"Oh dear, I don't know! *Blackhaven*," Miss Benedict said with the same kind of distasteful dread as she might have mentioned London stews, or even hell. "You had best speak to my brother first. I don't think..." She trailed off, choosing to finish her luncheon rather than her sentence.

It was while Caroline was correcting Rosa's arithmetic that the unfamiliar sound of carriage wheels on the stony drive attracted them both to the schoolroom window. A smart, familiar carriage was driven up to the overgrown front terrace and a coachman got down to open the door and let down the steps.

Lady Serena, now Lady Tamar, emerged, closely followed by her sisters, Maria, Alice, and Helen. Caroline's heart lifted at once.

"How wonderful!" she exclaimed.

But of course, she could not run down there to greet them, no matter how much she might wish to. She was the governess. Lady Tamar might or might not have come to see her, but if she had, no one would admit it. Caroline would have to wait and simply hope that the Benedicts would receive Lady Tamar and then, perhaps, summon Rosa and Caroline...

Rosa gazed at her, brows raised in interrogation.

"My old pupils," Caroline said warmly. "With their sister, Lady Tamar."

Rosa walked back to her desk, but not before Caroline had seen the familiar, anxious look on her face. Rosa didn't like change or the prospect of it.

It seemed to be difficult for both of them to concentrate after that, so it was a relief in several ways when the maid stuck her head around the schoolroom door. "Miss Benedict says will you and Miss Rosa join her in the drawing room."

Rosa dragged her heels a little. "You will like the young ladies," Caroline assured her. "Lady Helen is only about a year older than you."

And doubts Caroline might have harbored as to how the Braithwaite ladies would regard her after the countess's unfair dismissal, fell apart at once.

She had no sooner entered the drawing room and glimpsed the lovely Lady Tamar seated beside the vague and fluttery Miss Benedict, when a Helen-shaped cannonball hurtled into her. There were no ladylike curtsies and handshakes as she'd taught them. Even Lady Maria, almost sixteen, hugged her with enthusiasm.

Caroline emerged from the multiple embrace with self-conscious laughter. "So much for discipline and self-restraint," she said severely.

"We are sadly in need of you," Lady Tamar said warmly, although she offered her hand in a more civilized manner than her siblings. "How are you, Miss Grey?"

"I am very well, as I can see, are you!" She turned to find Rosa shrinking back against the wall, and held out her hand, beckoning. Rosa came with reluctance. "Will you allow me to present my new charge, Miss Rosa Benedict? Rosa, this is Lady Tamar and her sisters, Lady Maria, Lady Alice, and Lady Helen Conway."

With a kind smile, Lady Tamar held out her hand, and Rosa curtsied slightly grudgingly.

Miss Benedict, meanwhile, was sipping her tea, watching Rosa in a worried kind of way. In Caroline's experience, children were better sorting out their own relationships, so she merely said lightly, "Don't overwhelm Rosa all at once. And she does not speak, so you must observe how she does communicate."

With that, Caroline crossed to Miss Benedict and thanked her for the opportunity to meet her old pupils.

"Well, I can see how fond you are of each other," Miss Benedict said sadly. "Tea, Miss Grey?"

Caroline accepted a cup and sat opposite Miss Benedict and Serena, who occupied the sofa.

"How is Lord Tamar?" Caroline asked politely and was touched to see a hint of color tinge Serena's creamy skin.

"He is very well and sends his regards."

"And your lady mother and his lordship?"

"Ah, they are well, too, and set off yesterday for London at last."

"Ah." So, she'd simply been abandoned to her fate after all. Curiously, it didn't hurt as much as she'd expected it to.

"But he has not forgotten his obligation to you," Serena said hastily. "In fact, that is one reason I came to call on Miss Benedict. We would very much like you to return to Braithwaite Castle at your earliest convenience."

Caroline's eyebrows flew up. This was not how she'd expected things to happen. She searched Lady Serena's open face. "Ah. I think this is your idea and not Lady Braithwaite's."

"Miss Grey, Braithwaite and I both know my mother will relent in the end. In fact, if my brother chose to lay down the law, he could— and will if it becomes necessary. My sisters need you."

Serena knew how to tug her heart. She glanced to the other side of the room where the girls, kneeling on the Turkish carpet, were trying to teach a slightly bewildered Rosa a clapping game. The Conway sisters were all bright, lively, and good-natured. And Caroline missed them. She even missed Serena's company, for she had become almost a friend in the month or so before her wedding.

Here, she had a troubled pupil who would not speak and the company of a slightly dotty, middle-aged lady who occasionally lost her temper and threw cake at her brother. And as for that brother…he was nothing but mystery and danger. And whenever she thought about it—which was often—she could still feel last night's kiss upon her lips, his powerful arms clasping her close to his hard, wet body…

But Javan Benedict was not the issue here. Rosa was. Rosa, so isolated that she was lost in the company of other children, and terrified of being abandoned by the adults in her life.

"Please come back," Serena pleaded.

Caroline drew in her breath. "I don't believe I can. Certainly not on our old terms. My first duty is here."

Miss Benedict's face split into smiles.

Lady Tamar, whose will was not often crossed, looked flabbergasted. "But I will be going to Tamar Abbey quite soon, now. Someone needs to care for the girls."

How about their mother? She who was so quick to judge and dispose of me? She bit back the ill-natured taunt. None of this was Serena's fault. In fact, to some degree, it was Caroline's. Concerned for own position and her family, she hadn't truly considered the effect of her arrangement with Lord Braithwaite on either her old pupils or her new.

"I'm sorry, my lady," she apologized. "I may be able to help in some way… Allow me to speak with Mr. Benedict."

"Now?" Serena said hopefully.

Caroline blinked. "No, not now." A memory came to her. "But it seems I have a day to myself on Saturday and was planning to be in Blackhaven. I could call at the castle—"

"I shall meet you in town," Serena said firmly, appearing to see nothing outlandish in consorting with a governess. She sat back a little, including Miss Benedict in the conversation. "I have been telling Miss Benedict that Tamar and I are planning to hold some kind of party before we leave. I'll send cards and hope to see all of you there."

Serena stayed only a little longer, making civil conversation while her sisters did their best to include Rosa in their chatter and games. For most of the time, Rosa looked more bewildered than happy, but Caroline felt her heart contract when Rosa returned Helen's grin with a tentative but sweet smile.

BEFORE SHE AND Rosa began their customary afternoon walk, which was generally in the company of Mr. Benedict, Caroline took her courage in both hands and decided to beard the lion in his den.

A knock on his study door elicited no response. Since she could hear no movement inside, she assumed he must be elsewhere, so her second knock was half-hearted and purely token.

"Blast you, come in," his voice growled from beyond the door. It did not bode well, but she could hardly run now.

Drawing a breath, she opened the door and entered.

Javan Benedict sat at his desk in his shirt sleeves, a magnifying glass in one hand and several plant specimens laid out in front of him. A notebook to his right displayed drawings and writings. All this, she took in at a glance before he stood up and reached for the coat on the back of his chair.

"I beg your pardon," he said. "I assumed it was Williams." He did not, however, sound terribly apologetic, more irritated. And his frown seemed chasm-deep. Any illusions she had harbored about a new closeness between them were being quickly eroded.

"I apologize for the interruption," she said stiffly. "I merely wished to speak to you before I mention the scheme to Rosa."

His frown deepened impossibly. "What scheme?"

"You suggested I go to Blackhaven on Saturday to buy new boots."

The frown eased slightly. Beneath it, something flared in his grey eyes that caught at her breath. "I remember."

"With your permission I would like to take Rosa with me, let her—"

"Out of the question," he barked.

Caroline blinked. "I'm sure she would enjoy a day out, looking at shops and such, and there is an ice parlor in—"

"I said, it is out of the question." He sat back down at his desk and picked up his pen.

Caroline struggled to control her indignation. "May I know why?" she managed.

He stared at her. "No. It is not your concern."

Common sense dictated she leave it there but she couldn't. "I beg your pardon," she retorted. "I understood care of Rosa was specifically my concern!"

"*Teaching* Rosa is your concern. Her care is mine and mine alone."

"Then I take leave to tell you, sir, you need to do better," Caroline burst out. "The child does not speak and she is so isolated she does not even know how to play with others. How do you expect her to grow into a happy, responsible adult?"

He shot to his feet, his face white, his eyes blazing with fury—and behind that some awful pain that doused her temper like a bucket of water.

"Forgive me," she muttered. "I know there are circumstances of which I have no knowledge and have no right to speak. But please, believe I wish to help."

His lips twisted. "By taking her shopping?"

"Yes, and other mundane and hopefully amusing pastimes. I believe she should be allowed to grow used to people, to be with other children. You may not be aware that Lady Tamar called this afternoon with her young sisters—"

"I am well aware."

Then he had merely lacked the civility to greet them.

He pushed the book across the desk, crushing papers in the process. "I am also aware you cannot...*fix* Rosa in whatever few days you have left here."

"I do not claim to—" She broke off, searching his face with a first hint of understanding. "Are you dismissing me?"

"You are on loan, are you not?" he snapped. "I presume Lady Tamar came to take you back. I'm only surprised you didn't jump in her carriage at once."

Caroline flushed under the contempt in his voice. "If it weren't for

Rosa, I would have. It is certainly not the courtesies of my employer which keep me."

"Then it must be the boots."

She frowned. "The boots? I—" She met his suddenly tranquil gaze, and in spite of everything, had to bite back a surge of laughter. "Yes, of course it is the boots."

"You're not going back to them, are you? And yet I heard her— Lady Tamar—ask you to."

He had been as close to the drawing room as that, and yet he had not come in? Because Lady Tamar had asked her to go back.

"I find I cannot go back," she said now with difficulty. "Not until it might be possible to teach Rosa along with the Braithwaite girls." She raised her hands to prevent the inevitable outburst. "Please don't bite my head off, I am well aware that time is not yet, and is not my decision to make either."

"You are a very *managing* female," he observed.

"It is a useful quality in a governess," she replied with dignity.

"Do you normally feel called upon to manage the families of your charges, too?"

"Frequently."

A faint smile played about his lips. "You made a poor job of it with the Braithwaites."

"On the contrary, I made an excellent job of it, up until a rare moment of weakness. It won't happen again."

"We'll see." He moved from behind the desk, advancing upon her. For a moment she couldn't breathe, until he walked past her toward the door. "Fetch your cloak, Miss Grey, I believe it's time for Tiny's walk."

Chapter Seven

T HE FOLLOWING AFTERNOON, as part of the music lesson, Caroline sang out a note, and Rosa had to find the corresponding key on the piano. Rosa became adept at this very quickly. She seemed to like the way the human voice blended with the piano and urged Caroline to sing along to the scales she was practicing, which became amusing when Rosa's finger slipped, and Caroline mimicked the corresponding discord.

Caroline was just calling things back to order when something made her glance at the doorway to the drawing room. Javan Benedict stood there, leaning against the door, his face inscrutable as he watched them. Her heart gave the funny little leap it always seemed to when she saw him.

Rosa immediately showed off her scales with more care and received her father's as well as Caroline's approval.

"Go and find Tiny," he told his daughter. "I want a word with Miss Grey."

Rosa, like any child, looked delighted that lessons were finishing early and skipped off with great glee.

"It gets dark so early now," Mr. Benedict remarked in an excusing kind of way. To her surprise, he moved to the piano. "I've been thinking about what you said." He depressed the last key and wrinkled his nose before sinking down onto Rosa's vacated stool. If Caroline had moved, she'd have touched him. As it was, his warmth radiated through her.

"I shall accompany Rosa," he said abruptly.

Caroline smiled. "Tomorrow?"

"Yes, tomorrow. But I don't care to spend my day in a lady's shoe shop. Besides, it would cause talk, and it is your day off. We shall all go in the carriage to Blackhaven, and you may go off and do as you wish, and then return with us. Or the carriage can come back for you."

Caroline murmured her thanks and waited.

He continued to stare at his large hand, his fingers moving silently back and forth across the same keys. "You are right," he said. "She is too little with other people, especially children, but it must be done gradually so as not to overwhelm her."

"That seems a very sensible course," she allowed.

His lips curved as he cast her a caustic glance. "Careful, Miss Grey. Agreeing with me might become a habit."

She raised her brows. "I thought, sir, that *you* were agreeing with *me.*"

The smile in his eyes deepened, which did strange things to her breathing. "You are an insolent baggage, and I shall probably dismiss you tomorrow."

Surprised laughter spilled from her lips, but footsteps sounded in the drawing room beyond the open door, and he rose as quickly as he'd sat down.

"Sir?" came the voice of Williams the manservant.

Mr. Benedict strode into the drawing room. "I'm here, what is it?"

"Miss Rosa opened the door and the dog's off on his own," Williams said apologetically.

"Well, he won't go far without us. Come along, Miss Grey, time for some more managing."

Obediently, she hurried after him. At the drawing room door, he paused and glanced back at her over his shoulder. "It was a joke, before you go running back to Braithwaite Castle."

"Ah," she retorted. "I thought you were merely keeping me *up to scratch.*"

"Both." He walked out of the room. "Though I trust you don't use such cant to my daughter."

"Oh no, sir. My position is too valuable to me."

He glanced at her as she caught up with him. "Then why do I get the feeling you are mocking me?"

"I expect you have a guilty conscience about mocking the governess."

The laughter was back in his eyes. Butterflies fluttered in her stomach.

"I expect I have," he agreed. "You really aren't afraid of me, are you, Miss Grey?"

"Should I be?" she countered, as they came to the stairs.

A quick, almost savage laugh broke from him. "Oh yes."

Her foot faltered for the barest instant, and he ran downstairs ahead of her. When he moved like that, there was no sign of lameness.

SATURDAY DAWNED BRIGHT and fair with a hint of frost still on the ground as the Benedicts' carriage bowled out of the overgrown drive and along the road to Blackhaven. Since Miss Benedict also accompanied them, the carriage was cramped, with the excited Rosa and her aunt facing the direction of travel, and Caroline and Mr. Benedict seated opposite.

Caroline could not but be aware of his presence beside her, his arm brushing against her shoulder with the lurching of the carriage. It gave her a secret, wicked pleasure.

"So what diversions do you recommend, Miss Grey?" Mr. Benedict inquired.

"The ice parlor at the top of High Street," Caroline replied promptly and won a huge grin from Rosa. "There are shops selling just about everything, and an art gallery with a mixed selection of paintings. And you might like to visit the circulating library, where they have a surprisingly good collection. Also, the harbor is very pretty, and the beaches pleasant if the tide is far enough out. The church is several centuries old and very picturesque. The vicar, Mr. Grant, welcomes visitors, whether he is there at the time or not."

Miss Benedict beamed. "Why, you are as good as a guide book, Miss Grey. How long were you at the castle with the Braithwaites?"

"A few weeks only," Caroline admitted. "But they are lively girls."

"Well, we've told Williams to come back for us at one o'clock," Miss Benedict said. "He'll wait for us in front of the church. If you aren't there, then, we'll send him back for you at, when? Four o'clock?"

"That would be most kind," Caroline said. "Thank you."

Williams halted the horses opposite the church, and Mr. Benedict immediately pushed open the door and climbed out to let down the steps. He swung Rosa out in a large spin that made her smile and clutch on to him, and then, more civilly, handed out his sister and Caroline.

"Off you go, then," he said to her. "Enjoy your liberty."

Rosa, who showed a tendency to cling to her father as people passed in the street, reached out and seized Caroline's hand.

Caroline clasped her fingers with what she hoped was a reassuring smile. "I shall see you again this afternoon—at the latest. For the town is so small we may well bump into each other again at any time."

Rosa released her reluctantly and with a jaunty wave, Caroline walked away toward High Street. Today would surely be good for Rosa, moving among people, seeing other children. And she would see also that adults who left her came back again.

When she reached the shoemaker's shop, she was surprised to find Lady Tamar already there.

"Tamar is painting sunrises," she explained. "So, I was abroad early. And look, I have found you the sweetest little boots ever!"

They were indeed beautiful, made of soft kid and almost as dainty as dancing slippers.

"They are delightful," Caroline allowed. "But they would not last one muddy day at Haven Hall. I need something much stouter!"

"But not hideous," Serena insisted, pulling her past a display of plain, solid boots. "Let us speak to Mr. Nulty."

In the end, Caroline settled for something both pretty and comfortable, and Mr. Nulty the shoemaker promised to send them up to Haven Hall on Monday.

"Excellent," Serena approved. "Have you breakfasted, Miss Grey? For I'm famished! Let's go to the hotel."

Caroline accompanied her willingly enough. "Will people not think you very odd for being so much in the governess's company?"

"Well, they already think me odd for my marriage, and I can't say I care about that either. Besides, apparently you're not *our* governess anymore."

"I'm sorry," Caroline said with genuine contrition. "If I could continue teaching your sisters, I would."

"Is that what you intended to speak to Mr. Benedict about?"

"Yes, and perhaps by the time the countess relents, the time will be right."

"But the girls miss you now."

"As I miss them." Caroline hesitated. "I love your sisters, my lady, but Rosa needs me more. I hope to coax her back into the way of company, and maybe even a return to speech. I would love to find a way to teach them all together. I believe that would be best of all for Rosa. But I do understand that you want a governess now. I shall quite understand if you engage another."

Serena smiled wryly and sailed through the door of the hotel. "That is my lady mother's concern, not mine. But I don't like to leave them with only Mrs. Gaskell."

"Could you take them with you to Tamar Abbey?" Caroline asked once they were seated at a table in the quiet dining room and had ordered coffee and breakfast.

Serena wrinkled her nose. "Tamar says not. I don't think he wants to take *me* until he's beaten his brothers and sister into submission. I suspect it's all pretty ramshackle, and as you know, his brothers are not at all the thing."

"Well, neither was Lord Tamar until he married you."

"No, but he was always sweet-natured. I'm not sure that applies to his siblings. Anyway, neither of us is prepared to risk mine until I've met his for myself. And we may be trapped down there for the winter, so as I say, it's a fine excuse for a party." She delved into her reticule and produced a little packet which she set in front of Caroline. "Cards of invitation for the Benedicts and you."

"For me?" Startled, Caroline paused with her hand on the packet. "You don't invite the governess to parties!"

"I invite *you*. Besides, there will be children present, so I have an ulterior motive. I hope they will bring Rosa."

"I think that might be moving too quickly," Caroline said ruefully. "She will need to get used to one or two children before she can manage lots in a houseful of strange adults."

"Will her father not agree to that?"

"He might, now…to be honest, they have all got out of the way of company." And quite deliberately, from what Caroline could gather.

"Well, you must write to me. I could bring Helen over by herself one day and then you could bring Rosa to the castle. If he agrees." She waited until the waiter had set the coffee pot and cups on the table and departed, before she asked bluntly, "What is he like? Cold and terrifying?"

"Not at all," Caroline objected. "Nor does he eat children or keep his wife locked in a tower."

"I hope not if the poor creature is dead."

"It is Betty Smith's theory that she isn't, and that Miss Benedict is really Mrs. Benedict!"

"Betty Smith always made up stories. They entertained Frances and me when we were young, but I'm not sure that one is so funny. Are you happy there, Caroline? Or is it just your need to help that keeps you with them?"

It was the first time Serena had used her Christian name. The significance wasn't lost on Caroline, although Lady Tamar herself didn't appear to notice.

Caroline shrugged. "Both, I suppose."

Serena gazed thoughtfully into her steaming coffee and added a little cream. "Does he grieve still for his wife?" she asked.

It was a good question. "Certainly, he grieves for something. I suppose it must be her, though he doesn't speak of her. No one does." Which was odd. Miss Benedict never referred to her. Nor did any of the servants who must have known her.

Serena's eyes brightened. "It is a house of mystery," she said, all but rubbing her hands with glee. "Most definitely I must bring Helen next week. Though the others will hate me for leaving them behind."

They talked of other things while they ate breakfast. Serena, bright and animated as she generally was, seemed to have an extra brilliance about her, an inner glow that Caroline eventually put down to happiness. She hoped Lord Tamar would never let her down, for Serena clearly loved him to distraction. And although Tamar always appeared to be equally enchanted by his wife, Caroline did not have a high opinion of men's constancy.

"Well, well," a man's jovial voice interrupted their chatter. "What a bevy of beauty to greet my old eyes this morning!"

Caroline looked up to see the white-whiskered Colonel Fredericks, the retired commander of the 44th regiment barracked in Blackhaven. Serena had known him since childhood and immediately invited him to join them.

"Very happy to," he replied gratefully, easing himself into the seat opposite them. Colonel Fredericks gave a good impression of being merely a kind old gentleman well past his prime, though in fact, if one looked closely, his eyes were sharp and perceptive and, according to Serena, he still had charge of some intelligence matters relating to the never-ending war with France. He was also entertaining company, and Caroline was quite happy to spend half an hour drinking more coffee with him.

"So, you have both managed to lose your charges for today?" he said at last.

"Do you mean my husband?" Serena teased.

"I do, of course! And to a lesser extent, your delightful sisters."

"I left the former painting and the latter sleeping," Serena informed him. "But Miss Grey no longer looks after them. She has another position."

He seemed genuinely surprised. "Do you really? Well, well. Still in Blackhaven, I trust?"

"Haven Hall," Caroline replied.

The colonel raised his eyebrows. "Indeed? Who is it who has the hall now? Tenants never seem to stay there."

"Mr. Benedict and his family," Caroline murmured.

He cocked his ear. "I beg your pardon? I'm a little deaf."

"Mr. Javan Benedict and his family," Caroline repeated more clearly.

His eyes widened and focused more firmly on hers. "Javan Benedict?" he exclaimed. "*Colonel* Javan Benedict?"

"Oh no," she said at once. "I don't think—" She broke off, frowning. "They never call him that," she finished lamely. And yet it would explain so much: his travels, his injuries…

"Well, it is an uncommon name," Fredericks pointed out. "I would be surprised if it weren't him. How is he?"

"Convalescing, I believe," Caroline managed. "Are you acquainted with him, Colonel?"

"Only by repute."

"Who is he?" Serena asked with much more blatant curiosity than Caroline felt comfortable betraying. "What happened to him?"

"Oh, he commanded a crack unit under Wellington for a long time. Special duties, often behind enemy lines by all accounts. Was very good at it, too, or so I heard. But his luck ran out eventually, and he was captured. Months later, he escaped, but he was still direly wounded and he sold his commission almost immediately. Wellington himself regarded it as a severe loss, I'm told, but couldn't convince him to stay."

"Goodness," Serena said in awe. "A hero in our midst and we're listening to stupid and frankly ugly gossip about him! I shall make it my business to turn *that* on its head."

"Don't," Caroline blurted.

Serena blinked at her. "I beg your pardon?"

"I don't think he wishes to be discussed at all," Caroline said with difficulty, "let alone be recognized. Even the servants he brought with him never refer to him as *Colonel* Benedict. Neither does his sister. He obviously wants it that way. If it *is* him." It was. She knew suddenly that Fredericks was right.

"I suspect Miss Grey is correct," Colonel Fredericks said apologetically.

"Incognito," Serena murmured. "Who am I to upset a hero? My lips are sealed on the subject." She smiled at Caroline. "At least I can stop worrying about you at that place now."

AFTER PARTING FROM Serena, Caroline walked round to the circulating library and borrowed a novel and a book on botany, a subject on which she knew little. She then walked through the street market to the harbor, wondering if she should meet the Benedicts at one o'clock, or spend the afternoon searching for an inexpensive new gown to alter or to make up for herself.

The trouble was, she mistrusted her motives for this sudden desire for new garments. Of course, she disliked her dull old gowns—who wouldn't? But working for the Earl of Braithwaite, her dress had never concerned her. Why now, when she was employed by the most casual of families who barely noticed what they wore themselves? She refused to think of a reason, merely repeated to herself that it didn't matter. And it didn't. She just fantasized a little about appearing not to be dull. Just for an hour or two...

As though she'd conjured his reality by refusing to allow thoughts of him into her head, Javan Benedict stood by the harbor wall, gazing out to sea. She recognized him easily from behind, even in his unfamiliar tall, beaver hat. There was something in his straight posture, in his stillness. It couldn't have been anyone else.

Her step faltered. There was no trace of his family nearby.

She hesitated. She had long made the decision in her mind that if she came upon any of the Benedicts in town, alone or singly, she would merely wave—if she couldn't immediately duck out of sight. He didn't see her. He had no idea she stood behind him. She had only to spin around and walk smartly back to the market, or swerve left and walk down the row of fishermen's cottages where Lord Tamar had his studio.

But why should she change her plans? Just because one man stood more or less where she had intended to. There was room for both.

I'm fooling myself, she acknowledged as she walked on toward the harbor wall. *I was always going to do this.* Not that she expected a particularly warm response.

She stood beside him, looking out to sea, over the fishing boats tied up, to the larger vessel drifting past in the distance. The sea was a brilliant, frothy blue, reflecting the sunny sky. The whole view could have been one of Lord Tamar's more beautiful paintings, only the salty spray was damp on her skin and the scent of the sea strong in her nostrils.

Although she'd meant to greet him politely, she said nothing, merely stood beside him until she was aware of his head slowly turning and taking her in. At least he didn't swear, although he did turn back to the sea again.

"Is it normal for you just to stand there, oozing comfort?" he said at last.

She flushed. "I hope it's not normal for me to ooze anything at all. But if it helps, I'm content."

He didn't respond, merely gazed out to sea for a while longer, before he asked, "Was your business in Blackhaven successful?"

"I have ordered new boots and I breakfasted at the hotel with Lady Serena—Lady Tamar," she corrected. For some reason, it seemed too much information to mention Colonel Fredericks. "Have you sent Rosa shopping with Miss Benedict?"

"I sent them on to the ice parlor without me. Once was enough for me, even for the pleasure of watching Rosa's face as she eats."

"Two ices in one day! You are an indulgent parent."

"Well, I was never very moderate myself. I sympathize."

She could imagine it. Carefully, she avoided looking at him. Somehow, she knew it would make it easier for him to answer. "Are you quite well, sir?"

"*Not* quite," he replied. "But I'm getting there."

"Is that why you feel the need of comfort?"

"No, it's my self-pity that requires it. But I've done now."

"Then for your health, might I recommend the Blackhaven waters?"

He glanced at her with amusement. "A little harmless trickery?"

"Oh, there's no trick. It's only mineral water from the hills, which trickles underground and comes out at the Pump Room. But many people have noticed improvements in their health."

"Any reputable physicians?" he asked wryly.

"I don't know. But when Lady Serena was very down a month or so back, she took the waters and is now quite restored." She didn't mention that she was also restored to Lord Tamar, which was probably at least as much to do with the improvement. "But if you feel a physician would benefit you more, I believe Dr. Lampton is very well thought of."

"By the rich troubled with nervous disorders?"

"By everyone, I think. I believe the 44th use him, too, now that their surgeon is abroad. It would do no harm if you asked Dr. Lampton to call. And in the meantime, it would *certainly* do you no harm to drink the waters."

He regarded her with some amusement. "Very well," he said unexpectedly. "Take me to your wretched waters."

As they walked, a few acquaintances greeted her, one or two by name. All looked askance at her scarred escort. She wondered if the limp made him appear more or less of a threat. But since his temper was erratic at best, she was just grateful no one stopped to make conversation. Until, within sight of the pump room, they encountered Mrs. Winslow and Miss Muir.

Mrs. Winslow's eyes lit up at once. Fresh grist for her rumor mill, Caroline realized as she paused politely to greet the ladies. And as they both waited agog, there was nothing for it but to introduce her companion.

"Allow me to present Mr. Benedict of Haven Hall, who has recently employed me to teach his daughter. Sir, Mrs. Winslow, the squire's lady, and Miss Muir."

"Oh my," said Miss Muir, who was deaf as a post and often spoke without seeming to realize other people could hear her.

"What a surprise," Mrs. Winslow commented after exchanging distant bows with Benedict. "And do we not get to meet the new pupil?"

"One day, I'm sure," Caroline said hastily. "She is currently in the ice parlor with her aunt."

"Ladies," Mr. Benedict said coldly, raising his hat and walking on.

With an apologetic smile, Caroline hurried after him. "There is the pump room," she said as they reached the entrance with its fake Grecian pillars. "I believe you can swim. Or simply drink the water."

"Thank you," he said gravely. She nodded and turned away. Mrs. Winslow and Miss Muir were still gazing in her direction. "What will you tell them about me?"

"That you are grumpy and afraid of doctors," she said and walked away.

His surprised laughter followed her and made her smile as she raised a hand to the ladies and cut up the side road toward High Street.

Chapter Eight

C AROLINE DIDN'T RETURN with the family to Haven Hall. For one thing, she needed time to think about Colonel Fredericks's information, and for another, she felt unaccountably guilty that she hadn't already told her employer what she knew. Nor did she understand why any of this should be so important to her. Her employer's private life wasn't really any of her business, except insofar as it affected her pupil.

"I'm sorry to bring you out again," she said to Williams when she finally met the carriage at four o'clock in the gathering dusk.

"Don't be," Williams said cheerfully, stepping down from the box to open the door and let down the steps. "It's good for me *and* the horses."

Although it was dark by the time they reached home, it was hardly late, and Caroline wasn't prepared for the whirlwind that flew across the hall and into her arms with enough force to make her stagger. Tiny lolloped at her heels, barking. Caroline fended him off with one hand, distractedly ruffling his head while she hugged the child.

"Rosa, what on earth's the matter?" she demanded, peering down into her face.

Rosa shook her head, smiling through dried tears.

"You thought I wouldn't come back?" Caroline guessed.

Rosa nodded.

"Well," Caroline said. "I wouldn't be a very pleasant person if I just wandered off without saying goodbye to you. Or to your father and aunt. Am I so unpleasant?"

Smiling again, Rosa shook her head violently.

"There you are then." She hugged Rosa again, then released her. "Come, I think it's time we both washed and changed for dinner."

As she turned to the stairs, she saw Mr. Benedict watching them from the corner of the passage that led to his study. He stood in the shadows, as if he hadn't intended to be noticed, one shoulder leaning against the wall. Her heart gave one of its all-too-frequent lurches, but she carried on as if she hadn't seen him.

Twenty minutes later, having refreshed herself and changed into her slightly less dull gown, she straightened her shoulders, picked up the packet of invitations, and went downstairs in search of her employer.

Caroline always preferred things to be straightforward and open. And yet, even as she sought to make them so, she was aware she now had her own secrets. She could never reveal the effect he had on her. She didn't even know what it was. She just hoped it would pass, for it was entirely uncomfortable. And totally wonderful.

I'm addled. I'm madder than all the Benedicts put together and I must pull myself together.

With this stern admonition to herself, she raised her hand and knocked smartly on the study door.

"Come in," said the distracted voice beyond.

Had she really hoped *not* to find him? No, but she wasn't looking forward to the difficulties of the coming interview.

Opening the door, she walked into the study. From the hearth, Tiny didn't trouble to even lift his head this time, though he did thump his tail on the floor a couple of times by way of welcome.

His master kept on writing busily. "I thought it would be you," he observed as his pen flew across the page. Impatiently, he dipped it in the ink and scribbled another couple of words, added a definite full stop, and all but threw the pen into its stand before he rose to his feet.

"Miss Grey," he acknowledged. "My train of thought tends to wander these days. I need to write it down while it's still lucid. What can I do for you?"

She set the packet of invitations on the desk in front of him. "Lady Tamar gave me these for you and your family. And me. They are invitations to a party at the castle."

His lip quirked. "I shall not stop you going."

"You are kind. But I wanted to talk you about taking Rosa."

"No."

"That's not really a discussion," she observed. "Sir, I do not wish to simply drop her in there and leave her to cope alone. I have a plan to build up her tolerance and even appreciation of company."

To her surprise, he gestured her to the sofa and came out from behind his desk. He limped over to the decanter and poured a glass.

"No, I thank you," she said hastily when he cocked an eyebrow in her direction.

Taking his glass, he sauntered over to the sofa and sat beside her before taking a mouthful of brandy.

"Very well," he said wryly. "Now I'm ready."

So, she outlined her proposal to introduce Rosa gradually to greater intimacy with Helen and then with her sisters, and to the castle, all before the party which she hoped Rosa might actually enjoy, even for an hour or two.

He was frowning by the end, though not, it seemed, from anger. "And you think that this will somehow encourage her to speak?"

"I don't know," she replied. "But I think it might help. It strikes me that she is too...*comfortable* not speaking. Here, we don't just accept her silence but largely understand her meaning. She doesn't need to speak. My highest hope is that she will recognize how much more fun her relationships could be if she joins in normal chatter. But even if she doesn't, if it doesn't happen so quickly, she will at least be more comfortable in company."

"And if the company is...unkind to her?"

"Unkindness is something we must all get used to. But in this case, I see no reason why anyone would be. The Conway girls are very good natured, and in Blackhaven, even other children tend to follow the castle's lead."

He waved that aside. "Children's unkindness is one thing."

Caroline stared. "You cannot imagine adults would be unkind to her?"

"I cannot imagine *you* have not encountered unkindness in adults," he retorted. "If you hadn't, you wouldn't be here."

She flushed. "I am the governess. Rosa is a gentleman's daughter."

He fixed her with his harsh gaze. "You don't know anything about this *gentleman*."

"I know a little," she said with difficulty. "And I suspect more."

His eyes narrowed. "Such as?"

She held his gaze. "That you are an officer, a soldier."

He never blinked. "What makes you think so?"

"Colonel Fredericks, who is an old family friend of Lady Tamar's, thought he recognized your name. Are you Colonel Benedict?"

He threw the rest of the brandy down his throat and stood up. "I was. So the story is out."

"I don't believe so. Colonel Fredericks is a man of understanding and discretion. Of necessity, I gather."

He flung over to the decanter and sloshed another generous measure into his glass. "And Lady Tamar will tell no one such a juicy piece of gossip?" he mocked. "She would have to be inhuman!"

Caroline frowned, uncomprehending. "I don't believe it is *juicy gossip* to discover a man is a respected officer who escaped a French prison."

He stood by the sofa, staring down at her. "Is that what he told you?"

"Isn't it true?"

He threw himself onto the sofa. "So far as it goes. Did he say nothing else?"

"What else is there?"

"Family scandal," he said bitterly. "*That* is what I'm trying to protect Rosa from. That is why we came here to the middle of nowhere and why I never use my former rank."

"Colonel Fredericks said nothing like that."

"He wouldn't to you and Lady Tamar, would he?"

"I suppose not," she said honestly. "But then, I don't believe Colonel Fredericks is a gossiping kind of gentleman. Nor would he spread tales about a man he respects."

"Respects?" He laughed, a harsh, grating sound. "My dear girl, there is nothing to respect."

She didn't know if she hurt for him believing such a thing, or for herself in case it was true. "Why not?" she asked unsteadily.

He took a gulp of brandy. "That is a story for another day. For the rest, you'd better hear it from me because I don't want a whisper to reach Rosa from other sources." He gazed toward the fire, as though seeing his story in the flames. "I came home after more than two years abroad, sick and injured, to discover my wife expecting another man's child. Not only that, he was living in my house. I threw him out, and the next day, my wife and her unborn child died."

Caroline swallowed. Everything in her ached. "I'm sorry," she whispered.

"Why should you be sorry? The news was all round London within hours. So as soon as my wife was buried, I took Rosa and left."

Caroline nodded slowly. "But it wasn't that tragedy that deprived her of speech, was it?"

He shook his head. "No. She'd stopped talking almost a year before that. No one could tell me why. Even my wife."

"You carry a lot of guilt," Caroline said quietly, "for something that wasn't your fault."

He glanced at her. "I've given up apportioning faults. I have my share of them. For one, this isolation is not just for Rosa's sake. *I* need it."

"I gathered that."

A smile flickered across his face and vanished. "Of course, you did. But I accept that I am a selfish bas—" He broke off. "A selfish *man*. Begin your plan for Rosa if you will. On one condition."

"That if I catch one whiff of the scandal you mentioned, we do not attend the party?"

"What a superior governess you are. Except that you may, of course, attend the party under any and all circumstances. You never know, you might find a prince to sweep you off your feet."

"My feet remain firmly on the ground," she said dryly.

He sat back, regarding her over his brandy. "Come, Miss Grey, is there no romance in your cynical soul? You are young and attractive. You can't have given up hope of a better life than governess to someone else's children."

"It is the life I have chosen," she said stiffly, rising to her feet. "And I am perfectly content."

"Why do I not believe that?" he murmured.

"I have no idea. I have given you no cause to doubt my honesty or my commitment."

She swung away, hurrying to the door before she said more, or, worse, succumbed to the emotion suddenly tearing her up. She didn't expect him to move, let alone do so with such speed that he suddenly blocked her passage to the door.

"Don't run away. I was only teasing in my clumsy way. I did not mean to make you angry."

"I would not presume," she muttered.

His lips curved. "Yes, you would."

She hiccoughed an unexpected laugh, and his smile broadened encouragingly.

"I'm sorry for upsetting you," he said ruefully.

"I am not upset," she said, drawing in her breath. "Not really. Merely, I gave up all notions of marriage and motherhood before I took my first position."

He searched her eyes. "Someone let you down."

"It is a common story. Unfortunately, I am not a woman who changes her affections with ease."

"Then you still love him?"

It was a pain she had lived with for so long that she was almost surprised to find it lessened. To find *him* lessened to something almost paltry. It was the damaged man before her who filled her mind. And her heart.

No. Please no.

"I don't think of such things," she said desperately. "They mean nothing to me now. Excuse me."

She bolted ignominiously from the study, resolving never to be alone with him again.

"YOU GOT HIM to drink the waters," Miss Benedict said in a stage whisper. "Thank you!"

Caroline, who'd just taken her seat at the dinner table, flushed. "I merely showed him the way to the pump room."

"Well, I'm sure I see an improvement already. You must go every day, Javan."

"Must I?"

It was on the tip of her tongue to ask exactly what his injuries were, but since it was none of her business, and might, besides, upset Rosa, she swallowed back her questions and concentrated on her dinner.

Miss Benedict chattered about what a pleasant town Blackhaven was, and it was finally borne in upon Caroline that none of them had ever been there before today.

"Miss Grey, how is your handwriting?" Mr. Benedict asked in a rare pause.

"Legible, I believe," she replied. "Why?"

"I have an additional task for you, if you wish. I would pay you extra for it, of course."

"What would it entail?" she asked suspiciously.

"Making a fair copy of my semi-illegible notes."

"Ah, your book," she guessed. "Is it finished?"

"Almost."

"I would be happy to help," she said. "If I can."

And her heart beat and beat because it would involve spending more time in his company. Despite what she'd promised herself barely two hours before.

JAVAN BENEDICT WATCHED his daughter until she fell asleep. Because of her excitement during the day and her fear of Miss Grey not returning, it took her longer than usual, but he didn't mind. The governess was correct. Rosa did need to do normal things, to grow used to such minor expeditions today's. And she should not be so terrified of losing the governess she'd known less than a fortnight. Her morbid fear of abandonment had probably been heightened by the fact she had so few people around her.

There was more to bringing up a child than merely protecting her.

His heart was full as he gazed at her sleeping face. Marjorie thought he was too good to sit with his daughter every night. But it was no hardship to him. She was the comfort at the end of his day, his reason to begin another, a reminder of the rare goodness and sweetness in the world. She was his only joy and it broke his heart to think he might not be doing the best for her.

He had his reasons, of course. Reasons Miss Grey would surely discover in time. His revelations about the scandal had seemed to inspire more understanding than contempt or pity, neither of which would have been bearable from her.

Inevitably, his thoughts lingered on the governess. If he had guessed she would become such an obsession, he would have turned Braithwaite down. He hadn't wanted a young, beautiful female to teach Rosa. He'd wanted a sensible older woman, strict but kindly, a motherly figure—which her true mother had never been—not this *girl* who disturbed his thoughts and his lusts. He'd held her in the rain, and in the grip of his waking shock had kissed her soft, startled lips, in terrible fear that he'd hurt her.

He hadn't wanted to hurt her. He'd wanted to take her in the rain, in his bed, before the fire in his study, anywhere she would have him.

She wouldn't, of course, for she was a well-bred lady dependent on her pure reputation. And in truth, he would never take that from her, no matter how urgently his body demanded it. He had just been without a woman too long not to fantasize.

But that was too easy an excuse, unworthy of her, or even him.

As Rosa's fingers released his in sleep, he rose and walked across the room, conscious of new excitement in his heart. Caroline Grey would come to his study now, to be introduced to the work he'd so foolishly offered her.

Something had changed. Leaving Rosa, he no longer felt merely *prepared* to face another day. He *wanted* to.

His gaze fell on the door to Miss Grey's bedchamber, and his whole body tightened. Was she there now? Waiting for the sounds of him leaving, which she must surely hear. In many ways, it would be so much more natural to knock on her door and ask her to accompany him to the study. He wanted to see her in her own, personal room, about whatever tasks she gave herself—scrubbing the mud from her everyday gown, writing to her family... But that wouldn't be fair or right. He *liked* that she wasn't afraid of him.

Leaving by the passage door, he picked up the candle he'd left there and walked purposefully to the stairs. His left leg still didn't work as well as the right and had to be treated with care lest it collapse. Or lest he forget himself and groan from the pain.

In the evenings, when he was tired, the stairs were a challenge, but tonight he seemed to overcome them easily. Because he was remembering the way Miss Grey had come and stood beside him at the harbor. She hadn't needed to. He hadn't seen her approach. Equally, she could have greeted him and passed on.

He had known it was her as soon as she came up to him. He knew her clean, fresh scent, her presence. Although every nerve had been aware of her, he'd found a strange peace in her just being at his side. He'd almost been afraid to speak.

He walked into his study, leaving the door open. Tiny got up and loped over to lick his hand before returning to the hearth. There was only one lamp burning on the desk. Benedict lit a spill from his candle which he blew out before using the spill to light the other lamps and candles. Then he walked around the desk, arranging his notes into the order he wanted for the first few chapters of his book.

He strained every sense as though awaiting a lover instead of a secretary. At least he could laugh at himself.

Her quick, light footsteps along the passage brought a smile to his lips, though he'd banished it before she arrived.

"Ah, Miss Grey," he greeted her with briskness.

She blew out her candle and set it by his at the door. "Sir."

She crossed the room, looking as neat and efficient as always. She wore her drab grey gown with grace.

He hefted the pile of paper in his hands. "These are what I would like you to copy. Can you decipher my writing?"

She bent over the top sheet, scanning the words. "Yes, for the most part. If I come to a word I'm unsure of, I shall ask rather than guess."

She raised her eyes to his. They were a soft, yet brilliant blue, her lashes several shades darker than her hair, which she wore in too severe a style. He couldn't think of anything except removing her pins and shaking her lovely dark blond locks loose about her shoulders. As it had been that first night, when she'd followed Marjorie's crying and he'd somehow escorted her back to her chamber without touching her.

Under his continued gaze, her skin flushed. "Is something wrong, sir? Would you like me to copy a page to be sure I am up to the task?"

"Yes," he said, in an effort to make his brain think again. "If you please,"

Clearing a space on the nearside corner of his desk, he set down his papers, and took a large new notebook from the drawer on the other side. He found a chair by the window and set it by the desk. He even trimmed a pen for her and passed the ink.

This was ridiculous. He felt like a tongue-tied schoolboy, and yet he was only too aware that he was the one who held all the power, all the authority, and he could not approach her as an equal.

Approach her? he mocked himself as he strode back to the window. *With what? My late wife's money? My damaged child and my soiled honor?* Anger and shame and desire clashed in him, exploding in a turbulent mess that had him leaning his arm against the window for support.

Behind him, her pen scratched against the paper, the sound comfortingly normal. And it happened again. The strange peace she'd seemed to bring him by the harbor began to wash over him once more. No wonder Rosa found her so necessary so quickly. He was in danger of finding the same.

He let his arm fall to his side and walked to the desk. She laid aside the pen and sat back while he bent over the book. Her writing was neat and legible with just a hint of flamboyance in the loops. He could smell lavender from her hair, hear her every breath as though it were his own.

"Perfect," he said straightening. "There is no huge rush for this work, so just come here and continue whenever you wish and your duties with Rosa allow. Whether I am here or not."

Deliberately, he did not ask her to stay right now, merely walked around the desk to his own chair and sat down to continue with his final chapters. After a moment, she picked up her pen again and began to write.

It was a sweet torture, one he was happy to endure.

Chapter Nine

THAT SUNDAY, LADY Serena was as good as her word and rode over from Braithwaite Castle with Lady Helen. When Williams admitted them, Caroline was crossing the hall in the direction of the study and paused to greet them. Helen ran at her, and Serena hastily pressed a letter into her hand.

"It was delivered to the castle yesterday," she murmured.

Caroline's heart lurched in fear, for it was her mother's hand which had scrawled the wrong address. The reasons for such carelessness were truly terrifying. Fortunately, Williams took Serena and Helen straight up to Miss Benedict in the drawing room, so Caroline was able to flee to the quiet of the study.

She knew the room would be empty, for from her chamber window, barely twenty minutes ago, she had seen Mr. Benedict walk into the woods with Tiny. By past practice, he would not return for hours.

With her heart in her mouth, she tore open the seal, sinking onto the sofa. But there was no way to prepare for the blow she feared.

For a few moments, the words danced before her eyes, making no sense. Then she realized what they were saying and reread them properly, tears streaming down her face.

"Thank God," she whispered. "Thank God."

She didn't even hear anyone come in, but suddenly, Tiny's head was in her lap, and Mr. Benedict knelt at her feet, frowning into her face.

"What is it?" he said urgently. "What has happened?"

She smiled through her tears. "Peter is well. He was probably

never in any real danger, but when they didn't write I was so afraid…"
She dashed her hand against her cheeks in a belated attempt to hide
her emotion, but to her surprise, he caught her hand and held it.
Suddenly she was blurting out the whole story of Peter's illness, the
cost of the doctor, and her managing to send the money home via
Lord Braithwaite, only to hear nothing at all of his health since.

Mr. Benedict gave her a large handkerchief. Only as she took it, did
she realize she was clutching his hand. She released it with a hiccup of
apology and hastily wiped her face and eyes.

"I'm sorry," she muttered. "You must think me very foolish to be
crying over such happy news."

"Not foolish. I can see you care a great deal for the child." He
caught her gaze. "Tell me truthfully. Is he really your nephew?"

She stared at him uncomprehending. "Really my…oh!"

She jumped up, narrowly missing the dog's great feet as she
backed away from Benedict.

"Of course he is my nephew," she said stiffly. "Do I have your
permission to take Rosa to the drawing room to meet Lady Helen? I
thought Lady Tamar and I could take them for a walk."

"Of course," he said impatiently. "I told you so yesterday. Miss
Grey—"

"Thank you," she interrupted and stalked out of the room. *How
dare he? How dare he even think Peter is mine? What does he take me for?*

She'd run to her bedchamber, splashed water on her face and tow-
eled it dry before she admitted to herself why she was so angry. The
way he'd looked at her occasionally, with that wild, exciting heat. His
words that first night—*"Go in before I forget I was once a gentleman."* His
apparent favor to her, allowing her to copy out his book, thrusting her
more into his company… Was it all a ruse because he imagined she
had a child out of wedlock and was therefore easy pickings? A light-
skirted female who'd already tried to seduce Lord Braithwaite—and
succeeded for all Benedict knew.

"Dear God, it was a mistake coming here," she whispered. But she
had come, and she had her duties. She threw the towel onto the table

by the washing bowl and walked into Rosa's room.

Rosa sprawled on the bed, reading. She seemed more nervous than delighted by the treat of Lady Helen's company, and showed a tendency to cling to Caroline as they went to the drawing room.

"I don't go about much," Miss Benedict was saying to Serena. "I haven't for a long time now, but I must say your party sounds delightful. And here is Rosa."

Rosa curtseyed to Lady Tamar as Caroline had taught her.

"Goodness, you curtsey much better than I can," Helen observed.

"That's because you're in too big a hurry," Caroline said, "and only pay about a quarter of the attention necessary."

"Well, it's not a very interesting thing to learn," Helen complained.

Caroline had to allow her that one. It even won the glimmer of a smile from Rosa.

"But it is necessary if one moves in polite society," Caroline said primly. "Or any society, really."

"Quite," Miss Benedict said with a sage nod.

"Shall we take a walk while the sun is shining?" Serena suggested.

"Perhaps we can take Tiny," Caroline suggested.

"Who is Tiny?" Helen asked, bewildered.

Rosa smiled mischievously and beckoned the other girl from the room.

It was a start.

In the end, not only Tiny, but Tiny's master chose to accompany them. He appeared around the corner from his study, his coat fastened and his cravat tied carelessly about his throat. Helen, pinned to the wall by Tiny, stopped laughing to stare at Benedict in awe. Even Serena's breath caught at her first glimpse of the legendary tenant of Haven Hall.

And he did look dangerous in the shadows of the back hall, his long, jagged scar standing out lividly across his saturnine face. Until Rosa and Tiny both bounded at him.

"I see you've met Tiny," he observed.

"Lady Tamar, allow me to present Mr. Benedict," Caroline said as calmly as she could. "Sir, Lady Tamar and Lady Helen Conway."

Benedict bowed with unexpected elegance. "I hope you realize there are no formal gardens here. The grounds were thoroughly overgrown when we took the place, and I confess I've done nothing about them."

"We enjoy natural beauty," Serena assured him.

"Well, we have the natural in abundance. Heel, Tiny," he added severely, and opened the door with one hand while he unhooked his old coat and hat with the other. No one could have accused him of currying favor with the beautiful young marchioness.

Inevitably, Tiny shot out of the door like a cannon ball, both girls at his heels.

Caroline, thrown by this sudden turn of events, hoped Benedict's anxiety for his daughter wouldn't inspire him to interfere and keep too close an eye on the girls. And indeed, he did begin by walking beside them while she and Serena followed some distance behind. He threw a stick for Tiny, who seemed to fly through the air to catch it at its height, before landing on his feet again. Helen clapped her hands with delight and laughed at whatever Benedict said to her.

After that, he veered off the path and the girls ran off after the dog to throw the stick for him again.

"Well, he's not what I imagined," Serena murmured.

"Because he hasn't yet eaten the children?"

"Pshaw. I thought he'd be much staider and colder. Or at least grumpier."

He emerged back onto the path a little further on and walked with the ladies, responding civilly to Serena's conversation, with occasional sardonic asides that seemed to amuse the marchioness. Caroline added very little. Already angry with Benedict, she was appalled to discover the added pain of jealousy, because beside Lady Tamar's vitality, charm and beauty, Caroline was nothing.

And what exactly is it you want to be to him? she asked herself furiously.

Perhaps fortunately, the walk was not a long one, for the rain was threatening. They repaired to the house to have tea with Miss Benedict before Serena's carriage was summoned. The two girls seemed comfortable with each other, if not yet bosom friends, and Caroline thought that it had been a good day's work for Rosa.

Mr. Benedict had retreated once more to his study or elsewhere, but his sister and Rosa accompanied Caroline to the front door to wave goodbye to their visitors.

"Come over to the castle if you can," Serena invited as she climbed into the carriage. "We can dress up!"

"What does she mean by that?" Miss Benedict wondered.

"I expect she means to find me one of her old gowns," Caroline replied frankly, "so that I might not afflict her party with drabness."

"My dear, you are not remotely drab!" Miss Benedict protested. "You have brightened us up wonderfully!"

"Then you are quite happy for me to attend with you and Rosa?"

"Of course. Perhaps, since it is an early party, we do not need Javan's escort?"

Miss Benedict, clearly, assumed her brother would not go. Caroline, who had once thought of persuading him, said nothing. Following Miss Benedict back inside, she resolved to go for a longer walk, alone, to clear her head. So, she merely passed through the house to the side door, resumed her cloak and bonnet and went out again.

She hadn't gone far before a crashing in the undergrowth heralded the appearance of Tiny, who greeted her like a long-lost friend.

"You're not out on your own, are you?" she murmured, pulling his ears. And of course, he wasn't, for a few moments later, Mr. Benedict also emerged from the undergrowth, frowning over two plant cuttings in his hand as he walked.

Despite Tiny, Caroline would simply have hurried by with a quick, "Good afternoon, sir," and indeed, she walked faster to do just that. However, Mr. Benedict, glanced up and saw her.

"Miss Grey," he said at once, stuffing the plants in his pocket. He took a step nearer, blocking the path. "I have to apologize for my misunderstanding, and the offence I have given. You should know that I thought no less of you, whatever I imagined."

"I cannot believe that is true," she said flatly.

He looked surprised. "Can't you? You would not have been the first gently bred girl betrayed through no fault of her own. Despite what I once said about Braithwaite's mistress not being fit to teach my daughter, I regarded your situation—what I imagined was your situation—quite differently."

"I doubt the rest of the world does!" She drew in a breath. "However, I, too, must apologize for losing my temper. In truth, I was angry because…because I *do* almost regard Peter as my own. In my worst moments, I have *wished* he was my own,"

Frowning, he began to walk. "Why?"

"Because his father was once my whole world," she blurted. "I was young and naive and we were engaged to be married. And then he met my sister and married her instead. I used to torment myself with the belief that he should have been mine, that if Theo had married me as he'd promised, and not Eliza, then he *would* have been mine."

She would not look at him, but his gaze burned into her face.

"And yet," he said, slowly, "now you work to keep your sister and the child who should have been yours. You are a lesson in duty."

"No, just necessity."

He walked on in silence. "Do you miss him?" he flung at her at last.

She thought about it, then shook her head. "Not really. In fact, I believe we would have been most unhappy together, for he was a shallow and feckless man who left my sister without a penny. Imagine the disillusion of discovering such a thing of your spouse rather than of your sister's spouse."

He let out a short laugh. "I don't need to imagine. It seems we have both been deceived."

"Did you love your wife very much?" she asked before she could stop herself.

"Once," he replied. "For five minutes or so. I was not a very satisfactory husband."

Shocked, she waited for more, but that appeared to be the end of his confidence.

"Then we are still friends?" he said, casting her a sideways glance.

"No, sir," she replied firmly. "You are my employer. And I am your daughter's governess."

Her skin flushed under his continuous scrutiny, but she would not meet his gaze.

"And in spite of our better understanding," he said, "you still refuse to believe why I seek your company."

"And why *is* that, Mr. Benedict?" she challenged.

His lips quirked. "Because I like you, Miss Grey," he said softly. "Because I like you." He tipped his old hat to her and sauntered off down the other path toward the woods.

"*THAT IS THE* one," Lady Tamar said warmly.

They stood before the glass in her bedchamber, where Caroline had tried on several of the marchioness's evening gowns. On the other side of the room, Rosa and Helen were doing likewise—except where Serena snatched certain gowns from their grasp. The children did not appear to mind. There were plenty to choose from. At the moment, Helen sprawled on the chaise longue in a caricature of a fashionably languid lady. She wore a slightly torn but gorgeous yellow silk that trailed so far beyond her toes that Rosa knelt beneath her on the floor, wrapping the train of the gown about her shoulder. They both found this exquisitely funny, and Caroline smiled to see them laughing together.

With an effort, Caroline dragged her gaze back to herself in the glass. She was a little thinner than Serena, who gathered the fabric of the gown at her back to portray a better fit. It was a high-waisted, delicate peach silk, worn over an under gown of a slightly deeper color. Although the low-cut neckline was not quite immodest, it exposed far more of her chest and shoulders than she was used to. Still, it did not look ill. Instead, it seemed to bring out the creaminess of her complexion and the brightness of her eyes.

"I don't look like the governess," she said flatly. "People will talk, say I'm encroaching and giving myself airs."

"Well, they might if you covered yourself with diamonds, too, and walked about with your nose in the air as if you were too good for Blackhaven. Those who know you will be glad to see you looking so well and enjoying yourself. Those who don't, will never guess that you're a governess."

"Except that I'll be with the children," Caroline said.

"Well, they pretty much look after themselves," Serena argued. "There's no need for you to be with them *constantly*. Let me just pin this, and I'll have Mrs. Gaskell take it in at the waist and alter the length."

"I don't know," Caroline said doubtfully. "When you held your midnight revel, I wore my own clothes."

"Well, no one wore their best because we were on the beach," Serena pointed out. "And besides, at night by the sea, with lit braziers and burning torches all over the place, the children *did* have to be watched more closely. But I don't see why you have to play the governess all the time."

Caroline blinked. "I'm not playing. I *am* the governess."

"Will he come?" Serena asked.

Caroline didn't need to ask who. "I don't know," she replied candidly. "But Miss Benedict is eager, and he has no objection to my going, with or without Rosa." In fact, he hadn't brought the subject up recently, even in the evenings they spent in his study.

Those evening hours had secretly become Caroline's favorite part of the day when she sat only feet from him, conversing little, as a rule, but simply soaking up his silent company, his very physical presence as he worked. He drank brandy constantly and yet never seemed inebriated. Nor did his manner to her ever change below the civil. And yet, she surely didn't imagine the sense of intimacy between them—inappropriate, dangerous, but still unspoken.

Last night, as he'd poured himself another glass of brandy, she'd blurted, "Why do you drink so much? For the pain?"

His eyebrows had flown up and he'd gazed at the glass in his hand, as though wondering how it had got there. His lips twisted. "Old pain and habit. I suppose it dulls the edges."

"Of pain?"

His gaze had lifted, devouring her. She had never seen such hunger in a man's eyes. It was dizzying, frightening, and yet wickedly exciting.

A short laugh had broken from him. "Pain, yes. Let us call it that."

He had sat back down at the desk, the glass by his elbow. But the thrill of that look, of the fierce desire it revealed, still churned inside her.

"What do you think, girls?" Serena asked the children, turning Caroline to face them while still holding the dress material in at the back.

The girls untangled themselves from the yellow gown and regarded Caroline with unexpected awe.

"Why, Miss Grey, you're beautiful," Helen said, while Rosa nodded slowly.

"If only I'd known," Caroline mourned. "So many wasted years! All I've ever needed is one of Lady Tamar's gowns."

Lady Tamar gave the gown a little twist to tighten it. "*Any* gown rather than the ones you have. I can't believe they ever became you."

"They weren't meant to," Caroline said. She'd chosen them, altering them from her mother's unworn collection, for precisely that reason. She'd thought being plain and dull would mitigate against her youth when looking for a position.

"Well, you were always beautiful," Serena retorted. "Ugly dresses and severe hairstyles do not disguise the fact. Trust me, you have been noticed,"

Disconcerted, Caroline twisted around to look at her. "By whom?"

"It doesn't matter," Serena said hastily. "I merely wish you to know, to make you comfortable going into society in this capacity."

"I don't think it does make me comfortable," Caroline murmured. "I think I will just wear the brown—"

"No!" Serena and Helen exclaimed together, and Caroline laughed self-consciously.

"Come, let's go and find the others and take a walk…"

Chapter Ten

W HEN SHE WAS dressed for Lady Tamar's party, Caroline took a moment to gaze at herself in the glass. She had pinned her hair in a higher, softer style than usual, and Serena's peach gown had been altered so that it fit Caroline perfectly. She thought she looked rather well and refused to admit why she cared. Instead, she spent half a second wishing she had some jewelry to set off her fine appearance. The few pieces she'd been given or inherited had been sold long since.

Shrugging, because it truly didn't matter, she walked through to Rosa's room and found Rosa sitting cross-legged on the floor in her new dress, playing with Tiny. With a sigh, she chased Tiny and brushed the dog hair off Rosa before accompanying her downstairs to meet her father and aunt.

Rosa was delighted that her father was escorting them and discovering him and her aunt at the foot of the stairs, she ran down to hug him.

At first, Caroline could not bring herself to look at him, afraid of what she might see or not see. Since that moment in the study, she had never again surprised the wild hunger in his eyes, which piqued her far more than it should. She had almost convinced herself it had all been the fevered imagination of a lonely spinster. She tried to focus her attention on Rosa who was now leaping around her aunt, but inevitably, her eyes strayed to the still, tall figure beside them.

Her heart leapt into her throat, for his gaze was rivetted to her, and it was very far from indifferent. It held…wonder.

Her foot faltered on the stairs and he took a step up, offering his hand to steady her. She could not refuse. She didn't want to. As she laid her hand in his, his strong fingers curled around it, and his gaze dropped to her mouth and lower, deliberately covering her throat and breast, her whole person. And when it returned to her face, the awe had given way to something much more predatory.

Shaken to her core, she slid her hand free and made a point of asking if Miss Benedict would be warm enough with just her shawl, or if Caroline could fetch her a cloak for travelling. She could not look at her employer again until she had regained some composure.

It was only when the carriage halted at the castle and he handed her down that she finally found the courage to meet his gaze. At last, she took in his smart black coat and pantaloons, his simply-tied cravat snowy white against his swarthy skin, and his raven hair brushed back from his face. Her foolish heart turned over because he looked so handsome. Even with the disfiguring scar and the limp, there was something very gallant about him. Despite the rumors, there would be many ladies here desperate to make his acquaintance. The knowledge made her heart ache.

"Quite an impressive pile," he remarked, scanning the castle as they walked together to the front door.

Lady Tamar's party was a rout with the atmosphere of a family gathering. There was a quartet of musicians playing in the long gallery, where there would be dancing later. In the large drawing room, there was to be poetry and music from whichever of the guests felt so inclined. In the smaller, card tables had been set up. Toys and books were scattered in various places, along with bowls of sweetmeats, and children of all sizes ran around the adult guests with great excitement. Caroline expected to be kept busy.

As with most Blackhaven social events of this kind, the guests were a mixture of local gentry and visitors to the town, most of whom came either to drink the waters for their health or to accompany someone else who did. And since the party was Lady Serena's, everyone invited had jumped eagerly at the opportunity.

Caroline noticed a few outraged glances by those who recognized her, though they appeared to be mollified whenever she was with children. Fortunately, Helen had decided to include Rosa in everything she did, so she was rarely alone unless she chose to be. The other children present seemed to regard her as a curiosity at first, but then accepted her naturally into their games. And Rosa herself, used to the Braithwaite girls, didn't develop the blank, hunted look she'd worn the first time Lady Tamar visited.

What did surprise Caroline, was her anxiety for the adult Benedicts. She was afraid her employer would get bored and sneer, which was quite likely considering the many curious glances cast his way, many of them blatant to the point of rudeness. Or that his frailer sister would shrink into loneliness. Not that she expected Marjorie to start throwing cake at the castle guests, but Caroline felt almost motherly toward her. In fact, she glimpsed Mr. Benedict once in conversation with a few gentlemen and then again entering the card room. And Miss Benedict seemed to make friends early on with the deaf but amiable Miss Muir who was a conduit to the rest of native Blackhaven society.

Through it all, Caroline endeavored to keep the children entertained without them running too wild. Occasionally, Lady Tamar brought a young man to make her acquaintance. Two of them beat a hasty retreat when they learned she was a governess, the third, a Mr. May, showed a tendency to linger until his mother summoned him away.

"Who are these gentlemen you're bringing to me?" she asked Serena under her breath as she conducted a small group of children to the dining room. "Are you actually *match-making?*"

"Oh no, I'd never presume," Lady Tamar replied in shock. "They are simply gentlemen who asked me for an introduction. You do look stunning, you know." She drifted on to greet the vicar and his wife who had just arrived, leaving Caroline gazing after her with a mixture of amusement and annoyance.

"Have you lost Rosa?" enquired a familiar voice behind her. Mr. Benedict.

"She's in the dining room," Caroline said, dragging her gaze to her employer and lowering her voice. "She seems to coping and is quite happy."

"And you?"

Her brows lifted in surprise. "I?"

"Are you happy? Or are you merely a drudge for lots of children instead of one?"

She smiled. "Oh no, I don't feel like a drudge at all, I like children—most of them!—and everyone is being kind to me." She inclined her head in response to the bow of the passing young man, Mr. May, who had been introduced to her earlier. He had been approaching the dining room door, though he now veered away toward the drawing room as though alarmed by Benedict's presence.

"I would not call it kindness," Mr. Benedict said wryly, watching this progress.

"Then what would you call it?" she challenged.

His gaze returned to hers. "Lust. Attraction, to give it a gentler name."

She flushed under his highly improper words but refused to look away. It was he who did that, gazing instead toward Lady Tamar. Their hostess had been joined by her slightly erratic husband, and together, they were now welcoming another newcomer, a handsome but frail looking gentleman. Perhaps thirty years old and pale skinned, he carried a walking stick.

Caroline felt Benedict's shock as though it were her own. His whole body went rigid and still. And the object of his attention, having smiled and moved beyond his hosts, glanced inevitably along the gallery. His gaze clashed with Benedict's, and he stopped dead. He even wobbled a little, leaning on his cane for support. For an instant, fear stood out in the stranger's eyes, in his whole, appalled face. Then it smoothed quite deliberately and the man turned and walked back the way he'd come. Leaning on his stick, he walked past Lord and Lady Tamar who were laughing with someone else, and headed for the stairs as though he were leaving.

Beside Caroline, Benedict drew in a breath that shuddered.

"Who is that man?" she asked urgently.

"Someone who must never, ever be anywhere near Rosa," he said harshly. "Do you understand me?"

"Perfectly. May I know your reasons?"

"No."

Stung by his sudden cold withdrawal, she inclined her head and stalked into the dining room.

"Wait." He followed her to the doorway. "I'm sorry," he said with apparent difficulty when she glanced back at him. "I will tell you, but not here."

Diverted by one of the Winslow boys trying to hog an entire plate of pastries, Caroline dashed to restore order before anyone else could object. By the time she looked around again, Mr. Benedict had left the room.

Out in the long gallery, dancing was beginning and Caroline suggested the children form a set of their own for the country dances. Inevitably, she was drawn into it, if only to show Rosa and some of the others what to do. She led them to the very end of the gallery, so they didn't get in the way of the adults but could still hear the music. A somewhat hilarious dance ensued, formed of an uneven number of boys and girls. Caroline found it great fun and even the adults in the set closest to them smiled at the children's antics.

Breathless but laughing, Caroline emerged from their midst, only to be accosted by Mr. May.

"Miss Grey." He bowed. "How kind you are to look after the children."

"Not kindness, sir," she assured him. "Party pleasure and part duty. I am a governess,"

"Not to all of them, surely!" He sounded so appalled that Caroline couldn't help laughing.

"Of course not, but the young Braithwaite ladies are my former pupils, so I am happy to be of assistance."

"Do your duties allow you to stand up with me for the next

dance?"

Caroline had no idea what to say to that. Due to the informal nature of Lady Tamar's party, there were no dance cards and dancing with anyone but the children had never entered her head. She opened her mouth to refuse on the grounds of being away from the children for too long.

But Lord Tamar, being dragged along the gallery by Helen at the time, murmured mischievously, "Of course you may dance. In fact, we insist."

Lord Tamar was not her employer, but somehow, she could never bring herself to ask Mr. Benedict for permission to dance. In fact, she was making too much of it, for he would not care...

"Thank you, Mr. May, you are most kind," she said civilly and received a beaming smile in return.

"Allow me to fetch you a glass of lemonade," he begged.

While he was gone, Caroline went in search of Rosa. She found her in a quiet corner of the drawing room with Lady Alice. The two girls appeared to be drawing each other while Miss Winslow sang and played on the pianoforte. Exchanging smiles with Rosa, Caroline passed on, pleased for the girl, and quickly toured the other rooms to make sure none of the children were getting up to mischief. Helen was organizing their next dance set, to include both Lord and Lady Tamar.

By the time she returned to the gallery, Mr. May was there with her lemonade, looking disconsolately around for her. She took pity upon him and approached him.

During the dance, she caught fewer disapproving looks from the Blackhaven gentry than she expected to, although Mr. May's mother scowled blackly enough for all of them. Caroline didn't mind that. It was time he stood up to his mother.

Afterward, he was clearly lost as to his next move. She supposed he was used to dancing with debutantes whom he returned to their strict guardians afterward. An older, independent woman of such flexible social position as Caroline obviously flummoxed him. Caroline took pity on him and excused herself to check on Rosa and the other children—who'd enjoyed a rather more boisterous dance with Lord Tamar egging them on.

In the drawing room, Rosa had returned to sketching with Alice. A couple of the other children had joined them to admire and advise, but Rosa still looked fairly contented, possibly because her father sat on a sofa nearby. He appeared to be deep in conversation with an unusual and beautiful lady—Mrs. Gallini, the Italian singer Lady Tamar had secured to make her party the event of the winter. Caroline hated the spurt of pointless jealousy which clawed at her, but it seemed there was nothing she could do about it except ignore it. In time, this foolish obsession would pass.

As she was about to retreat, he stood with his companion, who with a gracious smile, walked over to the piano to be introduced by Lady Tamar for her final song of the evening.

"Miss Grey," Benedict said formally, politely gesturing to the sofa.

Poised between flight and obedience, she remembered her place in time, and sat.

The singer was more than good. With passion and presence and the voice of an angel, she moved hearts. In spite of her feelings, Caroline could not help but listen in awe, although the song heightened rather than suppressed her powerful awareness of the man at her side.

After several moments, he murmured, "Are you happy with Rosa?"

"Very," she managed. "But I think perhaps this is long enough. If you wish, I shall take her home and send the carriage back for you and Miss Benedict."

"No, I think we should all go," he replied, "but not just yet."

"Of course not. After the performance."

"Indeed, and one more dance, which I hear is the waltz. Unless you are promised to the young man making sheep's eyes at you from across the room."

"Mr. May," she said with dignity, "does not have sheep's eyes."

"Lamb's then. So, are you committed for the waltz?"

"No," she said. "I can leave whenever—"

"Good," he interrupted and relapsed into silence for Mrs. Gallini's climactic finish.

Caroline could do no less than applaud with enthusiasm.

Mr. Benedict said, "I'll just speak to Rosa..." and moved away.

Somewhat confused by Benedict's remarks about the waltz, Caroline wondered if he actually meant to dance with the singer, which she doubted was socially acceptable. Such niceties would not weigh with him. She rose, thinking to go in search of Miss Benedict and warn her of the planned departure. But before she reached the door, the musicians had struck up the opening strains of a waltz and as she stepped into the gallery, an arm at her back swept her along the floor among the forming couples.

Shocked, she gazed up into the scarred face of her employer. "Oh no," she blurted. "You mustn't. People will talk!"

"People will always talk."

Her hand was lost in his. He stepped back, and she had to follow. "But your wounds—" she said anxiously.

"If I collapse at your feet, you must run for help."

She scowled at his flippancy. "You won't listen to anything I say, will you?"

"I listen to everything you say."

"And immediately discount it!"

"Quite the contrary."

She could think of nothing to say to that. Her normally sharp mind seemed to have lost track of everything except the dance. Surprisingly, despite his lame leg, he moved with grace and sureness of foot, as if the rhythm of the dance helped rather than hindered him. And for all her genuine objections—on his behalf and hers—there was something unspeakably sweet about dancing in his arms, about being so close to him for so long. His eyes held hers, a faint smile playing about his lips that looked faintly predatory, and yet even that excited rather than frightened her. It felt almost as if she was *meant* to be there...stupid, dangerous thought.

"You waltz well, Miss Grey."

"Thank you. I have to teach the steps to my pupils. What is your excuse?"

"It was my duty. All Wellington's officers have to waltz."

"Even when injured?" she challenged.

"Especially when injured. There's no mollycoddling in his lord-ship's army."

Something in his tone made her say, "You miss it."

"I was a soldier for eighteen years, so yes, I suppose I miss it."

"Couldn't you go back?"

"No." A flash of pain and something far more corroding darkened his face, and then his eyelids swooped down and his lips untwisted into a smile. "No, I can't go back. One never can, you know. The trick is to look forward. You have taught me that."

Her eyes widened. "I have?"

"We were standing still at Haven Hall, locked in the isolation of the present. Protected, safe but…"

"Bored?" she suggested.

A breath of laughter escaped him, warming her skin. "And stagnat-ing. I was protecting Rosa, but *you* are helping her."

She thought of the stranger who, at sight of Benedict, had fled the party he'd only just arrived at. He had to be something to do with the family's past, something to do with his protection of Rosa?

"Thank you," he said softly.

It wasn't so much his words but the warmth in his eyes and voice that made her flush to her toes.

"Thanks are not necessary," she managed. "If I have helped, then I'm glad."

"You are, aren't you? What a selfless little creature you are."

Her flush deepened. "You needn't make fun of me."

"Oh, my dear, I wasn't."

"Don't call me that," she all but hissed.

"Then you do not regard me as a father figure."

She blinked. "Father? There cannot be more than ten years between us!"

"I suppose that answers my question."

Before the thrilling heat in his eyes, she dropped her gaze to his chin. She hoped it was the dance that made her breathe so quickly.

It isn't. It's him...

She didn't want it to stop. And yet she knew this was madness. For one thing, although he took long walks, the continuous movement of the dance could not be good for his injured leg.

"I should go and find Miss Benedict and Rosa," she said breathlessly. "I think this is long enough for her."

Slowly, reluctantly, it seemed, he released her and offered her his arm until they had walked clear of the dancers. She could not look at him as she all but fled into the card room.

Miss Benedict had, fortunately, just finished a game of whist with Miss Muir and a couple of her friends and seemed happy enough to depart. They discovered Rosa and Mr. Benedict in the larger drawing room, making their farewells to Lady Tamar.

To Caroline's surprise, Serena hugged her, a faintly anxious look in her eyes. "Take care," she murmured. "And remember where I am."

"When do you leave for Tamar Abbey?"

"Oh, who knows? We're not sure about going at all, now." She walked with them downstairs and sent servants scurrying for their carriage and their cloaks while Miss Benedict fluttered about what a charming time she'd enjoyed and what a kind hostess Lady Tamar was.

"You must call on us when we're quieter," Serena invited. "One day next week, perhaps? You are all welcome."

For Caroline, the world had taken on a strange sense of unreality. Perhaps it was to do with the speed of her heartbeat, with the shrinking of her world into the few people now surrounding her, and .her over-sensitive awareness of Javan Benedict beside her.

Handed into the carriage, she again took the seat facing away from the horses, as befitted her lowly position. She didn't know if the journey would be harder with him beside her, all but touching her, or opposite her where she could see him.

He placed Rosa opposite her and sat beside her once more. Rosa threw herself back in her seat, smiling contentedly at everyone. She took her aunt's hand and closed her eyes, exhausted by the day's adventure.

While Miss Benedict chattered, Caroline concentrated with difficulty. Although Mr. Benedict seemed to be leaning the other way to avoid any accidental contact, there seemed to be invisible strings binding her to him. Every nerve, every sense, quivered with awareness.

Only as they finally drove up the neglected road from the gates to the house, did Williams cause the horses to swerve, no doubt to avoid a particularly hideous bump, and Caroline was thrown against Mr. Benedict. There was the shock of his hard shoulder and thigh, his warm hands catching and righting her.

"Sorry!" she gasped.

"Are you hurt?"

"No, no. Are you?"

"Of course not. You're little heavier than Rosa."

It was as if he was reminding himself that they were not alone. Tension coiled inside her. She couldn't help but speculate as to what would have happened if they were alone. She wondered how he would kiss when not soaked to the skin and terrified he'd hurt her in a dream...

No, no, and no!

The carriage pulled up at the front of the hall. Mr. Benedict leapt out almost before the horses had stilled and handed down his sister and Caroline. When she stole a glance at him, his eyes seemed to burn, but it might have been the fault of the carriage lanterns and the light blazing from the open front door. She hurried up the steps while Mr. Benedict swung Rosa out—in a huge arc judging by the child's joyous gasp.

"Are you hungry?" Caroline asked Rosa as they entered the house. "Shall I ask Cook to bring something up to the schoolroom before bed?"

Rosa shook her head and ran for the stairs. She needed some time alone after her unprecedented companionship that day.

"I'll come in shortly," Caroline called, beginning to follow her.

"A word with you first, Miss Grey, if you please," Benedict said abruptly.

Obediently, she took her foot off the step and followed him as he snatched up a candle and limped speedily toward the study.

He knows. He's going to send me away, or tell me off in some unbearably humiliating way...

Knows what? she answered herself aggressively. There was nothing to know.

He opened the study door. The fire was lit and another glow emanated from a lamp near the desk. That was all she saw before he kicked the door shut behind her and seized her in his arms. His mouth came down hard on her gasping lips, kissing her with a strength and desperation she'd never imagined.

When she could do more than hang in his arms, shock melting into hot, thrilling pleasure, she struggled to free her hands, which were pinned to her side. At once, his grip loosened, but she only flung her arms up around his neck, drawing him back to her, and he pulled her flush against his body, ravishing her mouth with long, invasive kisses.

Devastated, aroused beyond belief, she dug her fingers into his hair, stroked the rough skin of his face and the jagged line of his scar. She kissed him back with ever increasing urgency—though for what, where it was all leading, her befuddled mind neither knew nor cared.

Without conscious volition, she rubbed herself against him like a kitten. When his caressing hand found her breast, she let out a moan of delight and need.

"Christ, Caroline," he whispered. "Have you any idea how much I want you? Here and now?" He gave her no time to reply but buried his mouth in hers once more, lifting her right off her feet in his passion.

Beyond the study, a continuous knocking grew louder and more imperious, gradually breaking through Caroline's haze of blissful desire. Abruptly, the knocking stopped and voices could be heard in the hall, talking loudly.

Benedict's lips stilled. She opened her eyes, staring into his.

He raised his head very slowly. "I think...you might just have been saved. But damn and blast him to hell, whoever he is. Wait there. Better still, run to your room and lock the door. All the doors." He pressed another quick, hard kiss on her mouth and released her.

He threw open the study door and strode up the hall with his uneven gait.

"I insist on seeing your master this instant," came an imperious male voice. "Of course, he has not retired. The man never sleeps!"

Caroline, who had never had any intention of obeying him in this, followed him with her heart in her mouth. She wondered if it was the man who'd fled the castle party at sight of him.

Chapter Eleven

S HE'D ALMOST CAUGHT up with him by the time he rounded the corner into the main entrance hall.

He swore under his breath. "Richard," he said aloud. "What the devil do you want?"

The visitor, a gentleman in a smart, many caped driving coat, spun around. He was a handsome man, his dark hair cut fashionably short. His face broke into a grin. "There you are, Javan, gracious as ever. Since you ask, a bed for the night would be appreciated. And a shipload of brandy. Companionship in drinking the same is optional."

Benedict let out a short bark of laughter and strode forward with his hand held out. "You are a glutton for punishment."

The two men clasped hands warmly. Caroline, relieved to see that this was a friend, would have crept away at this point, but over Benedict's shoulder, the newcomer saw her.

His eyes widened. Dropping Benedict's hand, he walked toward her. "Surely not the second Mrs. Benedict?" he exclaimed.

"No, sir, the first governess," she replied tartly, although she softened the words with a curtsey.

"Are you, by God?" the visitor said, his gaze raking her. Too late, she wondered about the state of her hair after those wild minutes in Javan Benedict's arms. And, of course, she still wore Lady Tamar's altered gown. "I never saw a governess like you before."

"There is not another like her," Benedict said shortly, moving forward to stand protectively between them. "This is Miss Grey," he introduced her, "who joined us from the Earl of Braithwaite's household. Miss Grey, this, sadly, is my cousin, another Mr. Benedict."

His laughing eyes alight with curiosity, the newcomer bowed to her.

"Javan?" came Miss Benedict's voice from the staircase. "Who was knocking so loudly? Is someone here?"

"No, it's only Richard," Javan replied.

"Richard who?" Miss Benedict demanded.

Richard Benedict sighed. "How quickly one is forgotten, even by family," he mourned.

"Cousin Richard," Javan said dryly.

"Richard!" Miss Benedict exclaimed. "Goodness, how are you? What brings you here? Come up and tell me everything! I'll ring for a cold supper..."

"What of little Rosa?" Richard asked as he walked toward the staircase with his cousin. "Is she well?"

"Better," Javan said. "But she's had a busy day. You'll see her tomorrow...unless she wants to join us? Miss Grey, perhaps you'd go and see? Bring her to the drawing room if you think she's up to it."

Caroline bowed her head in acknowledgement. She was the governess. Whatever had provoked the madness in the study, it was over as if it had never been. And it never *should* have been. They had both forgotten themselves.

Silently, she hurried past them, upstairs and along the passage to the schoolroom.

FOR JAVAN, JUST at first, it almost felt like his military days again, dealing with several crises at once. His blood, already on fire from holding and kissing Caroline, flowed faster, and he had to think on his feet. But of course, there were no enemies here but his baser instincts, and no one was going to die.

The intrusion of Richard at that precise moment had seemed unbearable, and he had truly considered sending him about his business, before shame brought him back to his senses. It was true he'd come here to escape everyone who knew him, but Richard was more than family. He'd been his friend for as long as he could remember.

So, while Marjorie chattered and fussed over her order for a cold supper to be set up in the drawing room, he pulled himself together and found he was glad to see Richard.

As for Caroline…this between them had been building all day. All week. Since he'd first seen her, really. God knew there was more to the attraction than being too long without a woman. She was not simply any woman who'd seemed to notice him. She was not even simply a *beautiful* woman—although today in her fine gown with her hair in that softer style, she had shone. He had not been the only man who'd noticed, either…

But there was something about her that had got under his skin. Her stillness that seemed to radiate calm and comfort. Her wit, the way she understood his jokes… And the way her breasts rose and fell when he came near her. She was not frightened and she was not indifferent. There was passion in her he longed to explore, for she excited him as no woman ever had.

As if his thoughts had drawn her, she walked into the drawing room with Rosa, who ran at once to Richard. Clearly, she remembered him with affection. Richard caught her and swung her high into the air as he'd done when she was tiny, and Javan couldn't help smiling.

Caroline—he couldn't think of her as Miss Grey any more, not after she'd kissed him like *that*, caressed him with her delectable little body—turned to go.

Stay!

Fortunately, he didn't bark the word aloud. To everyone else, she had to appear merely Rosa's governess. Even though there had never been anything *mere* about Miss Caroline Grey.

"Oh, don't leave, Miss Grey," Marjorie said. "Stay and drink tea with us and have a little supper."

She looked around, as though searching for a place at the back of the room, as far away from everyone else as possible. And yet, Javan knew she'd occasionally kept Marjorie company here—only when Marjorie requested it, of course, she never presumed. No doubt experience and humiliating accusations of encroachment had taught her that. Or perhaps it was just her character. She gave everyone room and yet would always be there when needed. He wasn't quite sure how he knew that, but he did.

In the end, Rosa ran back to her and dragged her by the hand to sit with her on the sofa closest to her uncle.

Javan walked to the cabinet and poured two generous glasses of brandy. "So," he said, handing one glass to his cousin and clinking it with his own. "What brings you out into the middle of nowhere, Richard? Apart from the sudden desire for our company, of course."

"Like you, old boy, I've bolted."

"From what?" Javan asked, amused.

Richard wrinkled his nose. "Marriage," he said distastefully.

"You're married?" Marjorie squeaked.

"No, thank God, that's why I'm here, looking for cover."

"Is she so ferocious?" Javan mocked.

"Never met the woman and never want to," Richard assured him with a shudder. "It's the whole idea that appalls me. I'm a young man with wild oats still to sow."

"You're three and thirty years old," Javan pointed out. "Past time to get an heir, for I certainly don't want to be Bart."

Caroline's head lifted, and her mouth opened as if she was about to ask what he meant. Then she closed it again.

"Baronet," Marjorie explained kindly. "Richard's father, Sir George Benedict, is head of the family. Javan always called him Uncle Bart because when he was a child, he once saw a letter addressed to Sir George Benedict Bart, without the proper punctuation. Richard is his only son and heir."

"I shall one day be Cousin Bart," Richard said flippantly. "But I have no intention of producing baby Bart just yet."

"Take your medicine like a man," Javan advised, throwing himself into the chair beside Marjorie. "And don't be put off by my experience. Some people have quite pleasant marriages, I believe."

"You're not going to throw me to the wolves, are you?" Richard asked.

"Not as long as you didn't tell anyone you were coming here."

"How are my aunt and uncle?" Marjorie asked.

As the conversation flowed, Rosa's head began to droop slowly onto Caroline's shoulder.

"I think I should take her up to bed," Caroline said quietly.

"Come back for supper," Marjorie said brightly, for the servants were bringing in an array of dishes as Caroline gently woke Rosa and urged her to her feet. Javan knew she wouldn't come back.

WHEN HE ENTERED his daughter's room, as he did every night, he caught a whisk of peach silk as Caroline vanished into her own bedchamber.

The soft click of the latch echoed in his mind. He sat on the edge of Rosa's bed and she took his hand, smiling happily. Rosa was ready to face life again. He rather suspected life had found him, too.

The figure of Marcus Swayle swam before his eyes, all smiles and charm as he'd greeted Lord and Lady Tamar at the castle...until he'd seen Javan.

Javan was grateful for that hasty retreat. Thank God, Rosa had been elsewhere at the time. He hoped to hell the bastard had abandoned Blackhaven, for he wouldn't have the poisonous little toad spoiling the life he'd only just begun to enjoy.

Rosa was fast asleep in no time. Detaching his hand, he stood and walked to the passage door, carefully not looking at the one connecting to the governess's chamber. And yet, as he limped down the passage, he couldn't help pausing at her door. She was in there, alone, and she wanted him. Perhaps she heard him, knew he stood there unmoving, swamped by temptation.

He could take her. He could give her a night of joy, oh but he could, and his own would light up the heavens.

He squeezed his eyes shut. She was no lightskirt, and no sophisticated lady protected by her husband's name either. But she *was* a lady and she deserved marriage, or at the very least, an unsullied reputation in order to maintain herself. He could only give her the latter.

Determinedly, he walked on.

When he reentered the drawing room, he knew Marjorie and Richard had been talking about him. It was inevitable.

"Is she settled?" Richard asked lazily.

"Out like a light," Javan replied. "I expect Marjorie's been telling you of our full day of company—our first such since we came here. And I think it's been good for her. Only..." He took the glass Richard thrust into his hand and sank into the chair by the fire. "I might as well tell you both at once. Marcus Swayle was at the castle."

Marjorie's eyes boggled.

"Sophia's lover?" Richard said, stunned. "Good God, what brought him here? Did he track you down?"

"That was my first thought, too," Javan admitted, "though I can't think what good it would do him. Besides, he looked so stunned, so appalled to see me that he bolted. It seems to be merely some unlikely, not to say unkind, coincidence."

"What was he doing there?" Marjorie demanded. "He is not some friend of the Tamars' surely?"

"They are friendly people," Javan said impatiently. "Were they not, *we* would not have been there. Swayle didn't look well. I suspect he's here to drink the waters."

"You can go together," Richard said flippantly. "Wouldn't that be a cozy party?"

"Not once I'd run him through or strangled him to death in public," Javan retorted. "And so I shall avoid him. I want to be sure you know to do the same. On no account must he come anywhere near Rosa."

"You think he's fond of her?" Richard asked doubtfully.

"No." Javan knocked the brandy down his throat. "I think he hurt her."

"AND WHAT OF the governess?" Richard asked. It was much later and they had begun on a fresh decanter. Marjorie had long since left them to it.

"She is good for Rosa," Javan said. "In more ways than simply educating her."

"Is she good for you, too?"

Javan curled his lip. "Stupid question."

"Is it? My dear fellow, I could cut the tension between you like a knife. What's more, when I first arrived, she looked very like a girl who's been thoroughly kissed, if not tumbled."

Javan jerked the glass to his lips. "Don't *ever* repeat that. She's untouched by me or by anyone else, I'd wager."

"Ah, then she is good for you."

"That isn't the point, is it? I would certainly *not* be good for her. Change the subject, for God's sake."

Richard gave an annoying, lazy smile, but at least he obeyed. "Very well. What is to do in the neighborhood? Apart from drinking water and very excellent brandy?"

"I believe these are the town's chief claims to fame. How long do you plan to stay?"

"Until marriage with me is farthest from my would-be-bride's mind."

"Have a heart, Richard. She can't be more in favor of this than you."

"Are you saying I'm not a good catch?"

"I'm saying you're a deplorable catch. I'm sure she'd cry off if she only met you."

"I missed you, Javan," Richard said affectionately.

"I know. And incidentally, if you're in Blackhaven, I too am Mr.

Benedict."

"Not Colonel," Richard said carefully.

"Absolutely not Colonel."

"Could we demote you? Just to distinguish you from me?"

"No. For Rosa's sake, I want no connection to the scandal."

"I doubt anyone remembers it now," Richard said casually. "It was a long time ago in the world of gossip."

"I'm not prepared to take the chance, not until she's older and would understand."

"She may understand more than you think, Javan. It's hard to tell when she doesn't speak."

"Well, her excellent governess has a plan for that. My money is on her."

"So is mine," Richard murmured, though in connection with what, he did not reveal.

WITH SO MUCH going on in her mind and heart, Caroline could not sleep late as she'd been kindly bidden by Miss Benedict. Instead, giving herself a brisk, no-nonsense talking-to on the subject of her employer, her duties and her own foolishness, she rose at her usual time. Having washed and dressed in her Sunday gown, she peeped in on Rosa, who still slept peacefully. Caroline hesitated only a moment before going alone to the kitchen for breakfast.

"No Miss Rosa today?" asked Williams, who appeared to be heading outside with a hunk of bread and butter clutched in one large hand.

"She's still fast asleep after her adventurous day. Williams, if Mr. Benedict is awake, could you ask him if I might walk into Blackhaven this morning to go to church?"

Church was just what she needed today. Mr. Grant, the vicar, had a way of lifting one's mood, of encouraging one to do better without judging one's past.

"You'd have to run, not walk, Miss," Williams said doubtfully. "Tell you what, though, if you don't mind the cart, I'm driving a few of the servants to church. You could come with us. He won't mind, if you don't."

"That would be ideal," Caroline said warmly. "Thank you."

"I'll be leaving in about half an hour," Williams said, nodding as he clumped out the door.

"Do the family never go to church?" Caroline asked Nan the kitchen maid. She hadn't had the courage to ask before.

"No, Miss, not that I know of. They're good people but keep themselves to themselves."

That much, Caroline already knew.

Since she only possessed the one cloak and bonnet, she retrieved them from the hallstand by the side door, and then wondered what to do with herself for the next thirty minutes.

It was, she supposed, an ideal time to work a little on Mr. Benedict's book, He would not be up and about, and if she worked on it now, she could avoid doing so later when he was in the same room. Avoiding him would be sensible for the next few days at least.

The study door stood open, so she walked in.

Mr. Richard Benedict stood by one of the glass cabinets, examining the samples. Impeccably dressed in buff pantaloons and a blue superfine coat, with a dazzlingly white cravat intricately tied about his throat, he looked far too fashionable for the over-casual household of Haven Hall.

Caroline halted in surprise.

He glanced up with a quick smile. "Miss Grey. Good morning."

"Good morning, sir."

"If you seek the master of the house, he is not an early riser like you and me."

"Oh, I am aware, sir. I came to work on some copying I have undertaken for him, but I shall come back another time."

Richard waved one expansive arm. "No, no, feel free. I am just curious as to what he's been doing with himself this last year."

Caroline draped her cloak and bonnet over the back of her usual chair and sat down at the desk, opening the notebook. She reached for her pen.

"It always amazed me," Richard continued, "how he managed to bring live plants home from the most obscure and war-torn areas of the world. Intact, too, usually. I would have expected his mind to be on other things. I expect it was his way of dealing with situations most of us would have found intolerable."

Caroline suspected it still was. She worked in silence for a few minutes.

"You have been good for them all, I hear," Richard murmured.

"I hope I have taught Rosa a little, but I have not been here long."

"I don't just mean Rosa. Marjorie, for example. I find her much brighter, and she likes you."

"The two aren't necessarily connected, but I'm glad if I've found favor with her."

There was a pause then, "You're being very proper, aren't you?" he said with a hint of amusement. "Don't you wish to ask me about Marjorie? Most people would."

"Miss Benedict has shown me nothing but kindness," Caroline said. "I have no intention of discussing her with a stranger, even one who is related to her."

"*Very* proper," Richard drawled. "It's a melancholy," he added after a moment. "It has afflicted her periodically since she was a young girl little older than Rosa. Sometimes, she takes to her bed for weeks on end. On top of everything else, Javan found her like that when he came home and Louisa died. No one was looking after her except servants. I include myself, by the way. I was in the country at the time. Javan took her with him when he left London. Everyone thought Marjorie a poor choice to care for Rosa, but that was never his reason. He looks after both of them, even locks Marjorie in her room when things are bad and she is liable to hurt herself."

"I know." If she hadn't *known*, she'd certainly guessed. She looked up from her writing and set her pen aside before she looked at him directly. He leaned one hip against the farthest corner of the desk, watching her. "Why are you telling me this?"

"Because Javan is one of the very few men I admire. I am curious as to how you regard him."

"As my employer and Rosa's father," she said coolly.

"And how does he regard you?"

"As Rosa's governess." The words didn't come so easily this time as she struggled to prevent the color seeping into her face. "If you wish more information, you must apply to Mr. Benedict himself."

"Oh, I have and I will," Richard said.

Caroline couldn't help it. She laughed. "Mr. Benedict, are you warning me off? I'm afraid you must trust me when I say that I am well aware of my own position in life and his." She stood, reaching for her cloak and bonnet and allowing him to see her in all her dowdiness. "I am no Circe, am I?"

"Oh, I don't know. The rumor is Lord Braithwaite found you tempting enough."

Caroline closed her eyes. "He did nothing of the kind. Repeating such rubbish is unkind, both to me and to Lord Braithwaite. I shall not discuss the matter with you. If Mr. Benedict is satisfied with my work and my past, I see no reason for you to cast aspersions."

Richard threw up his hands. "Acquit me, dear lady. I merely seek out the lie of the land."

"Allow me to leave you to your seeking while I go to church." It was an excellent parting line, though she would have been happier with it if she hadn't heard his breath of laughter behind her. In that, he reminded her of Javan.

Chapter Twelve

BLACKHAVEN'S PICTURESQUE LITTLE church was packed for the Sunday service, Mr. Grant being a popular vicar, both with gentry and lesser mortals. Caroline barely managed to squeeze onto the end of one of the back pews. Behind her, several people, including the servants from Haven Hall, were standing.

When Caroline had been before, she had occupied the Braithwaite pew at the front of the church. But while her current position was less comfortable, it afforded her a better view of the congregation. Half way through the first hymn, as she gazed about her, she glimpsed the pale man who had run from the castle party at sight of Javan Benedict.

He sat across the aisle from her, as though he, too, had squashed himself in at the last minute. Under her scrutiny, he glanced around and met her gaze. Somewhat to her surprise, he inclined his head. She returned the gesture and hastily averted her gaze to the vicar. For the rest of the service, she made a point of never glancing in his direction again.

And yet, as she emerged from the church, feeling somewhat stronger than when she'd entered it, thanks to Mr. Grant's uplifting sermon, she knew this man followed behind her. He was there when she paused to speak to Mr. Grant and to Mrs. Grant who was admiring a fisherman's baby close-by.

In the street, Williams and the cart—already full of the hall servants—waited for her. Some distance from them, Serena and her sisters waved madly at her. To go to them, Caroline walked across the grass toward the side gate.

"Excuse me," a male voice said politely behind her.

Caroline turned and faced the pale man, who bowed to her.

"Forgive me," he said humbly. "I know we are not acquainted, but I understand you are Miss Grey, Rosa Benedict's governess."

"I am."

"My name is Swayle. Marcus Swayle." He seemed to expect the name to mean something to her. When she only gazed at him somewhat blankly, he said anxiously, "Please tell me...how is she?"

Caroline frowned. "How is who, sir?"

"Little Rosa."

"She is very well," Caroline replied.

Mr. Swayle smiled deprecatingly. "I can see you are wondering what business it is of mine, and legally speaking, the answer is none. However, you should know that I regard Rosa as a beloved daughter."

"You do?" Javan's warning about this man echoed through her mind. *"Someone who must never, ever be anywhere near Rosa.*

"This is hard," Mr. Swayle said ruefully. "I can only imagine what that man has told you about me."

"To the best of my recollection, he has never mentioned you at all."

This seemed to take Mr., Swayle aback, though only for a moment. "I expect he is ashamed, for I know all. The cruel way he treated his wife and daughter."

"Cruel?" she repeated, startled. Even when she'd first known him, his only sign of gentleness had been toward his daughter. "Sir, you are mistaken."

She began to turn away, but he flung out one hand to detain her, only swiftly withdrawing it again with a hasty apology. But belatedly, his possible identity struck Caroline with all the force of a hammer.

"You were her—" she blurted, only just breaking off before she uttered the word lover.

"Her lover?" Swayle said bitterly. "That is what he told you? It is true I loved her before he even met her and forced her to marry him. He wanted her money, for she was a wealthy heiress. You may think this wrong of us, but it was such a relief to us when we thought he was dead. I *married* her, was living with her as her husband. She and Rosa and I were a happy family at last and blissful that she was expecting my child. And then *he* came home. Clearly not dead at all. Enraged at finding us together, he beat me, half-killed me—as you see, I am still recovering. That, I can forgive. But Louisa's death, that of my unborn child, that is firmly at his door. And I fear so for Rosa."

Caroline's ears rang with his terrible accusations. She felt almost dizzy. Williams strode purposely through the side gate, glaring at her.

"Care for her, I beg you," Swayle said urgently. "And please, should you need help, or just wish to know more, you may find me at the hotel. Goodbye, Miss Grey."

Bemused, she stared after his retreating back as he walked back toward the church, leaning heavily on his cane.

"We're going home, Miss," Williams said abruptly.

"Of course." She turned with him to walk to the side gate.

"What did *he* want?" Williams demanded aggressively.

"You know him? I wondered if he was a little mad."

Williams snorted. "Not he. Nor even deluded, though he pretends. Best if you ignore him. What did he say to you?"

"He asked after Rosa," Caroline replied vaguely. "Mainly."

Williams paused. "You do know you mustn't let her see him?"

"*Let* her see him?" she repeated. "Does she want to?"

"No," Williams said flatly. "And don't believe a word that bas— that *man*—says."

MARCUS SWAYLE WALKED directly from church to the rather disgusting town tavern. Although he wasn't much of a man for slumming it—he liked his comforts—this was the second time in two days he'd found himself there. The first was yesterday after coming upon Javan Benedict at the castle rout.

He knew almost at once that he shouldn't have fled the castle, leaving Benedict, as it were, in possession of the field. But the shock had been great. And in truth, he was physically afraid of the man. It was only in the tavern, drinking a restorative brandy, that the possibilities for revenge had begun to percolate.

After the death of Louisa, Benedict had seemed to disappear from the face of the earth. Nursing his bruised body and aggrieved by the removal of Louisa's funds from his reach, Swayle had merely been glad of his enemy's absence. By the time he had recovered enough to re-enter London society, the juicy gossip of Benedict's return to England had almost died down—until Swayle had added fuel to the flame.

It had begun as mere vitriol against the man who had taken everything from him. And yes, perhaps there was a little shame in being beaten so comprehensively in a fight with a man who could barely stand. So, he never mentioned Benedict's injuries in his version of events. And it was then he had invented two ingenious fictions—that he and Louisa had been so convinced of Benedict's death that they had married, and that he feared for Rosa's life at the hands of her monstrous father. Society had lapped it up greedily. Only when Richard Benedict had returned to London, had Swayle felt it politic to depart the capital for the sake of his "shattered health".

He'd never expected to find the Benedicts here in Blackhaven, of all places. He was short of funds and in search of a wealthy woman to part from her fortune. Preferably a sickly widow, since she was likely to be more grateful for his attentions. And of course, she might die and leave him free to enjoy his inheritance unencumbered. Having obtained an introduction to Lady Tamar, he had expected her rout to be the best place to begin his search...until he had looked into the cold eyes of his enemy.

Well, his departure had been more of a tactical retreat than a defeat. For in the tavern, he had heard all Blackhaven's rumors about the family at Haven Hall. And had begun to tell his old stories.

Today, he had almost missed Miss Grey as the cart in front of him had disgorged several female servants. It had taken several seconds to connect her dowdy, respectable person to the beautiful lady he'd seen with Benedict last night. He'd followed her into church from instinct, listening and learning as he went.

Oh yes, there were possibilities there. Smiling, he raised his brandy to his lips just as someone large and clumsy bumped into him. Remembering where he was, he slapped his hand to his pocket and caught a grubby hand. It belonged to the man who had bumped into him, a big, villainous looking individual with his hat pushed to the back of his unclean head.

Swayle did not underestimate the difficulties here. The landlord didn't like trouble and apparently, he didn't take a moral stance over events like this, just took the quietest way out. Swayle was likely to be thrown out for any accusations of theft. Or the villain could simply stab him where he sat and walk away.

He suspected the man thought about it. Then the brute grinned. "Can't blame a man for trying," he observed. "Not when he's hard-up."

An idea began to dawn in Swayle's head. He would find a way to a devastating revenge on the man who had humiliated and impoverished him. But he would need help.

"Hard-up," Swayle repeated. "Then you are a man open to earning a little money, with no questions asked."

The large man pushed his hat even further back. "Might be," he admitted. He smiled in what he probably imagined was an ingratiating manner, but in fact was quite terrifying. "They don't call me Killer Miller for nothing."

"I WAS THINKING," Miss Benedict announced at luncheon.

"Congratulations, Marjorie," her brother said provokingly.

She cast him a quelling look.

"What were you thinking?" Richard asked.

"That we should invite Lord and Lady Tamar to dinner," Marjorie said in a rush.

Javan laid down his knife.

"Ah, the mythical Lord Tamar," Richard observed, "who turned out not to be a myth at all. Did he really marry Braithwaite's sister?"

"Yes," Caroline said since no one else answered him.

Javan's gaze was locked with his sister's, though he looked more stunned than annoyed. Eventually, he picked up his knife again. "Ask the Grants, too, if you like. He's a good man for a vicar."

Marjorie's jaw showed an initial tendency to drop at this easy victory. Then she frowned. "You confuse me. Isn't a vicar *meant* to be a good man?"

"Never confuse your definition of the word good with Javan's," Richard advised. "The Reverend Mr. Grant will no doubt be discovered to be a man of wit and sound strategic knowledge in military matters. And probably learned in botany."

Javan raised his wineglass to him.

"I hope they have well sprung carriages for getting up the drive," Richard added wryly.

"Try to contain your concern," Javan said. "I have some men coming over to clear and repair it next week."

"Have you?" Marjorie said in surprise.

"They should be here first thing in the morning, so there's no cause for panic if you hear a racket."

"Goodness," Marjorie said, clearly impressed. "What evening shall I invite them, then?"

"Whichever suits. I have," Javan said self-deprecatingly, "no unbreakable plans."

"Wednesday?" Marjorie suggested. "Richard, you will still be here, will you not?"

"I wouldn't miss it," Richard drawled.

"Excellent. Miss Grey, should we invite the Braithwaite children?"

Rosa's head snapped up as she smiled from her aunt to Caroline and back.

"They are quite civilized," Caroline replied, "and will be thrilled to attend an adult dinner. Especially with Rosa. I'm sure Lady Tamar will be happy to bring them."

Miss Benedict beamed.

After lunch, Caroline and Rosa went for their daily walk. As was usual, Javan and Tiny accompanied them, although rather to her surprise, Richard did not.

"Does Mr. Benedict not care to walk?" Caroline asked lightly.

Rosa grinned, pointing to her feet and then leaping back as though horrified by the mess appearing on her boots.

Javan laughed. "You think he's afraid of dirtying his fine footwear? He has a very superior valet to clean his boots. I expect he's just tired after his journey. It's a long way from London."

Rosa shrugged and ran ahead with Tiny. Silence lapsed between Caroline and Javan, but in truth, she only noticed when he said, "You are quiet. Are you wondering how to treat me after yesterday evening?"

Caroline drew a breath for courage. "Actually, no. I have been wondering whether or not to worry you with something else entirely."

"My shoulders are broad," he said flippantly. "Go ahead and worry me if you can."

"I spoke with Marcus Swayle this morning."

Although she was gazing deliberately straight ahead at Rosa throwing a stick for Tiny, she was aware Javan's head turned toward her, almost felt the new tension tighten within him.

"More accurately, *he* spoke to me," she corrected herself. "Outside church."

"What did he say?"

"He asked about Rosa." At last, she met his intense yet veiled gazed. "And he warned me against you."

Javan curled his lip. "I would expect nothing less. I'm sorry he chose you to bleat at, though. I was hoping he'd fled the country."

"He said you beat him to within an inch of his life."

"A slight exaggeration. Given what I suspect now, I wish I'd hit him harder. What else?"

"That you...that you forced your wife to marry you for her money and that you were responsible for her death."

He kicked a stone out of his path. "Perhaps I was," he said moodily.

"And he said that you mistreat Rosa," she blurted.

He glanced at her with contempt, though for what or whom she could not be sure. "And you believe that?"

"No. I suppose I *might* have believed the rest if it hadn't been for that, but I know nothing could induce you to harm Rosa."

"You can't know that," he snapped. "One never knows what *oneself* is capable of, let alone what another person is. What you mean is, you *hope* I would never harm Rosa, because for some reason I have yet to fathom, you like me."

"And that is why you hired *me*?" Caroline retorted. "In the mere hope that *I* would not harm her?"

A smile twisted his lips. "Exactly."

She waved one dismissive hand. "You are impossible. Sir, if Mr. Swayle took the trouble to speak to me in this way, he may well be traducing you in Blackhaven to anyone who will listen."

"I'm sure it's all grist to the rumor mill," he said without interest. "Which, judging by the way you looked at me when we first met, has already been working hard."

"I had no idea who you were when we first met."

"Do you know any better now?"

She held his gaze, watching with fascination as the icy contempt and fury behind them drained into something far warmer. "A little," she whispered. "I think."

His hand brushed her wrist among the folds of her cloak, and his fingers threaded through hers. "How did I exist without you, Caroline Grey?" His fingers curled convulsively. "How *will* I exist without you."

Her heart beat so fast she felt dizzy. She was afraid to breathe, to say or do the wrong thing. But she could not prevent her hand clasping his.

"I will not leave unless you bid me." The words came out hoarse, almost broken.

Abruptly, she was half-pushed, half-dragged off the path and into the trees until she felt the roughness of bark at her back and the hardness of his body pinning her there. His eyes blazed down into hers.

"You should not say such things to me," he whispered.

"You should not *do* such things to me," she returned shakily.

A warm smile flickered across his face. "No, I shouldn't." But he remained thrillingly pressed against her, forcing her to awareness of his muscled thighs, his hips, and the hardness that grew between. Delicious weakness held her still. Desire raged through her.

Slowly, his forehead dropped to hers and rested. "I wish…"

"What?" she asked desperately, and as suddenly as he'd seized her, she was freed.

"One day I might tell you that, too," he flung at her as he broke back on the path. "Until then, you should avoid being alone with me because it seems I can't keep my hands off you. Rosa! This way!"

Her trembling knees were reluctant to hold her up as she trailed after him to meet Rosa, struggling to work out what had just occurred.

AT LUNCHEON THE following day, Miss Benedict happily revealed that she had received notes of acceptance to her dinner from both Lady Tamar and Mrs. Grant. And that Lady Tamar would gladly bring her younger sisters—news which made Rosa clap her hands, her face lit up with delighted expectation.

As they returned to the schoolroom, Caroline said lightly, "You're looking forward to seeing the Braithwaite girls again."

Rosa nodded.

"You enjoy their company," Caroline observed, "as they enjoy yours. I'm glad you have found ways to communicate with them so that you can join in."

Rosa's smile faded. She looked away.

"You can't always join in?" Caroline asked gently.

Rosa shook her head. A single tear squeezed out of the corner of one eye and trickled down her face.

"Rosa." Caroline put her arm around the child, hugging her to her side. "No one thinks less of you for it. Your family loves you. I love you. Your friends will love you whether or not you speak. I just wonder if you wouldn't have more fun if you could bring yourself to say the odd word here and there. We grow too comfortable sometimes, with the way things are, but we can always make them better. Like your father and your aunt giving up solitude for company."

Rosa smiled wanly. For a moment, she clung to Caroline, and then broke free, and ran to the schoolroom.

Later that afternoon, while Rosa was lost in her painting of a bowl of fruit, Caroline was drawn to the window by the clop of hooves on the drive. Dr. Lampton, Blackhaven's preferred physician, dismounted, and, leaving his horse with Williams, walked up the steps to the house.

Anxiety flooded Caroline. Was Marjorie taken ill? Was Javan? She thought his appetite had been a little better this last week or so, but she'd no real idea what his injuries entailed.

More than half an hour later, Dr. Lampton still hadn't ridden away, and Caroline had to force herself not to pace and thus disturb Rosa's concentration with her own worry. Ginny the maid stuck her head around the door.

"Master asks that you bring Miss Rosa to the drawing room, Miss."

Rosa heard that at once, hastily shoving her painting to one side.

"That's very good," Caroline observed. "We'll take a look at the light when we return."

Javan Benedict was discovered in the drawing room with Dr. Lampton who, since his wife's death, had developed a rather forbidding aspect to go with his already cynical humor. He did at least relieve his scowl as they entered, presumably for Rosa's benefit, after she pulled up short at the sight of the unexpected stranger with her father.

Caroline's anxious gaze could find nothing ill or even out of the ordinary about Javan. Dr. Lampton gave her a slight bow but came to shake Rosa's hand when her father introduced them.

"How do you do, Miss Rosa?" he said gravely. "Your father tells me you haven't spoken a word in two years and would like to see if I can fix whatever is wrong, so that you can speak to him again. Is this a good idea?"

Rosa gave a little shrug, which he appeared to take as assent.

"So, do you feel ill? In pain? Unhappy?"

To each of his questions, Rosa shook her head.

Dr. Lampton then asked permission to examine her mouth and throat, then turned her toward the light from the window.

"Will you let him examine you, too?" Caroline asked.

"He already has. And Marjorie. I got a special price for a family group. He'd probably throw you in for free if you'd like a quick—"

"Thank you, I am never ill," she interrupted. "Please don't be flippant. Did he find you...well?"

"I believe so. He gave me some ointment and a vile tasting tonic, and some exercises to strengthen my leg. He seemed to be a sensible man so I let him talk to Marjorie and Rosa."

Caroline, who hadn't expected to learn even those few details from him, cast him a quick glance, but his attention was all on Rosa. While he examined her, Dr. Lampton asked her a lot of questions, even fished a notebook from his bag and a pencil and asked her to write down answers that required more than a nod or a headshake. It was, however, doubtful she would write anything new. Javan had already questioned her in this way and learned very little from her short, evasive answers.

While Rosa wrote, Dr. Lampton walked across to Javan and Caroline.

"She's frightened," he said abruptly. "And is either afraid to speak of it, or simply doesn't wish to remember. Therefore, she doesn't speak at all so that she can never speak about *that*. I suspect she'll speak again when she's ready, for her understanding seems to be quite superior for a child of her years, and I can find no physical damage. If you want to encourage her to speak…my advice would be to confront her—while she feels safe in your protection—with a dilute form of whatever frightened her in the first place."

"I don't know what that was," Javan said miserably. "I was not in the country when she first stopped speaking."

Dr. Lampton shrugged. "Then give her time. For what it's worth, I believe you are doing the right things." His gaze flickered over Caroline.

"And my sister?" Javan asked with difficulty. "Can you suggest anything other than bleeding her?"

"Bleeding her will only weaken her," Dr. Lampton snapped. "I would not suggest it at all. I have found a regular infusion of St. John's wort to help in many such cases. Lavender also. And persuade her to take more exercise or she will atrophy."

The doctor took a breath, perhaps realizing he had sounded too short. "Forgive my blunt manners."

"I prefer them to any other," Javan replied.

"I do not belittle your sister's condition," Lampton said. "In fact, you were right to consult me on all three cases, and if you are agreeable, I would like to see you all again in one month. Or earlier, if you feel the need. Good day."

He collected his notebook from Rosa with a surprisingly kind smile and took his leave. Rosa and her father both gazed after him.

"I'm glad you consulted him," Caroline said.

"Well, now that we have, let us see who can winkle Marjorie out for a walk with Tiny. My money is on Rosa."

Chapter Thirteen

O N THE AFTERNOON of the dinner party, Caroline changed quickly into her brown dress, and discovered Marjorie in the dining room, supervising the table setting.

"Might I help with anything, Miss Benedict?" she enquired.

Marjorie glanced up in clear relief, and then squeaked at sight of her. "No, no, the other gown, Miss Grey! The pretty one. Hurry."

Only when Caroline had changed again was she put to work, arranging table decorations and candles, while Marjorie gazed out of the window, anxiously watching the darkening of the sky.

"Oh dear, I think a storm is coming," she mourned. "They will not wish to come here in a storm, in case they cannot get home…"

However, despite the fast-worsening weather, the Grants arrived in good time and were shown into the drawing room.

"How wonderful," Marjorie exclaimed. "We were afraid you would not risk it in this wretched weather."

"Oh, we'd never do anything in Blackhaven if we let the weather dictate," Mrs. Grant said cheerfully. "And it is so kind of you to invite us."

While Marjorie was still introducing Richard, Rosa insinuated herself in front of Mrs. Grant, gazing up at her.

"Rosa," her father said, placing his hand on her shoulder to pull her back.

But Mrs. Grant only smiled. "You're wondering where your friends are, aren't you? They'll be here, soon. Serena—Lady Tamar—is never punctual, and time is somewhat *stretchable* to Lord Tamar!"

The Grants were both sociable people and excellent company. Richard and Mrs. Grant turned out to have many London acquaintances in common. In fact, Richard claimed to have worshipped her from afar for years without ever speaking to her, although Mrs. Grant took that with a laughing pinch of salt.

Before dinner had to be put back, the castle entourage arrived. By then, the weather had grown truly filthy, although Serena optimistically maintained the sky would be clear again by nine o'clock.

They ate dinner to the accompaniment of the howling wind, rattling window panes and the battering of rain on glass, but it was a merry meal. Javan, as he occasionally did, exerted himself to be entertaining, and made sure no one was left out of the conversation, for it was an informal table. Caroline was seated strategically between Richard and Rosa, on the fringes of both the adult and children's groups, and yet not truly part of either. Nevertheless, she enjoyed the fun of the children's conversation as well as the witty repartee of the adults, to which she only contributed when addressed directly.

Javan never spoke to her personally, although he laughed once at her jest with Serena. He seemed slightly taken aback when it was revealed Grant, too, had once been part of Wellington's army. But he did not disclose his own career, and neither Marjorie nor Richard tried to make him. For the first time, Caroline began to think seriously that there was more to his secretiveness than just preserving Rosa from the unkind gossip that might be associated with Colonel Benedict.

"You are right, of course," Richard murmured beside her.

"About what in particular?" she asked lightly.

"The gossip will begin anyway, with Swayle in town. When I was in Blackhaven yesterday, I discovered he has already started foul rumors. To be honest, I'm surprised to see our guests, for he is very plausible."

"Our guests pay little attention to gossip," Caroline returned, "having been at various times, the subjects of it themselves. Besides, they are too good natured."

"Everyone in Blackhaven is not," Richard said with a little grimness. "They cannot be. This is too bad, just when he's pulling himself out of—" He broke off abruptly.

Caroline waited, gazing at her plate while her fingers played idly with the stem of her wine glass. But he did not elucidate, and she would not ask. Eventually, she picked up her glass and under the cover of drinking from it, cast a quick glance up the table to Javan.

"There it is again," Richard murmured, even lower.

"What?" she asked.

"Concern. And yet you never encroach. If I wasn't the cynic I was born to be, I'd almost imagine you cared for him from afar and were content to do so."

Stricken, she stared at him. For an instant, he gazed back, then swore under his breath and laughed aloud. "Smile, Miss Grey," he said between his teeth. "For the benefit of all. I have the lie of the land now and shall act accordingly."

She smiled blindly, in case anyone was looking at her. "You mean to have me dismissed?" she whispered. Would Javan do that? For her own good? He must know better than Richard how she felt. And of course, she should not stay here feeling as she did for her employer, only...only she could not bear to leave him. Or Rosa. Surely there was a powerful, still-growing bond between all three of them...

"How would I do that?" Richard said reasonably. "I told you I have the lie of the land, and I won't hurt either of you."

Confused, she turned away to speak to Rosa and the other children who, at that moment, made more sense.

After dinner, the ladies repaired to the drawing room, leaving the men to their port. The girls were allowed to escape up to the school-room to play, although Maria, almost grown-up, opted to stay with the adults.

"The weather is atrocious," Marjorie said anxiously. "If anything, it's worse. I hate to think of you going home in that, in the dark. I wonder..." Her eyes glazed as she sank into thought.

"It is wild," Serena said from the window.

"We have space here, do we not, Miss Grey?" Marjorie said abruptly. "There are two guest bedchambers currently unused, although the young ladies…"

"The two younger ones could fit easily into Rosa's huge bed with her," Caroline said. "And we could make up the couch for Lady Maria."

"Oh no, it would put you to far too much trouble," Serena objected.

"Not at all," Marjorie assured. "I'll just see that the beds are made up and fires lit…"

"Let me do that, ma'am," Caroline said quietly, and Marjorie smiled gratefully, sinking back down into her chair while Caroline went down to the kitchen.

Two maids were easily pried away from washing up to help make up beds, and Williams went to fetch wood and coal for the fires.

When she finally returned to the drawing room, it was to find the gentleman had rejoined them, and Miss Benedict was about to pour tea. Quietly, Caroline took the cups and saucers from Marjorie and took them to the ladies and gentlemen.

"Efficient as ever," Javan murmured, when she served him last. "I suppose all our guests now have warm, clean beds to go to?"

"Well, the warming pans are still to go in," Caroline said apologetically, "but yes, they should be ready by the time everyone retires."

His lips quirked. "Thank you."

She searched his eyes quickly. "I hope you do not mind. It seemed the best solution"

"It is. Quite right." He rested his hip on the arm of an empty chair. Caroline was conscious of an urge to stay with him, to sit in that chair and feel the brush of his coat, his elbow whenever he moved, to simply soak up his nearness. Instead, she walked to the other side of the room and sat by Miss Benedict, where it was safe.

WITH ALL THE girls staying in Rosa's chamber, her father could not sit with her as he usually did. From bewilderment at her unprecedented company, she went to panic and ran to her father in the drawing room as though to prove to herself he was still there. After that, since Caroline was in and out organizing the girls, the fun of this novelty began to sink in.

By popular demand, Caroline read to them all in bed, and when she stood up to go, the Braithwaite girls all embraced her, declaring how much they missed her and how lucky Rosa was. Touched, Caroline hugged them back, ending with Rosa.

"Shall I stay until you're all asleep?" she asked, with a quelling look at her old pupils to prevent them ridiculing the idea.

Rosa hesitated, then shook her head and released Caroline to prod Helen in the back and make her squeal.

Without giving a reason, Caroline announced that the night light would remain lit, then left them alone. She read until they quieted down, and then undressed for bed. Despite the noise of the storm, she fell asleep almost immediately.

She woke in darkness to the shuffle of footsteps on the other side of the passage door. Her first thought was that it was the girls up to mischief. She shot out of bed, blundering toward the door and throwing it open before she realized she couldn't see who was in the passage without a light. Whoever was out there didn't carry one, but she could still hear the slow, shuffle of feet.

Her fingers were infuriatingly clumsy and slow with the flint, but at last the candle was lit. Seizing it, she hurried out the door just in time to see a male figure vanish around the corner of the passage toward the stairs.

Javan? Was he sleepwalking again? It had been stormy the last time he had done this... What if he went outside again? What if he fell downstairs? Even if he merely embarrassed himself in front of his guests, he would be mortified.

Caroline flung her wrapper around herself, and hastened along the passage, her candle light bobbing and flickering in front of her.

Javan stood with his back to the stairs, quite still, gazing straight ahead. She was afraid to speak to him or to touch him, in case he jerked backward and fell, for he was quite clearly sleepwalking again. Then, without warning, he moved away from her—or perhaps from the light, for he lifted one hand as though shading his eyes. He walked swiftly across the landing, Caroline at his heels.

Her candlelight flickered over the library door, and with relief, she recognized a safe place to wake him. If she could make him go in.

However, as soon as she opened the door, he turned toward the faint noise, as if his dreaming urge to escape was attuned to the sound. He walked straight past her into the room.

Hastily, she followed and closed the door, then set the candle down on the table.

"Sir," she said quietly, standing directly in front of him. "Sir, you must wake up."

At the first sound of her voice, he took a decisive step away from her, and yet he paused, looking back toward her, frowning in the dim light, his mouth twisted with some strange mixture of despair and hope.

"I told them," he said, in peculiar agony. "I told them."

"Sir, Javan, please wake up!"

He blinked several times and swayed. She caught his elbows and his arms swung around her as though holding himself up.

"Caroline," he whispered. "Caroline, are you real?"

She took his face between his hands. "Yes, yes, I'm here. You were sleepwalking again."

His arms tightened as though he'd never let her go.

ROSA RARELY WOKE in the night. When she did, there was always the faint, comforting glow of the nightlight allowing her to fall asleep again before the fears took hold. Tonight, too, the nightlight was there, along with the unfamiliar feeling of other people in the bed with her. Helen and Alice. And across the room was Maria. She liked all the girls. She was glad they were there, only…she wished her father was here, too.

At least Miss Grey was on the other side of the door she could just make out in the dim light. For she was sure she could hear distant footsteps. Not *him*. They couldn't be *him*, here at Haven Hall… Still, she needed Miss Grey to tell her so, or even just to see her would show how silly her old fears were. She stood up in the bed, stepped over Helen, and slithered on to the floor before padding across to the governess's door.

She opened it without knocking, taking the night light with her.

Miss Grey's bed was empty.

Rosa's heart began to gallop with fear. She clutched it, trying to calm it, to think. Miss Grey couldn't have left, wouldn't have left without saying goodbye. Where was she? Had *he* got her? *Was* he here in the hall?

Common sense told her that of course he wasn't, but still, she needed to know Miss Grey was safe. Had she the courage to go along the dark passage to Papa's chamber?

Leaving the door open, she returned to her own room. Her knees shook.

"Rosa?" Maria loomed up from the couch, whispering her name. "What is it?"

Without thought, Rosa took her by the hand and dragged her out of bed, and across to the open door, pointing at Miss Grey's empty bed.

"You want Miss Grey?" Maria murmured. "Now?"

Rosa nodded vehemently.

Maria thought. "She's probably with Serena. Come on." This time it was Maria who drew Rosa by the hand to the passage door and along past the landing toward the bedchamber given to Maria's sister and her husband.

As they passed the library door, Rosa was sure she heard a noise, and shrank closer to Maria.

FOR THE SECOND time in his life, Javan woke to find himself gazing into the eyes of Caroline Grey. She took his face between her hands, murmuring words of comfort, her eyes huge with care for him. And the contrast between the horrors of his dream and the sweetness of her presence, her caress, was too great. He pushed against her hands until his mouth found hers, and he kissed her as though he'd never stop. He never wanted to stop.

Somewhere, he'd registered that it was night and that they were in the library. Beyond that, there was only Caroline, the warm softness of her body pressed to his, her scent in his nostrils, her unique taste on his lips, his tongue. Her instinctive passion inflamed him, driving him beyond comfort to raging lust.

Something moved on the edge of his vision.

A familiar voice drawled. "You do know you're not alone?"

Caroline gasped under his mouth and sprang back.

Javan turned more slowly to face his cousin, who was looming over the back of the sofa, only just within reach of the candle's faintest illumination. "Richard, what the *devil*?"

"I was about to ask you the same question. I was here first."

"Well, what do you mean by skulking here with no light?" Javan demanded.

"I was on watch-for-the-intruder duty, remember? Well, I fell asleep and was having very pleasant dreams before you two battered your way in here and woke me up." Richard rose to his feet and ambled toward them, a smirk on his handsome face that seemed to betoken both amusement and pleasure. "May I be the first to bless you, my children?"

"Sir, Mr. Benedict was sleepwalking," Caroline said desperately. "He did not know what he was doing,"

Is that truly what she thought? Or was she simply trying to save the tatters of her reputation? She needn't have bothered. Richard might tease, but he would never blab.

Richard snorted with laughter. "Truly?" he said and took both her hand and Richard's and solemnly joined them. Javan would have pulled free and sworn at him had not the library door opened again to reveal a whole host of people.

Rosa pushed past Mrs. Grant and Lord Tamar to run to Caroline. Lady Tamar tried to stop her sister following, and the result was they all tumbled into the room. They had brought their own candles, and so and were afforded a clear view of Caroline in her night rail, stunned. One of her hands had been grasped by Rosa. The other was still held by both Javan and Richard, neither of whom, in their shirt sleeves, were properly dressed to be in a lady's company.

"Miss Grey!" Lady Tamar exclaimed. She sounded more astonished than shocked. "What on earth is going on?"

The matter was not beyond control. These people were Caroline's friends. The worst that could happen was that he would have to reveal his tendency to sleepwalk.

Until Richard said, "It isn't what you think."

And Lord Tamar, who seemed—damn him—to feel protective toward Caroline, pushed forward with a dangerous frown. "And what exactly is it I think?" he demanded.

"Rupert, the children!" his wife reminded him.

"What are you both doing here with Miss Grey?" Tamar asked bluntly.

Caroline pulled her hands free, furiously hugging herself, remembering no doubt the previous time she'd been accused of impropriety and lost her position. With sudden, blinding clarity, Javan knew how to put it right in the eyes of the word. Knew too that life could hold no greater happiness than being married to Caroline.

He looked from her appalled gaze to Richard's expectant one, and the words dried in his throat. She'd never believe he loved her now. In any case, was he not insane to put his heart and Rosa's care in the possession of a woman he'd known less than a month?

The silence stretched. Caroline would no longer look at him. He refused to do this in front of everyone.

"We'll sort this out in the morning," he said abruptly. "I suggest we all retire."

"I don't—" Tamar began furiously.

"After," Richard interrupted, "you all also congratulate me on my engagement to Miss Grey."

The blood roared in Javan's ears. *No!* The single word crashed through his head but remained unspoken, for Caroline was staring at Richard in shock.

"This isn't how we intended it to come out," Richard said glibly, "but Javan has just given us his blessing in this somewhat unconventional setting, so you might as well know now as tomorrow."

This was insane. He couldn't marry Caroline... But she suddenly grasped Richard's arm and at last the suspicion fell into place that such an engagement was not unplanned. His earlier remarks had been sarcastic, teasing... Richard was charming, undamaged, and the wealthy heir to a baronetcy. Javan was...less.

Somehow, he managed a bow. "Goodnight," he said and pushed his way out of the room, leaving Caroline being embraced by Lady Tamar and Mrs. Grant and Maria all at once.

Only fury kept the pain at bay.

Chapter Fourteen

IN CONSIDERATION OF the unexpected guests, breakfast the following morning was to be served in the dining room. After washing and dressing, Caroline woke the girls and left them to dress in their own time. Her plan was to eat breakfast alone and escape for a long, head-clearing walk before she was required to speak to anyone about anything that mattered.

However, in this she was foiled at the outset, for as soon as she reached the staircase, Richard Benedict strode out of the library and beckoned her inside. Being still furious with him, she hesitated before finally deciding to clear up this silly mess as soon as possible. With dignity, she followed him into the library, without closing the door.

"Don't look so fierce, Miss Grey. You should be happy on your betrothal day."

"I am not," she uttered, "betrothed. At the very least I insist on being consulted before the fact!"

"Well, I'd no time to ask you, and if I had, you would only have refused."

"And yet here we are, with everyone believing us to be engaged!"

"Including Javan."

Especially Javan. Pain racked her, like a dagger in the heart. How dared he believe it when she had only just kissed him? How dared he?

"Don't you see that this is the point, Miss Grey?" Richard urged.

"If there is a point, it is far too obscure for me."

"No one wishes you to be ruined."

"I would not have been ruined," she exclaimed. "Lady Serena

would never believe ill of me—"

"Not even after you were accused of a similar indiscretion with her own brother?"

Stricken, she stared at him.

Richard threw up his hands. "You may be right," he allowed. "But I could not take the chance. I waited for Javan to get in first, but he didn't."

The dagger in her heart twisted. "No," she agreed. "He didn't."

"And if he had, you would be thinking he did it merely from honor."

"It would have been the truth."

"Rubbish. It was not honor in his heart when he was kissing you in this very room last night."

She flushed to the roots of her hair. "He was confused, waking from dreams to find himself in a place he—"

"Yes, yes," Richard interrupted. "Miss Grey, if my cousin is not forced out of it, he will carry on believing he does not deserve happiness. It is your business and mine to show him he does."

She stared at him. "By us marrying each other? How much, exactly, does he want me out of his hair?"

"Don't be obtuse, Miss Grey, it does not suit you. Look, anyone can see Javan is in love with you. Except Javan, of course, who will have rationalized it so he can wallow a bit longer in the safety of his superior misery."

"That is hardly fair," she said coldly. "Or true!"

"The love is true," he insisted. "The rest may be exaggerated by my own frustration. The point is, he married Louisa in haste, encouraged by her parents and his own family, and he repented almost immediately. For good reason. He is determined never to make such a mistake again, particularly not when there is Rosa to consider. He needs a push to win you. I thought last night's discovery might do it, but he drew back at the last moment, so now we must resort to inspiring jealousy."

Caroline closed her mouth. "You are insane."

"I promise you it will work. He is already mad as fire."

She sank onto the window seat. "No, this is wrong," she said anxiously. "You cannot push people or their emotions about in this way. But more than that, I will *not* have Rosa believing I will leave her!"

This, clearly, was something Richard had not thought of. Though he quickly overcame the objection. "Never mind. Just tell her we'll live here for the foreseeable future."

She regarded him with fascination. "You have an answer for everything. But the truth is, whatever good you imagine you are achieving, you are doing ill by your cousin and by me. I will not *spoil* things with this dishonesty, and I will not deign to try this manipulation—"

"Now don't relapse into righteous indignation," Richard commanded. "Comfort yourself that you will never have to marry me and *trust* me. I've known Javan since I was born. It's harsh, but he does need a kindly kick. At the very least, you must not make me out a liar, so let us maintain the fiction for today at least."

"No longer," she muttered as she rose and walked out of the room.

As it turned out, she had little opportunity either to confirm or deny her supposed betrothal to Richard Benedict. By the time she returned from her walk, Javan had made his farewells to his guests and shut himself up in his study, leaving Marjorie and Richard to wave them off.

"I'm *so* glad for you," Serena said warmly, giving Caroline a final hug. "Though who will teach my wretched sisters now, I cannot imagine!"

The wretched sisters embraced her with equal enthusiasm and demanded to be invited to the wedding. Caroline actually sighed with relief when their carriages drove off out of sight. There was little sign now of yesterday's fierce storm, except the sodden, muddy texture of the ground.

Rosa's hand crept into hers.

She forced a smile to her lips. "Did you enjoy the night with your friends?"

Rosa nodded enthusiastically, although behind the remembered happiness, her eyes were full of questions Caroline could not answer.

"Run up to the schoolroom," Caroline said. "I'll be with you directly."

Rosa obeyed readily enough, and Caroline turned her feet in the direction of Javan's study. Richard leaned against the bannister, watching her. She ignored him.

A soft rap on the study door elicited no response. She knocked again, more loudly but again she was greeted with silence from the other side. She was sure he was in there and that he knew it was she who knocked. He simply didn't want to see her. Closing her eyes, she rested her cheek against the door for the tiniest moment. Then she walked away and climbed the stairs to the schoolroom.

CAROLINE FOUND HERSELF both dreading and longing for luncheon. She wanted to see Javan very badly, and explain, whatever the outcome.

But when she entered the dining room, Miss Benedict was crying with joy and embracing Richard amidst much congratulation. Caroline stopped dead, gazing upon the scene with consternation. This was becoming ridiculous. She would not lie to these people who had been so kind to her. How Richard could, was beyond her.

Miss Benedict flew to hug Caroline, too. "Oh, I am so pleased!" she exclaimed.

Over by the window, Javan stood with his back to the room, apparently paying no one any attention. Was he truly hurt? Her guilty heart ached for him…but still he did not turn to see her pain. And it came to her, with considerable pique, that she should *not* be pitying him. If he truly cared for her, *he* should have been the one leaping to her defense last night. He was the one who had kissed her, beginning the chain of ridiculous events that had led to this pretense. And yet there he stood, silent and superior, disdaining her and Richard.

"Thank you," she said to Marjorie. "I can scarcely believe it myself."

"It's so wonderful! Though what we shall do without you, I don't know!"

A quick glance showed her that Rosa looked stricken. Caroline started toward her, but Richard got there first.

"Don't worry," he whispered. "We won't leave you."

He might have meant it only for Rosa, but Javan suddenly looked across at him, as though he'd heard every word. He glanced from Richard to Caroline and then to Rosa.

A derisive smile curled his lips. "Really, Richard?" he mocked. "*Really?* Shall I build you a cottage in the grounds, with a rose garden?"

He knows, Caroline thought in fresh despair. *God knows what he thinks of me, now!*

IT WAS, OF course, impossible to tell. During his usual afternoon walk with Rosa, he treated Caroline much as he always did—with unconventional civility leavened by his own distinctive humor. Only the growing closeness between them had clearly vanished, and for that Caroline wanted to weep and to shout at him in fury. She refrained, however, and the matter of the engagement was never referred to. At least Rosa seemed to have abandoned her earlier fears.

At dinner, Richard announced that he had been to Blackhaven and bought tickets for the subscription ball at the assembly rooms next week, and for the theatre tomorrow.

"I'm sure you'll enjoy an excellent evening," Javan said politely. "On both occasions."

"I thought we could *all* go," Richard said.

"I'm not a dancing man," Javan stated. His gaze fell on Caroline, who remembered only too well dancing with him at the castle rout.

"I'd rather stay here with Rosa."

"Well, the theatre will not be too late," Marjorie observed. "I could stay in with Rosa if you wanted to go."

"I'll think about it," Javan said carelessly.

"I could not go without you, Miss Benedict," Caroline protested. "It makes more sense for me to stay."

"Good lord," Richard drawled. "Anyone would think the theatre was some kind of punishment. It's meant to be fun. Miss Grey—Caroline—the world is not so strict with an engaged lady. I believe the presence of your betrothed is propriety enough, but do ask a female friend to join us, if it will make you more comfortable."

"I shall take care of that," Javan said unexpectedly.

CAROLINE'S SENSE OF losing control of her life and everyone in it, was further heightened that evening when she discovered Rosa and Richard sitting on the stairs together. It must have been a somewhat one-sided conversation, but it made Rosa smile, and as Caroline passed them to go to her own chamber, Rosa jumped up and hugged her for no obvious reason.

In her own chamber, Caroline sat down at the desk and penned a note to Lady Tamar, begging for her company at the theatre the following evening if she had no better plans. Only, once she'd given it to Williams to be delivered first thing in the morning, did she bury her head in her hands and acknowledge that this was not solving the problem. She was merely covering the proprieties rather than simply ending this sham engagement.

Caroline had always tried her best to do right, and had stood stead-fast in her own sensible opinions, at least until she discovered evidence to the contrary. Yet somehow, she had allowed herself to be swayed by Javan's mischievous kinsmen into an unbecoming masquerade that had little to do with saving her reputation. Anger with Javan had mingled with the desire to win him, and somehow, she was engaged to another man she did not want. It made no sense and it was *wrong*.

Decisively, she jumped to her feet, seized her candle, and left her chamber. A quick glance showed her that the drawing room was empty, so she knew where to find Javan.

She knocked on his study door, and this time, after only the slightest pause, his voice bade her come in.

He was watering his plants as she entered and showed no surprise at seeing her.

"Miss Grey, what might I do for you?"

"I wish to speak to you about my engagement," she blurted.

He stilled for an instant before lowering his watering can and setting it on top of a cabinet. "I am no expert in such matters."

"Neither," she said dangerously, "am I."

He regarded her with faint amusement in his otherwise veiled eyes. "Go on."

She glared at him. "You know perfectly well this betrothal is a sham. Mr. Benedict pretended it only to save my reputation."

"Which was never at any risk," Javan said with a hint of contempt that stung. "If neither of you wanted it, you should have kept quiet."

"As you did?" she snapped.

He picked up the watering can. "Yes," he said, opening the next cabinet. "As I did. If you don't wish to marry him, be patient. He will leave soon enough and then you can just let if drop naturally."

She stared at his averted face. "*That* is your best advice?"

"If you don't like it, you don't need to take it." He walked around the cabinet until he stood too close to her. She refused to back away but met his gaze with seething indignation. With his nearness came the inevitable melting of her bones, and a twinge of hope. "What do you want from me, Caroline?" he asked softly. "Another proposal?"

Hope died in a fresh flurry of bitter anger. "Another? I have not received one yet!" With that, she flung away from him and out of the room.

JAVAN WATCHED HER go with raging disappointment and guilt. She was in an impossible situation, for a young woman in her position could not go about making and breaking engagements. And her engagement to Richard would be all around Blackhaven by now, perhaps even on its way to London and Richard's friends and family.

Caroline had come to Javan for help, and he had not given it, mostly because he wasn't sure it was what she wanted. He couldn't truly believe she was the devious schemer who had first gone after Braithwaite and then him, before she had settled on his wealthier cousin, a baronet's heir. The girl he knew would never behave so. And yet…she had not denied the engagement at the outset, although she must have known the compromising situation she'd been discovered in would never have gone beyond the Tamars and the Grants.

But could he blame her for wanting a better life than the drudgery of governessing? And Richard would make her a far better husband. Why then had she come to him about it now? He had always meant to offer himself as the alternative, if only she would come to him honestly. But then she had bolted before he could say the words. And doubts—not so much of her fitness but of his—kept him from following her.

I'm making a mess of this…

When the eerie howling began, he thought for a moment that it came from his own unhappiness and actually bit down on his lips to stop it. A bare instant later, he recognized it for the sound he'd been waiting for. Galvanized, he seized a candle and bolted out of the study and up the back stairs. As before, it was impossible to tell where the strange, echoing wail came from. Javan had no idea where the intruder was, but he knew where he would eventually have to go.

Approaching the library, he saw Marjorie's head poking out of her bedchamber door. "Javan?" she whispered, clutching his arm. "It's happening again!"

"I know," he said grimly. "But this will be the last time. Don't worry." He had no doubt of his ability to deal with whoever this turned out to be. In fact, he *wanted* to deal with them. He wanted to fight, to expend energy on something tangible—a battle against someone other than himself.

The library door was closed as normal, though not completely, for it opened as soon as he pushed it. Darkness shrouded everything within. All his senses alert, in case the intruder lurked there, Javan entered, raising his candle high and quickly searching every corner of the room. Empty...and yet he was sure he sensed something...

And then he saw it. Where the left-hand side of the fireplace should have been, the tiles had been replaced by blackness. A small man-sized hole. He took a hasty step toward it and a man's head poke out.

Williams. His old sergeant beckoned him with a grin. Javan advanced hastily, bent and entered the hole. For the barest instant, his candle flame flickered over Caroline's face, and then she blew it out.

"Is the whole household here?" he murmured.

"Just us," Williams assured him as another, more muffled howl reached them. "He didn't even see me lurking behind the sofa in the dark, just stepped out of here and went straight for the door. No light."

"He must know this house like the back of his hand," Javan remarked.

"Should do," Williams said sardonically. "He's here often enough. But look, he leaves his lantern here." Williams reached behind him and lifted something, a blanket, to reveal the lantern beneath. For an instant, the light glowed on a narrow stone passage within the walls, and steep steps leading downward. Then Williams dropped the blanket back over it.

"Useful," Javan commented.

"I must have passed him downstairs when I left you," Caroline whispered. "For I'm sure the first howl came from there when I was half way upstairs." In the cramped space, her breath caressed his ear with devastating effect.

"So you came in here to be safe?" he managed with cool sarcasm.

"To see how he got in," she corrected. "I thought it was the plan. Where is—"

He cut her short with a finger over her lips, for his ears, trained for so many years to pick up the faintest sounds, told him their man approached.

Her lips parted in shock at his touch. And God help him, it was sweet, even in this slightly ridiculous situation. Shrouded in darkness, awaiting the approach of the enemy, there was something unspeakably sensual about her soft, warm lips against his fingertip, her ragged breath stirring the tiny hairs on his skin. Even when she was engaged to his cousin. He did not move as the library door whispered open and breath panted in the room, advancing on their hiding place.

With reluctance, Javan let his finger slide away. He tugged the blanket off the lantern, grasped it and stepped out into the room, straightening at once.

A young man stood frozen in the light, his eyes wide and frightened. It was no great surprise.

"Tom Nairn," Javan said conversationally. "I thought it was you."

As though released from a bow, Nairn whirled around and bolted for the library door—but Richard now stood there, placing a candelabra on the table beside him. Brought up short, Nairn spun helplessly, looking for an escape that didn't exist.

At last, his shoulders slumped. He didn't even try to fight when Williams advanced and collared him.

"Any reason we shouldn't hand you over to the magistrate?" Javan asked sternly.

Nairn shook his head miserably. "I told him it was over. Said you came too close last time, which you did, and you weren't going to leave anyway—"

"You want us to go so you can buy the house cheaply?"

"It's for my ma. She used to work here, was lady's maid to Mrs. Gardyn, and always dreamed of living here again, only as mistress. And when my da came into some money..."

"If you had frightened my daughter, just once," Javan said coldly, "I'd kill you."

The boy blanched. "I told him that. I said you weren't like the other tenants and we were playing with fire, but he wouldn't give up. Said he'd come himself."

"Who? Your father?"

Nairn paused, then nodded.

But Javan had already picked up his hesitation. "Not your father?" he pounced, going closer, holding the youth's frightened gaze. "Come on, man, spit it out. It's your only hope."

"I'd talked my da round. He didn't like it, but he took my word eventually. Then he met this cove skulking around the farm and nearby land, and suddenly it was back on again. This cove don't like you, paid my da to scare you one more time."

"What cove?" Williams demanded.

"I don't know his name," Nairn insisted. "Not sure my da does either!"

"A slender, pale gentleman with a walking stick?" Javan hazarded.

Nairn blinked. "Oh no. He was no gentleman. Great hulking fellow you wouldn't want to cross."

Javan frowned. That, he hadn't expected. Although the boy might be lying.

"How do you open the passage from this side?" Caroline asked. "We found the lever inside the passage, but we couldn't find a way in from the room."

Nairn hesitated.

"Magistrate," Williams said decisively, tugging Nairn by the collar.

"No, wait!" Nairn resisted, desperately. "I'll show you and I'll swear on the Bible never to come here again if you just let me go. It'll kill my ma if I get sent to prison and—"

"Stop whining and show us," Javan interrupted.

Nairn drew in his breath, and Williams released his collar, allowing him to walk to the bell pull. Lifting the cord, he pulled it sharply to the right and the fireplace hole began to close with the same clanking grind Javan had heard so often before. Then Nairn pulled the cord to the left, and the secret door slid silently open again.

"Well," Caroline said, impressed. "None of us thought of that."

"I'll be blocking this off," Javan snapped. "At both ends. And you may tell your father I'll have you both up before the magistrate—who is a friend of mine, incidentally—before you can say 'help' if I catch either of you within a hundred yards of my house or my family again. Or, if I'm angry, if my daughter is frightened in the slightest degree, I'll just kill you where you cower. Do I make myself clear?"

He pushed the terrified boy back into Williams' hold to be marched out of the house by the front door.

Richard raised one eyebrow at him. "You're letting him go?"

Javan shrugged impatiently. "I don't want the fuss. Besides, it's over. He knew that before he came." He glanced around, frowning suddenly. "Where is Caroline?"

Chapter Fifteen

CAROLINE, ONCE SHE saw that Javan would not harm the boy, had simply picked up the abandoned lantern and stepped back inside the secret passage.

The tension in Javan had been wound so tightly she'd been sure at first that it would have to erupt into violence. But he was a soldier, with a lifetime of training, self-control and, probably, a deep understanding of the folly of young, badly behaved men. Reassured, she went exploring on her own.

Curiosity as to where the passage led, if it joined with others inside the walls of the house, propelled her onward, down the narrow steps. She expected the stone to be damp and dank, but in fact the passage surrounded the chimney, the warmth from which seemed to have kept it dry over the years.

At the foot of the steep steps she found herself in another cave-like room, similar to the one at the top. There was only one passage leading out of it. Above her, hurried footsteps clattered down the steps.

"Caroline?" Javan's voice, unexpectedly anxious.

"I'm here," she called, though part of her wished to punish him with silence.

She held the lantern high and saw that he'd come in such a hurry he'd brought no light of his own. The lantern cast a soft glow over his harsh features, and in spite of everything, her heart lurched just at the sight of him. "There seems to be just one way out," she managed, moving forward again. He said nothing, not even to chastise her for foolhardiness in coming down here alone, or to persuade her to return. He simply followed her.

Her every nerve seemed to tingle in awareness of his silent closeness behind her. At last she reached a dead end, the wall being a panel made of old, slightly warped wood. Javan brushed past her and found a lever similar to the one above.

"Stand back," he warned, pulling it. The panel swung open and he walked forward.

Following, she found herself in the chill of a natural cave. She could hear water close by, but she couldn't see it for the heavy fronds and thick tree roots that almost blocked the cave entrance.

"It must be in those rocks by the river," Javan said. He touched the boulder by his side. "I suspect they roll this across the entrance to hide the panel from casual view. A way out for priests, perhaps, or rebels in the civil war. Or Jacobites, maybe."

She shivered, imagining the tragedies and stirring escapes of long dead men and women associated with Haven Hall. "I would have expected this sort of thing at the castle more than here."

"The castle would have been a lot more secure than a mere country house. Come back. It's too cold out here." As if he'd forgotten their quarrel, he took her hand and drew her back behind the panel, which he closed again.

They stood too close, and he still held her hand. Her body, her whole being ached. He must have seen it in her face, for he dropped her hand at once.

"Christ," he muttered. "You are better with Richard."

"It appears I have no say," she retorted. "But, in fact, I do, and I want neither of you!"

"Good choice," he approved, and led the way around the winding passage toward the steps.

The lantern began to flicker.

"Stay close," he muttered. "I think it's about to go out."

It died, just as they reached the steps.

"Give me your hand," he said roughly. She obeyed, and he began to climb. She tried not to stumble as she followed. The pitch darkness was disorienting and yet strangely…liberating. She let her fingers cling to his.

Abruptly, he stopped and stepped back down, pinning her to warm stone wall. "You don't want me, Caroline," he ground out. "You don't. You deserve a good, clean man, unsullied by life and dishonor."

"Dishonor?" she repeated, startled. "You have every honor—"

"No."

She could make out only deeper blackness where he stood, but she could feel his hardness, his heavy breathing. This, she thought, whatever this turned out to be, was the root of his damage.

"Tell me," she whispered, raising their joined hands to his cheek.

"I betrayed the Fort of San Pedro," he blurted. "The French walked into it, chasing the British out, because of me."

The agony behind his short, abrupt tone made her want to weep. "How because of you?"

"I told them," he whispered. "I blurted it all out and I don't even remember."

I told them. The same agonized words he'd uttered in his dream last night. "Where?" she asked bewildered. "Where did you tell them this?"

"In my prison bed."

"You were asleep?"

"I told." He tried to push away, but she clung to him.

"I don't care, Javan," she said clearly. "I don't care whether that is true or not."

He stilled. "You should care." And with that, he stepped back, climbing onward and all but dragged her after him into the light of the library.

As she stepped into the carriage the following evening, she made to sit as usual with her back to the horses, until Richard urged her to the better seat facing the direction of travel and sat beside her. Javan slouched on the bench opposite, his scar livid in the gloomy shadows. She was sure it was his gaze that made her skin burn, and yet she refused to glance at him to see. If he truly wanted her, why was he tolerating, even urging her engagement to his cousin? To punish her? For what? Even last night's strange revelation seemed to have been made to drive her away rather than to ease his own soul.

Richard appeared unaware of the tension and conversed amiably for most of the journey without much response from either of his companions.

Caroline was almost relieved when Javan excused himself in the theatre foyer, leaving her and Richard to make their way to the box. As she took her seat, Caroline was only too aware of the scrutiny from many other boxes around the theatre. She was the governess who'd hooked a wealthy baronet's heir—after failing to secure her earl, she was sure it was said. Being used to the unfairness of life, she wouldn't have cared, except for the fact that she hadn't actually "hooked" anyone.

Fortunately, the arrival of Lord and Lady Tamar reduced the stares, although they must have been intrigued beyond endurance when the tenant of Haven Hall himself entered the box with none other than Mrs. Gallini.

Sought after by the highest hostesses in polite society, the singer was in something of a unique position. The tarnish of the stage did not quite cling to her—in Blackhaven at least—as it would have to a mere actress or dancer, and yet she was an odd choice to chaperone Caroline, if that had ever been Javan's intention.

Worse, just as the curtain went up, Caroline sensed a different kind of observation, and she glanced down at the pit to discover Thomas Swayle bowing to her. Her stomach jolted nervously, for she had no idea how Javan would react to his presence.

Although Caroline normally loved the theatre and rarely had the opportunity to indulge her passion, she could not enjoy this evening. Her nerves jangled too much and she simply wanted to go home.

Home. It seemed she regarded Haven Hall as home, despite Javan's recent behavior.

At the first interval began the true purpose of the theatre—visiting each other's boxes and comparing gossip. Tamar and Richard went off together, although Javan lounged in the back of the box, silent and brooding. While Serena exchanged conversation around the pillar with their nearest neighbor, Mrs. Gallini drew her seat closer to Caroline.

"Forgive me, Miss Grey, but I saw that man Swayle trying to attract your attention earlier. You must know he is the source of rumors against your employer."

"I can imagine," Caroline said with a sigh. "I can only hope no one believes such nonsense."

The singer shrugged. "Those who know him will not. However, he is also saying that you became engaged to Mr., Richard Benedict in order to avoid the lascivious attentions of Colonel Javan Benedict, of whom you are afraid."

Caroline's jaw dropped. "That is ridiculous! He cannot say such things!"

"I am afraid your waltz at the castle was noted by many. After all, he did not dance with anyone else. And now you are engaged to his cousin. It fits Swayle's story, which is always more interesting than the truth."

"I wish I had the luxury of not caring what people say," Caroline said intensely.

"So do I," Mrs. Gallini agreed. "Women who must work are at the mercy of all."

Caroline's smile was twisted. "What comforting thought you bring me, Signora."

Casting a quick glance behind her at Javan, the singer lowered her voice further. "I wanted to be sure you did not believe these calumnies against him. We are old friends, he and I, and after what he suffered at the hands of the French, it makes me angry if his own people abuse him, too,"

"He was a prisoner of the French, I believe."

"For several months." The singer's gaze was direct. "They tortured him."

The blood drained from Caroline's face. "Why?" she whispered.

Mrs. Gallini shrugged. "The kind of fighting he did. They assumed he knew secrets."

"Dear God..." No wonder he had nightmares from which he sought to escape. No wonder he had betrayed San Pedro or was afraid that he had.

And in reality, when he finally had escaped his terrible prison, when he reached home, he had found his wife with her lover, a daughter who couldn't speak, and a lot of vile rumors and accusations. With the flood of pity came the beginnings of an understanding. He doubted his worth.

"He is a proud man, Miss Grey," the singer said quietly. "But a lost one. I do not pretend to know what's going on between the three of you, but please, please do not let him down."

Whatever she had expected of Mrs. Gallini, it was not this. "How are you friends?" she blurted, for the first time doubting her assumptions of their past, if not present intimacy.

"In my profession, I travel," Mrs. Gallini replied. "I sang in Spain for Joseph Bonaparte...and for Lord Wellington, which is where I met Javan. He escorted me safely out of Spain, when it was time for me to return to Italy. And we met again after I escaped to England." She spread her fan, raising it to her face. "He is a fascinating man, Miss Grey, but he never loved me. And if I ever loved him, it was only a very little. I have a...weakness, it seems, for strong Englishmen."

Mrs. Gallini sat back, smiling, as Lady Serena drew away from the pillar and two gentlemen entered the box. As the world went on around her, Caroline felt a little as if she'd been struck on the head. Javan doubted her to some extent at least because he doubted himself. In his heart, he suspected she *preferred* Richard.

What she didn't know, of course, was how he felt about *her*. A few kisses to a man, a soldier, didn't necessarily mean anything. He'd been starved of female company for some time, and the times he'd touched her had been in moments of stress or drunkenness. Her heart tightened painfully. She didn't want to be just anyone to him. She wanted to be his all, as he, God help her, was hers.

Tears gathered threateningly in her throat, but fortunately, the curtain went up again and she could focus on the stage.

It was only as they finally left the theatre that the inevitable encounter between Javan and Swayle occurred. Although he'd wandered out of the box to stretch his legs a few times, he never seemed to have met the man he regarded as his enemy.

Perhaps Swayle grew too bold. Though he really didn't want to encounter Javan, Benedict's over-casual attitude must have given Swayle the wrong impression of his observational skills. In company with Serena and Tamar, Caroline was following the Benedicts out the theatre door when Swayle stepped up to her from the shadows.

"Miss Grey," he said nervously. He licked his lips, his gaze flickering to right and left. As well it might, for several people seemed to be avidly watching the encounter.

Caroline inclined her head and would have walked on, only he took a step nearer. "Please, Miss Grey, I wish only to be assured of your wellbeing."

To her relief, for she did not want there to be a fight, Richard had walked on without noticing. Javan, however, paused and turned slowly to face her and Swayle. The eyes of the two men met, the one large, scarred, and just a little frightening, the other slight and fragile and, apparently, bravely facing up to the monster.

Don't hit him. Please don't hit him…

With an effort, Caroline forced her shoulders to relax and bestowed the most dazzling smile she could summon. "As you see, sir, I am very well. Very well indeed." She stepped nearer Javan and set the tips of her fingers on his proffered arm. Paying no more attention to Swayle, she prattled, "Did you enjoy the play, sir? I found it quite charming."

"Nicely done," Javan murmured. "Thank you."

"It does not suit my dignity to be thought afraid of you," she said coolly.

"Nor mine."

There was time for little more. Lord and Lady Tamar were going to the hotel for supper, and so said farewell to Caroline and the Benedicts.

"Did that little slubber speak to you, Caroline?" Richard demanded as he climbed into the coach beside her.

"He timed it well. I think he meant to separate me from you both and see what trouble he could cause in front of the crowd."

"She sent him about his business with a most believable display of happiness," Javan observed. "I don't really understand why he's still here."

"I expect he thinks you won't hit him now that he has a walking stick," Richard said.

Javan curled his lip.

"Seriously," Richard added, "I think he's looking for revenge against you for making him look like the cur he is when Louisa died."

Javan scowled. "I don't want him skulking in Blackhaven when Rosa's there."

Chapter Sixteen

T HE FOLLOWING MORNING, for the first time in several days, Caroline woke with a feeling of optimism. The silly engagement to Richard could easily be fixed and the world made right if Javan only cared for her a little. And as she began to understand him more, she thought he did. Now, she could try to help him heal.

She sat up as the maid crept in with her washing bowl.

"Oh, you're awake, Miss," the girl said. "Good. There's a letter here, came for you yesterday, but you'd gone out already."

As the maid laid it on the bedside table, Caroline saw that it was from her sister Eliza, which was rare enough to intrigue her. Breaking the seal, she spread out the sheet and began to read.

A second later, she held the back of her hand to her cheek in fear and shock. Peter was worse, dangerously so, and more money was necessary for the doctor.

She was out of bed and throwing on her clothes before she'd even finished reading, let alone planned what she must do. It was still early, so if she could persuade Williams to drive her to Carlisle immediately, she might just catch the Edinburgh mail coach and be home by the evening. Hastily, she threw her spare gown and undergarments into her bag and left by the passage door.

Hurtling downstairs, she almost crashed into Richard, coming in the opposite direction.

"Woah, there," he exclaimed. "Where's the fire?"

"Home," Caroline said distraught. "I have to go home. Do you think I could borrow Williams to drive me to Carlisle? Oh, and if I don't have time to write, can you tell Rosa I'll only be gone a few days, and apologize to Mr. and Miss Benedict—"

"Slow down," Richard begged. "If there is a family emergency, of course I'll drive you to Carlisle—or all the way home, if you prefer. Let me get my man and then we'll go."

Caroline seized her bonnet and cloak from their usual place, ignoring the foolish ache as she glanced along to the study door. Alert for sounds of Richard's return, she dashed into the drawing room and scribbled a note to Javan. There wasn't time to write much. Richard clattered down the stairs and the clop of horses' hooves heralded the speedy arrival of his curricle in front of the house. In the end, she wrote only,

My dear Sir,

Forgive me, I have gone to Scotland. Please assure Rosa I shall return in a few days. My apologies to you and to Miss Benedict.

Yours humbly,
Caroline Grey.

She barely had time to fold it and prop it up on the mantle shelf before she ran out to join Richard. In no time, she was seated beside him, her familiar, battered carpet bag on her lap, while Richard, with a practiced flick of his wrists, set his spirited team of horses into motion.

As she drew away from Haven Hall, she had the peculiar fantasy that her heart was being ripped from her body.

MARCUS SWAYLE WAS barely awake when the villainous but useful Mr. Miller—Killer Miller to his friends—was brought before him. From his bed, propped up on pillows, Swayle regarded his most recent henchman with disfavor.

"They're on the move," Miller informed him.

"Who are?" Swayle demanded testily. He wasn't at his best before his morning cup of tea.

"Folks at Haven Hall. Two of 'em at any rate."

When no further information was forthcoming, Swayle snatched his tea from his valet and glared at Miller. "Which two?"

"Benedict and the young lady."

Swayle paused with his tea half way to his lips. "Indeed?" he said softly. "*Now* you interest me, my friend. And...er...where are they on the move *to*? Blackhaven?"

"No, sir, they took the north road."

Swayle almost choked on his tea and hastily set down his cup. "Truly? Then they are eloping? This is wonderful! He's got so angry that she engaged herself to his cousin that he's dragging her to Gretna Green!"

Miller scratched his head. "Glad we're pleased by the turn of events."

"We most certainly are. Now you must hurry, my man. Ride after them, and on a quiet piece of road, shoot her."

Miller blinked. "Shoot her? Got no call to go shooting women! I thought it was this Benedict we was out to get?"

"Idiot, sirrah! We *do* get him! The world thinks *he* shot her, just as he killed his wife, my sainted Louisa. At best, Benedict's hanged for it. At the least, he loses what's left of his reputation and is furious besides at losing his latest toy."

"Toy?" Miller said, bewildered.

Swayle scowled. "The governess, whom you will have shot."

Miller's low brow tugged further down his face as he stared at Swayle. "Can't go around killing gentlefolk," he said at last, with a trace of regret.

"She isn't gentlefolk, she's the governess!"

Miller appeared to be considering this while he stroked his unshaven chin. "Very well," he pronounced. "One thing you might not have considered."

Swayle almost laughed in his face. The very idea that the brutal imbecile Miller might have thought of something Swayle hadn't was really quite exquisitely humorous. But Swayle was in a good mood now. "What might that be?" he inquired with patience.

Miller let his grubby hand drop from his face. "Not entirely sure which Benedict it is. What if it's the cousin?"

Swayle's mouth dropped open. "The cousin? Richard? Don't you know?"

"No. Couldn't skulk in their stables, now, could I? They look the same over the kind of distance I was at."

Swayle finished his tea and rattled the cup against the saucer for more. As his valet obliged, pouring from the pot, he glared at his henchman, reminding himself that he wasn't called Killer Miller for nothing.

"It doesn't matter," he said at last. He opened the bedside cabinet and took out a monogrammed handkerchief. It bore the initials JB, lovingly embroidered by some dead Benedict no doubt. Swayle had taken it long ago, with many other things, when he'd lived in Javan's house. "Leave this close to the scene. It will be enough to prove Javan Benedict's presence there. He might just as well shoot the girl for eloping with his cousin. The important thing is she gets shot and Javan Benedict gets the blame."

Miller pocketed the handkerchief with a smooth, speedy movement that spoke volumes for his previous career as a pickpocket.

"Well, I will shoot her," he agreed at last. "But I ain't killing her if I can help it."

Swayle cast his eyes to heaven. "You *have* to kill her! Otherwise, she'll inform against you!" Or, at least, claim Javan's innocence, which didn't suit Swayle at all.

Miller looked back at him with unexpected contempt. "You'd better pray she don't. Because if I get collared for this, so do you."

With that, Miller sauntered out of the room. Swayle waved his hands urgently at his valet to follow and make sure the disreputable assassin left the hotel by the back stairs.

JAVAN WAS SURPRISED by a morning visit from his daughter before he had even left his bedchamber. Dressed in his old walking clothes, he was gazing out of the window, contemplating a long walk with Tiny to strengthen his injured leg, when Rosa burst in with barely a knock. She looked as if she were about to cry.

"What is it?" he asked, going to her at once.

For answer, she seized his hand and tugged him out of his chamber in the direction of the schoolroom. Happy enough to oblige—for it was time, past time, that he spoke to Caroline like an adult—he walked into the schoolroom.

Caroline was not there. However, the connecting door to her bedchamber was open, and Rosa dragged him toward it. Now at last, he pulled back.

"Rosa," he objected. "No. Is Miss Grey ill?"

Impatiently, she pulled free of his hand and ran into the bedchamber, waving her arms around to show him that it was empty.

"She'll be in the kitchen, eating breakfast and waiting for you," he said. "Go and find her."

Rosa shook her head vehemently, pointing at her eyes and then downward to show she'd already looked for her governess downstairs. Then she walked to Miss Grey's wardrobe and opened the door. Only the peach evening gown hung there. Of the other gowns he'd seen her wear, there was no sign. However, it felt quite wrong to be in the room like this, and despite a twinge of definite unease, Javan refused to go through her possessions, or allow Rosa to do so.

He pulled her out of the room. "You mustn't pry into her things," he said severely. "Perhaps she's gone for a walk. Tiny was barking earlier, so she might have taken him. Is your aunt up yet?"

Marjorie was discovered in the drawing room, staring at a sheet of paper which she held in front of her.

Slowly, she raised her eyes to Javan's and held the paper out to him. He strode forward and twitched it from his sister's fingers. A note from Caroline—brief, impersonal, and apologetic.

His ears began to sing. "Scotland…"

"She went with Richard," Marjorie said with difficulty. "I saw them from my window."

Javan gripped the letter so tightly that it began to tear. He sank onto the arm of the nearest chair. "What have I done?" he whispered.

He'd driven her away, made life impossible for her. She could have been his. He'd seen it in her eyes, gloried in it, and yet chosen to punish her for his own lack of confidence. *He* should have claimed her the night in the library. Instead, he'd let Richard be the gentleman. He knew instinctively she did not love Richard. So how had he let it get to this? He was destroying himself and everyone he loved all over again.

And God help me, I do love her...

Without a word, he walked out of the room and downstairs to his study. Tiny, lying in front of the fire, lifted his head hopefully, but Javan only closed the door and walked to his desk like some clumsy automaton.

I can live without her. I can live with this grief, too...

Only, why should he? Why should Rosa? Why should *Caroline*? She belonged to him and his family, and he would never be complete without her. But what propelled him into sudden action was the knowledge that neither would she be whole without him. A hundred tiny looks and smiles and blushes had told him that. The way she trembled at his touch and gasped at his nearness. He'd soaked them up like water to a drowning man and never realized how much he valued them. How much she had given him, how much she had risked because she couldn't help this love any more than he could.

With an oath, he strode out of the room, yelling for Williams and his horse.

"Rosa!" he called up the staircase. "I'm going to bring her back! Stay with your aunt and be good!"

WHEN RICHARD HAD gone, Marjorie sat down by the drawing-room fire with Rosa at her feet. They both gazed into the flames, each thinking, no doubt, much the same thoughts about the same people.

To Marjorie, there had always been something not quite right about Richard's engagement to Miss Grey. Not that the girl wasn't pretty, cultured, charming, and well-mannered in the quietly-spoken way Marjorie most admired, but it had seemed to her that any *tendre* Miss Grey might harbor beneath her severe and civil exterior, was for Javan. Not that she suspected the governess of inveigling him into marriage, as it was rumored she had tried with the Earl of Braithwaite.

Although that *had* been Marjorie's first fear, the day Miss Grey had arrived and she had thrown the cake... She'd known if it had missed Javan it was liable to hit the governess. Marjorie cast the troubled memory aside. That had been a bad day, but she'd recovered, and observed Rosa's growing brightness, and Javan's. Particularly Javan's. And she had discovered the new governess to be a kind and sensible young woman.

Somehow, Caroline Grey had got under all their skins. She was a comfortable companion, interesting to converse with, witty when she chose to be, and had enough fun in her ill-dressed person to appeal to Rosa. Marjorie was aware that theirs was an odd household full of damaged people, but Miss Grey had never appeared to judge. She accepted them all and quietly went about making things better.

Until this odd engagement to the mischievous Richard. Marjorie liked Richard, and she was aware he thought the world of Javan. Could he not see that his betrothal *hurt* Javan?

Marjorie sat up straighter. Of course he could see it. Richard was no fool. Was that his game? Was he trying to *force* Javan into action? After all, with his first, utterly disastrous marriage under his belt, Javan was understandably skittish about marriage and highly cynical of women on the so-called marriage mart. He might well *need* to be forced, although where on earth the rush was when Miss Grey hadn't been here a month...

Moreover, Marjorie balked at the idea of Miss Grey bringing shame on herself, her family, and her employer's family by eloping. One way or another, it would surely break her relationship with Rosa.

Nothing about Miss Grey gave Marjorie any reason to believe her a schemer, a fortune-hunter—the Braithwaite rumors notwithstanding.

Marjorie nodded twice. "Rosa," she said firmly. "Ring the bell. I think we need to question the servants."

"So," Marjorie said, ten minutes later, after she had spoken to the servants and dismissed all of them save Williams. "So, Ginny took a letter to Miss Grey and then Mr. Richard called for his curricle."

"He was going to take her to Carlisle, at least, or 'home' if she preferred," Williams repeated.

"And did you tell this to the colonel?" Marjorie demanded, forgetting that she wasn't meant to use his rank.

"No, he didn't ask, just rode off without a word."

"So, he thinks they've gone to Gretna Green. And in fact, they're going to her family somewhere else in Scotland. Or Richard will put her on the mail coach at Carlisle."

Williams inclined his head, while Rosa looked from one of them to the other.

"Does it seem to you," Marjorie asked, frowning, "that there is room there for lots more misunderstandings? And scandal? And in spite of all, the wrong marriage? At best, Miss Grey will need a chaperone."

Williams, who clearly hadn't thought of Gretna Green until Marjorie mentioned it, began to nod vigorously. He knew his master very well.

"Then we had better go, had we not?" Marjorie said.

"To Scotland?" Williams asked doubtfully.

"If we drive like the wind, will we reach Carlisle before the Edinburgh coach leaves?"

"Maybe. But it will rattle your bones."

"Well, what else do I use the old things for? Fetch the coach and the horses, Williams! We'll need food and a blanket."

THE WAY FROM Blackhaven to the Carlisle road was not great for carriage travel. Javan, riding across country, had every hope of catching up with Richard's curricle long before it reached the city. The road wound between hills and along the coast for part of the way. Javan cut off several miles by simply riding as the crow flies, over the hills and streams and through the forest, until, galloping fast, he caught sight of the road below him. A horse and cart ambled in the opposite direction. And then, around the corner, came a curricle containing two people, a man and a woman.

With some triumph, Javan turned his horse's head and galloped onward and downward to head them off. It was then that he noticed the fresh hoof prints again. He'd glimpsed them at various stages on the way without paying much attention, for he knew both his quarries were in Richard's curricle, not riding on horseback. He followed the hoofprints for a little, but as he came closer to the road, they carried on around the side of the hill while he galloped on downward toward the road and Caroline.

Now that the moment was almost upon him, he realized he'd no real idea of what he would do or say. Every speech he came up with made him sound like a pompous ass, a coxcomb or a pathetic whiner, none of which could he imagine appealing to Caroline.

The trouble was, words could not adequately express his feelings or his desires, or his care for hers.

He would have to wait until he saw her. Once he saw her face, he would know whether he was saving her to be with him, or simply to prevent a disastrous elopement and the damage to her reputation. Either way, he would fight to win her and be worthy of her, and he would never give up...

A flash from the hill above caught his attention. Almost at the road now, he turned and gazed several yards up and to his right, just above the next bend. The low, wintry sun was certainly glinting on something, something so familiar to him it was like coming home. A sword. Or a rifle.

He absorbed the terrain without really trying. From the glint, a sharpshooter had a clear sight of the road below, and yet had plenty of cover. From the road, and from where Javan observed, he could remain hidden. Any vehicle would slow drastically around that bend, giving a good shot his best chance.

Only, who would do such a thing? He hadn't heard of highwaymen in the area, though it was true he hadn't been in much of a position to hear of any that were. That, too, was the result of his chosen isolation.

By the time he stopped the curricle now, they would all be in the direct view of any sharpshooter. Before the thought was properly formed, he'd turned his horse's head, urging it up the hill as fast as it would go. All the time, he scanned the hills for signs of other weapons, other shooters.

By the time he threw himself off the horse, the rumble of the curricle's wheels seemed to fill his ears. Blending speed and caution, he crept around the rocky outcrop and saw what he'd become sure he would—one man stretched out with a rifle pointing below. The distance was perfect, and the curricle was rounding the bend with slow, smooth perfection. No one had ever accused Richard of driving badly.

"Good morning," Javan said to distract the shooter, because he wasn't sure he had time to jump on him before he shot. He hadn't, as it turned out. A mere instant before he landed on the shooter, the familiar crack of a rifle exploded and echoed around the hills.

The gunman heaved himself around almost in the same movement as he shot—not in time to save himself, but in time to see his attacker's face. "You!" he exclaimed as Javan landed on his shoulder and punched him hard on the chin.

The man's eyes rolled up, but he was clearly as tough as old boots, for he still managed to heft the rifle and swing the butt at Javan's head. Swearing, Javan seized it in both hands, bouncing as the gunman bucked beneath him in an effort to dislodge him.

"I don't have time for this," Javan said between his teeth, and brought up his knee sharply between his opponent's thighs. As the shock jerked the gunman's body into an attempted ball, Javan snatched the rifle and swung it sharply into the gunman's head. This time, he went out like a light.

Javan had no time for triumph. Taking the rifle with him, he began to run down the hill, whistling for his horse as he went. Now, at last, he could observe what had happened below. But if he'd hoped to see the curricle trundling on in blissful ignorance of the events on the hill above, he was doomed to disappointment.

The gunman had let off a shot, and it seemed he was good. For the horses and curricle stood still on the corner, and the female passenger lay spread out in the road.

Chapter Seventeen

THE EXPLOSION HAD come out of nowhere. One moment, Caroline was admiring Richard's skill in taking the corners on the appalling road, and the next, over the top of the pounding hooves and the rumbling wheels, an almighty crack sounded. At the same time, her arm jerked of its own volition, spinning her against the side of the curricle, and the horses screamed in fright.

"What the…?" came Richard's voice, then, "Dear God, Caroline!"

Somehow, he must have got the horses under control, for a moment later, she was lying in the road, with him looming over her.

"What happened?" she asked blankly. "How did I get here? Did I fall out?"

"Sort of," Richard said hoarsely. "It's as well I managed to halt them first. Be brave, my dear, I'm afraid you've been shot. It must be highwaymen, and one of them is running toward us."

As he spoke, he produced a pistol from the pocket of his overcoat. She could make that out although the fringes of her world were growing misty. It seemed to take a long time for his words to penetrate.

She frowned up at the sky. "I've been shot?" She turned her head toward the sudden, galloping pain in her arm. There was blood. "Oh dear, so I have. Am I going to die? I mustn't! Who will care for Peter? And I must not abandon Rosa. Oh, where is he?" Sudden, weak tears filled her eyes because she would die without seeing Javan again, without telling him…

"Oh, put the pistol away, you lummock, it's me," said an irritable voice, surely in her imagination, for it sounded like *his*. Hasty footsteps sounded on the road, and his face swam before her misty eyes.

"Help her," Richard's voice pleaded. "I don't know what to do."

Caroline smiled, reaching urgently for Javan with her good arm, because even if he wasn't real, she wanted his presence so much. But the skin of his neck was warm and firm under her hand, his deeply scarred face frowning and desperate.

"I have you, Caroline," he whispered, his rough fingers gentle and soothing on her face. "I have you. Hold on."

Enchanted by the warmth of his voice, she let the happiness explode within her. She tugged him closer, gasping his name as she pressed her lips to his. "I love you," she whispered.

She felt the aching, tender response of his lips for a bare instant. And then, his voice, "Then you'd better let me see that wound, so I can remind you of the fact for years to come."

"Years," she said blissfully. "Am I dreaming, Javan?"

"No, but I need somewhere cleaner and safer to get the bullet out of you."

His hands were beneath her, swinging her up across the sky, and then she seemed to be back in the curricle with Richard. She tried to ask where Javan had gone, and then she saw him on horseback, riding beside them. The world sped up and vanished into blackness.

WHEN SHE WOKE, she was between crisp sheets. She had a memory of excruciating pain that went on and on, relieved only by the sweetness of Javan's voice. She'd trusted him to make it stop. She must have been dreaming. The fierce ache in her arm told her it hadn't all been imagination. And behind that was some nagging worry that she had something important to do.

"Javan?" She turned her head on the pillow, searching.

A silhouette by the window stretched into the shape of a man springing to his feet. He strode toward her and she saw with wonder that it truly was Javan.

"It *is* you!"

"It is. How are you?"

There was something incredibly wonderful in him sitting on the edge of her bed. He touched her forehead, no doubt feeling for fever, and then moved on, stroking her hair.

"I'm well, I think," she replied, "though my arm hurts. Was I truly shot? And how in the world did you come to be there?"

"I was trying to catch up with you, came across that fellow with a rifle. I shall never forgive myself for not stopping him in time."

"I thought I might die," she remembered. "And it seemed so cruel without seeing you again, and then you were there."

He took her hand, his fingers curling around hers. "I'm sorry," he whispered. "I'm afraid I'm a mess of a human being. I didn't quite understand until you left how much you mean to me."

"I do?" she said, enchanted.

He smiled, raising her hand to his lips and kissing her fingers, then her knuckles. "I love you, Caroline Grey. Please don't leave me again."

She frowned. "I didn't leave you, precisely. I had to…" She broke off, her eyes widening. "Peter! Peter is ill. I *had* to go to him this time. Have I missed the mail coach? Where am I?"

She struggled to sit, but his hand on her good shoulder pressed her back into the pillows.

"Be still," he said severely. "I know, Richard explained to me. Yes, you have missed the mail coach, because we haven't yet made it to Carlisle. We brought you to the nearest inn, where, not three hours ago, I dug a rifle ball out of your arm. Which explains why you are not going anywhere for a couple of days."

"But I feel fine," she protested. "And Peter—you don't under-stand—he cries for me when he's ill, for my sister cannot abide sickness and goes to pieces and my mother… Well, she was used to servants doing her bidding and has no idea how to nurse, and Peter might die!"

"Drink this," he said, sliding one arm under her shoulders and holding a cup of water to her lips. She drank it obediently, though it tasted peculiar, for she was very thirsty. And besides, there was something beguiling in being held in his strong arm against his chest. It did strange things to her heart and her stomach.

"I understand from Richard," he said calmly, easing her gently back on to the pillows, "that your sister asked for money rather than your presence, so we doubt Peter is actually at death's door. However, since you are clearly worried, either Richard or I will go there for you if you wish and see what is to be done. For, as I said, *you* are not going anywhere until I am assured you are well."

She frowned, trying to make sense of all of this. Somewhere, she liked him commanding her, for though she was used to people's orders, they weren't normally given for her benefit. She found the novelty curiously sweet. However, in some things, she, too, was immovable.

"You are not a physician," she pointed out. She frowned. "So how is it you took the ball from my arm?"

"Practice," he said. "My men didn't always have access to a surgeon. Don't look so impressed. Once you've taken a ball out of your own body, extracting one from someone else's is a blessed relief."

In spite of herself, she laughed, just as the door opened and Richard sauntered in with a large tray of food.

"Ah, that sounds more like our Miss Grey," he said cheerfully, although his glance was piercing and more than a little anxious. "I've brought food."

"So I see," Javan murmured.

"The boy's following with drinks," Richard said. He cocked one eye at Javan. "Do you want to feed our prisoner?"

"Lord, no, let him stew."

"Prisoner?" Caroline asked, intrigued.

Richard's lips twisted. "Killer Miller," he said with contempt. "The man who shot you."

Her eyes widened. "You caught him? Shouldn't you have handed him over to the authorities?"

"Probably will," Javan said without much obvious interest.

"Is he an infamous highwayman?" Caroline asked, accepting a little bread and butter. The ache in her arm seemed to have eased just a little and she felt very sleepy, but there were things she needed to know.

"He's an infamous rogue for hire," Richard said grimly.

"But how did you capture him?" Caroline demanded. "I want to know everything!"

"Javan just rode up the hill and fetched him," Richard said. "Having taken the earlier precaution of knocking him cold with his own rifle. We needed to be sure there were no other gunmen around taking pot-shots at us."

"And were there?" she asked breathlessly.

"No," Richard replied, taking the tray of ale and coffee from some unseen person at the door. "You see, he isn't a highwayman, but a ruffian hired by our old friend Marcus Swayle."

"Who will pay," Javan said in a cold, dangerous voice, all the more chilling for its absolute certainty.

"We assumed this Miller had mistaken me for Javan," Richard said, "and hit you by accident. Turns out, his orders were to shoot *you*."

"Me?" She dropped her nibbled crust on the plate. "I'm the governess! Why would Swayle want me dead?"

"To further discredit Javan," Richard explained. "Put the blame on him and hope he hanged for it."

Caroline gazed from him to Javan. "But that's…"

"Unforgivable," Javan finished for her. "Even Miller seems to think so, for he's quite happy to land his paymaster in the soup. Apparently on Swayle's instructions, it was Miller who hired Nairn for one more howling at the hall. Also, according to Miller, he told Swayle he wouldn't kill you if he could help it."

"You would have made it easier for them by being there," Caroline speculated. She frowned at Javan. "*Why* were you there? Why were you following us?"

Richard grinned with unabashed mockery. "He thought we were

eloping."

A gurgle of laughter broke from Caroline. "Truly?"

"Truly," Javan said shortly. "And you needn't look so pleased about it because—"

She threw out her hand, effectively silencing him and his fingers closed around hers. "I'm so sorry about the engagement sham. I didn't know what to do for the best and everything seemed *wrong*."

"It was," Javan said ruefully. "It was I who should have claimed the betrothal."

"Yes, you should," Richard said frankly, "considering you were the one who was kissing her."

"I didn't want to be pushed," Javan muttered. His fingers tightened. "More than that, I didn't want *you* to be pushed. I don't want you to marry me to save your blasted reputation."

"Is it really that bad?" she asked.

A breath of laughter escaped Javan. "Your reputation? Hardly. I don't believe the Tamars or the Grants would have blabbed. I suppose we *should* care that no one realizes you are now travelling alone with *two* male Benedicts, but—"

"Actually, that doesn't seem to be strictly true," Richard said from the window. "Come and see this."

"Not you," Javan said severely to Caroline as he strode across the room to join his cousin. It seemed to her that his limp was less noticeable than when she'd first arrived at Haven Hall.

"Good God," Javan said in awe. "How the devil did she know? And she's brought Rosa!"

"Who has?" Caroline demanded. She really was very sleepy.

"Marjorie," Javan said. "It seems your reputation is saved. Although it will still seem odd, no doubt, when you return engaged to the other Benedict cousin."

Caroline frowned. "Neither of you ever considers asking."

"I'll ask," Javan said softly. He was standing by the bed again, leaning down to stroke her hair, and she couldn't help smiling through the waves of sleepiness. "When you're awake and well. Now, before you fall asleep, where exactly does your family live?"

She blurted out the direction, just as she finally recalled the odd taste in the water. "Laudanum!" she exclaimed, "You gave me laudanum…"

"You need to sleep," he said softly. "So, sleep."

She did.

JAVAN CROSSED INTO Scotland before nightfall and rode straight through Gretna Green, travelling a few miles east, off the main Edinburgh road, to the Rose and Thistle. This was a smaller inn he'd been told about by the landlord he'd just left. The two innkeepers were apparently related, and the English one was very proud of his Scottish cousin, who apparently had a business on the side, marrying people according to peculiar Scots law. More to Javan's immediate purpose, the inn was closer to the village of Ecclerigg, where resided Caroline's mother, sister, and nephew.

Although the taproom was busy, the innkeeper gave him a choice of bedchambers for the night and brought him a hearty dinner.

After a disturbed night—he worried too much about Caroline to sleep well—he ate an early breakfast and rode on to Ecclerigg. This turned out to be a small, picturesque village at the foot of two hills. The blacksmith was happy to direct him to Mrs. Grey's cottage.

The cottage was not large, but it looked well-cared for and had a neat garden. A child of around four played in the garden while a maid hung up washing and hummed to herself.

Javan dismounted and looped the reins around the fence before he opened the gate and closed it again behind him.

"Good morning," he said civilly to the maid. "Is Mrs. Grey at home?"

The maid, her humming cut off, showed a tendency to stare with her jaw dropped. It was the child who stopped galloping around the garden to say, "Yes, she is. Is that your horse, sir?"

"Yes. You can stroke him if you like. He's very well mannered."

Grinning, the boy ran at the horse, who eyed him disdainfully across the fence.

"Give him this," Javan advised, taking a lump of sugar from his pocket. "Flat on your palm like so. He will love you forever. Are you Peter, by any chance?"

The boy nodded absently, watching with awe as the horse lipped the sugar gently from his hand.

"And who might you be?" the maid demanded with a hint of aggression that might have been her way of protecting the child from a stranger.

Javan gave her a slightly crumpled card. He hadn't had any printed for some time. "Be so good as to take this to Mrs. Grey. She will know my name as her daughter's employer."

The maid's eyes widened. "Peter, come in," she ordered, seizing the boy by the hand. "You'd better come too, sir."

She showed him through the narrow hallway and into a pleasant parlor, then, taking Peter with her, she left him. He heard the clumping of her footsteps on the stairs.

Peter, clearly, was not at death's door. He was doubly glad he'd left Caroline on the other side of the border.

After several minutes, when he could hear voices upstairs, a flurry of feet coming down heralded the arrival in the parlor of a middle-aged lady in a cap, and a young and very beautiful lady who held Peter by the hand.

"Mr. Benedict," the elder lady said, curtseying. "I am Mrs. Grey. This is my daughter, Mrs. Dauntry."

Javan bowed civilly.

"How can we possibly help you?" Mrs. Grey asked anxiously. "Caroline is not here."

"I know. I came on her behalf because she seemed to believe Peter here to be...very ill."

"He has had such a terrible chill," the beautiful Mrs. Dauntry said a shade nervously.

"But that was weeks ago," her mother said. "He has been fine since. I wrote to Caroline and told her so." She frowned. "Though, do you know, I may have sent it to Braithwaite Castle! I am so scatter-brained...perhaps she never received it?"

"Oh, no, she received that letter. It was sent over from the castle. No, this was a later one, from Mrs. Dauntry. I believe monies were required to pay the doctor? Because Peter had relapsed."

Mrs. Dauntry cast a glance at her mother, half-imploring, half-frightened. "Oh no...that is, I was afraid he might..." As though recollecting herself, she cast a dazzling smile at Javan. "But sir, you are amazingly kind to take up my sister's cause and come here in her stead. We thank you from the bottom of our hearts."

Mrs. Grey didn't look grateful. She looked confused and not a little put-out.

Javan inclined his head slightly and waited.

"Please, sit down," Mrs. Dauntry urged. "Will you have tea?"

He met her gaze and read there the confidence of a beautiful woman who knew she could bamboozle and win whichever man she liked. What was it she'd wanted the money for? Another new gown with which to seduce the local gentlemen? Or just a better class of dinners? Clearly, it had never been for Peter. The mother knew it and was not best pleased. Which said something for her. Just not enough in Javan's opinion.

"No, thank you," he said. "I won't have tea. I came really, to bring you news of Miss Grey. Since neither of you have asked, it is my duty to inform you that she is not currently well. She left my house in desperate haste to see Peter and was injured on the journey. She currently lies at an inn near Carlisle, in the care of my sister. The direction is written on the back of my card, should you need it. Good morning."

"Wait!" moaned Mrs. Grey. "Sir, what has happened to Caroline? You must tell me!"

"She was shot," Javan said brutally, and was only slightly mollified to see the sister whiten as she sat down too quickly.

"Shot!" the mother exclaimed. "Dear God!"

"Will she die?" Mrs. Dauntry whispered.

Javan relented. "No, I don't believe so. I have some experience of gunshot wounds and providing we can avoid corruption, I believe she will recover well. But I am glad to be able to relieve her mind over Peter."

"What were you thinking of, Eliza?" the mother burst out. "Do you think a governess earns so much—?"

"I was selfish," Mrs. Dauntry whispered, bowing her head. "You know I have been dull since I returned from Edinburgh and...and I so wish I hadn't written that stupid letter. Truly, I did not think it would matter. This is all my fault."

"Yes, it is," Mrs. Grey snapped. "Go and pack your bag and Peter's—*one* bag, Eliza! Sir, might we request your escort to my daughter? If you are returning there."

"I am. And I would be happy to escort you. I believe we can hire a chaise for you at the Rose and Thistle."

"Then we shall meet you there," Mrs. Grey said decisively. "We can borrow a conveyance that far at least and I know you are riding."

He bowed again, and began to walk away, but to his surprise, she caught his arm. "Sir, I thank you for your care of my daughter."

"It is the least I can do, ma'am. Her condition is more my fault than yours."

A frown flickered across her face at that. "I don't know how that may be. But you must find us selfish and neglectful. In truth, we have grown to rely too much on Caroline. She was always our strength, and Eliza has always been too indulged...that is my fault, for I imagined she would make a splendid marriage which would save us from penury when my husband died. But in truth, there is no excuse for her writing such a lie to Caroline."

"I do not judge either of you, ma'am," Javan said, not entirely truthfully.

"Thank you, for Eliza is not truly bad-natured. Just impulsive and inclined to selfishness, as are we all."

"As are we all," he agreed. He smiled faintly. "Except for Caroline."

Chapter Eighteen

A LONE IN THE inn's coffee room, Javan wished he had never agreed to escort Caroline's family. By four o'clock, they still had not arrived at the Rose and Thistle. It would be too late to start out now, especially with the child. He almost went alone, for his need to see Caroline all but overwhelmed him. However, being a man of his word, he resolved to leave it until evening and then send over a note to the effect that he would leave at first light, with or without them.

The matter was no sooner decided than he heard the rumble of a vehicle entering the inn yard. Rising to his feet, he walked to the window.

Not one carriage, but two were crossing the yard. Moreover, the first was only too familiar and driven by Williams, who jumped down as soon as the horses came to a standstill. Leaving them to the ostlers hurrying toward them, he opened the carriage door and let down the steps.

Swearing beneath his breath, Javan all but ran across the room and out into the yard, where it was beginning to rain. Caroline had emerged from the carriage, leaning on Williams' arm while Marjorie and Rosa jumped down beside her.

Rosa ran to him, and he caught her in one arm while striding toward Caroline with furious anxiety. His gaze lashed Richard who emerged from the other carriage with their captured assassin.

Refusing to be distracted for long, he searched Caroline's pale face as he took the final few paces to her.

She smiled at him, melting his heart all over again. "Don't be angry. I felt perfectly well and I'm afraid I insisted."

"She slept well all night," Marjorie added, as proud as if it had been her own achievement. "And had breakfast in bed, though she insisted on rising for luncheon and then felt so well that we gave in and brought her."

"We thought the journey would do her less harm than continued anxiety," Richard put in.

Caroline cast him a glance of respect, and suddenly Javan wanted to laugh because they were all trying to manage him and the truth was, despite his fear for her, his heart sang just because she was here in front of him.

He took her good hand from Williams, elbowing his old sergeant aside. "Then you'd better come inside and sit. Let me say at once that Peter is perfectly well. So are your mother and sister. In fact, they are expected here imminently."

The relief seemed to make her sag slightly. He flung one arm about her waist to support her and swept her inside, barking orders at the innkeeper and his wife as he went.

In no time, Caroline was ensconced in the best armchair before the coffee room fire, a soft cushion under her injured arm, and a cup of tea on the small table at her other side. Javan had pulled one of the large tables nearer her, and the rest of them—including Miller, who was tied to his chair—sat around it, drinking tea and ale and consuming a pleasant repast, tasty morsels of which were passed to Caroline.

Her wound did not appear to have reopened when Javan examined her dressing. In fact, she seemed none the worse for her journey, according to his close and continuous scrutiny. Which allowed him, finally, to concentrate on other things.

"What is *he* doing here?" he asked, jerking his head across the table to Miller, who was attempting to eat and drink with his hands bound together.

Richard swallowed his cold meat and reached for his ale. "Didn't know what else to do with him. He seems amiable enough when disarmed. And happy to daub Swayle in it. Expect he wants us to let him go if he does."

Miller gave what he probably imagined was an engaging smile. "Happy to help. Don't hold with killing women, certainly not gentlewomen, which anyone can see she is, governess or no."

"Didn't stop you, though, did it?" Javan retorted.

"Well, she ain't dead," Miller said incontrovertibly. "Is she?"

Whatever Javan might have replied became lost in a furor by the door.

"I *beg* your pardon!" exclaimed a strident female voice, "but this is a public coffee room and I insist on being allowed inside!"

"But I have quality in there, and a sick guest who needs quiet," insisted Archie the innkeeper. "Allow me to have your dinner brought to your room. It will be much more pleasant and private."

"My wife said the coffee room!" roared a male voice. There was a scuffle, as if poor Archie had been thrust aside, and then a man barreled into the coffee room, closely followed by his wife, two daughters, and a slightly stringy young man who might have been their son. The family halted and stared with dislike at Javan's party.

Miller got to his feet with the chair still tied to him and bared his teeth.

Led by the father, the family fled in silence. Grinning, Miller sat back down again and nodded at Javan. "You're welcome."

"Finally," Javan observed flippantly. "A man more frightening than me."

IT WAS ODD, but Caroline found the time at the inn curiously comforting and exciting at the same time. Apart from the pain in her arm, she truly felt well, and quite blissful in Javan's company. He sat close to her, leaning one elbow on the big table, the other occasionally brushing against her good shoulder. His nearness, of course, was the source of her excitement, adding to the pleasure of the other Benedicts' company. She was unspeakably touched by the way they all looked after her. That even Marjorie had followed and stayed with her…That Javan had gone to her mother just to relieve her mind of worry…That Rosa was happy to have them all reunited.

When her mother and sister finally arrived, Caroline and her companions were in the midst of an amusing and spirited discussion. She and Marjorie each had a ladylike glass of sherry wine, while the Benedict gentlemen had a bottle of brandy which was almost as good, apparently, as that found in Blackhaven. Rosa was playing cards with Miller.

Warned in advance, the innkeeper merely ushered his newest patrons into the coffee room. Caroline was smiling at Javan's laughter, because he laughed so much more easily now, when, over Richard's shoulder, she saw her mother enter.

"Forgive our tardiness, Mr. Benedict," her mother began. "The only available conveyance was a cart pulled by a very old donkey and it took forever just to—Caroline!"

"Mama!" She tried to rise, but Javan and Marjorie both pressed her back into her seat. As the gentlemen rose to greet the newcomers, Peter flew past everyone and threw himself onto Caroline's lap.

"Aunt Caro! Aunt Caro! You'll never guess! I saw the biggest, finest horse in the world *and* I gave it sugar! It was his," he added, grinning at Javan while Caroline hugged him in her good arm.

By then, Eliza too was kneeling at her feet. "You're here, Caro! Oh, thank God, I was afraid we'd find you wilting in bed, quite at death's door!"

Inevitably, there was a hint of accusation in among Eliza's genuine relief.

"Like Peter?" Caroline said before she could help herself.

Eliza had the grace to blush. "Well, I am sorry about that letter. It was a great mistake and I am thoroughly ashamed, but how was I to know you would gallop up here and get shot? Which Mr. Benedict said was *not* my fault."

"No, it was his," Richard drawled, waving one hand at Miller, who hung his head.

"Is that why he's tied up?" Peter asked, sliding off Caroline's knee to allow his grandmother to embrace her.

"Exactly," said Javan. "Ladies, allow me to present my sister, Miss Benedict, my cousin Mr. Richard Benedict, and my daughter Rosa. And Mr. Miller, of course," he added, apparently for pure devilment. "Known to his friends as Killer."

"Good Lord," Caroline's mother murmured. "Do you trust him?"

"God, no. Not unless he's tied up and has something to gain by cooperating. Please, sit down. A glass of sherry, perhaps? We're expecting dinner at any moment."

This was the time Caroline had been secretly dreading. She liked her sister to shine, but she didn't want to see the light of admiration in Javan's eyes when he looked at her. Her smile could dazzle the coldest hearted princes... Or at least it had dazzled Theo Dauntry. But she wouldn't think about him. She would only think of her pleasure in seeing her family. There was nothing she could do about anything else.

She knew she was quieter, more subdued at dinner, as she always was in her sister's company. And Eliza was in form, spreading her smile indiscriminately. "How handsome Mr. Richard is, Caro," she whispered. "And heir to a baronet, you say? Of course, the other is more romantic, but just a little frightening. Perhaps it is the scar."

She seemed to imagine she had her choice of them. Certainly, it never entered her head that either could be interested in Caroline. And of course, they indulged her. It took Caroline some time to realize that indulgence was all it was, like humoring a child by listening to her prattle. They both addressed frequent remarks to Caroline by name and gradually, Caroline began to reply more naturally until she realized it was Eliza who had grown subdued, stunned by the attention paid to her older, plainer sister the governess.

She chided herself for ill nature, but after Theo, it was sweet to see Javan's attention rarely straying from herself. She wanted to preen.

Since the inn only had three bedchambers, it was decided that Caroline would share one with Marjorie and Rosa. Her mother, sister, and Peter would have the second bedchamber, and the Benedicts the third. Williams undertook to watch Miller in the stables.

Javan conducted Caroline upstairs behind Marjorie and Rosa. Because it was sweet, she leaned on him just a little more than she needed to. And when Marjorie and Rosa went inside with their candle, Javan quietly closed the door on them, set his candle in the window embrasure, and there in the passage, took Caroline into his arms. She melted.

"Tell me now, Caroline Grey," he whispered into her hair. "Will you marry me?"

She inhaled the scent of his skin, let her lips open against his warm, rough cheek. "Do you love me?"

His mouth found hers. His kiss was long and tender and left her devastated.

"More than life," he murmured against her lips. "Never doubt it, for I shan't. It seems as if I've always loved you. I always will."

Never had she expected such a comprehensive declaration from Javan Benedict. She smiled without letting her lips leave his. "Then yes, I will gladly marry you. So very gladly."

He kissed her again. "Tomorrow?"

She laughed breathlessly at his eagerness. "I hardly see how! But as soon as it can be arranged, yes. Perhaps Mr. Grant could marry us."

"Perhaps," Javan said, kissing her lips and then her forehead. "Perhaps. Good night, my love."

"Good night," she said, so enchanted that she had to reach up and kiss him again.

Her mother's door further along the passage opened and Eliza looked out and saw them. Her mouth opened in shock.

"Good night," Caroline gasped and whisked herself inside her own room. As she leaned her back against the closed door, Marjorie and Rosa blinked at her in surprise. She could hear Javan's soft laughter and his footsteps as he ran back downstairs, no doubt to join Richard in finishing off the brandy.

WHEN SHE WOKE in the morning, her arm didn't feel quite so sore, perhaps because she was so happy that she couldn't stop smiling. She could still feel Javan's kisses on her lips. He loved her. He wanted to marry her. Never, since the day she'd discovered Theo's betrayal, had she expected to find this kind of happiness. And what she felt for Javan felt so much more than that ignorant, girlish love. More intense and overwhelming, as if she'd never stop falling and never wanted to. It was almost...*frightening*, because she couldn't control it and yet, she was delighted to follow where it led.

Marjorie insisted on her staying in bed to eat breakfast, which was no hardship since Peter and Rosa accompanied the maid with her breakfast tray. They sat on her bed while she ate, happily munching the pieces she allowed them. Rosa seemed to have found a new purpose in looking after the younger Peter, who gazed at her with awe a lot of the time.

Smiling, Marjorie left Caroline at the children's mercy and went downstairs to breakfast. Eliza wandered in a little later and also sat on the bed to tell her about her life in recent months, Peter's illness, and her stay in Edinburgh.

After a little, the restless children moved away, pointing and giggling at things they could see out of the window. Eventually, they ran off to play.

"So," Eliza said, fixing Caroline with a clear stare. "You and Mr. Javan Benedict. Your employer, Caroline. You are playing with fire."

"I know."

"You are the governess." Eliza rammed the point home with genuine concern. "Caro, he will not care for you. He is a hard man and will simply break your heart and cast you aside. I could not bear that for you again."

She had never before admitted that her marriage had hurt Caroline. Once, this would have mattered a lot more. As it was, Caroline felt touched by her sister's concern.

"Don't worry," she soothed. "It isn't as bad as it appears."

"Caro, you were kissing him!"

"I know. But I'm going to marry him."

"Does he know?" Eliza asked cynically. "Because I don't think much of anyone's chances getting *him* to do anything he has not chosen!"

"I believe he has."

Eliza's eyes widened. "Truly?" she said doubtfully. "Have you told Mama this?"

"No, there has been no time. But you are not hurrying home today, are you?"

"I don't know. Originally, we were coming to you on the other side of the border. It would be lovely to stay here for another day and night, but you know how money is."

"I'm sure Mr. Benedict intends to take care of all of that."

A frown puckered her brow. "Is he *very* wealthy?"

"I don't actually know," Caroline said in surprise.

Eliza laughed and gave her a quick hug. "Oh, Caro, you are ridiculous!"

Eliza left when Marjorie returned to help her dress and pin her hair.

"Not so severe today," Marjorie suggested as Caroline brushed her hair back tightly as usual. "You're not working, you know! More like you styled it for Lady Tamar's rout." She took the brush from Caroline, rolling and pinning her hair to her own satisfaction. "Much prettier. Although, to be sure, you always look lovely."

"I do?" Caroline said, startled.

"If one cares to look," Marjorie said vaguely. "Now, are you feeling strong enough? Shall we go down to the coffee room?"

Caroline agreed to this plan. Her heart beat faster, only because of the possibility that Javan was already there. Just being with him made her happy.

At the foot of the stairs, she encountered her mother, and Marjorie relinquished her, hurrying into the coffee room as if she had something important to do. It was sweet the way everyone seemed to assume she could not walk unaided. After all, it was her arm, not her leg, which had been injured.

However, she was content to take her mother's arm.

"You're looking very well," her mother murmured as they walked together. "Despite all the excitement, to call it no worse. You are happy at Haven Hall?"

Surprised by the anxiety in her mother's voice, she smiled reassuringly. "Yes, I am. I own I was devastated to leave Braithwaite Castle, but somehow, Haven Hall, though much less...*convenient*, has become my home." She squeezed her mother's arm. "We have much to discuss."

"Yes, we do," her mother agreed, walking with her into the coffee room and closing the door.

Caroline blinked because not only Javan but everyone else was there already—Marjorie, Rosa, Peter, Eliza, Richard, Williams, and even Killer Miller—most of them sitting not at tables but in chairs set out in a clear space before the fire. Archie the innkeeper was there too, facing them, while his wife and one of the inn servants skulked more in the background.

Javan advanced to meet Caroline. She met his gaze with bewilderment. He offered his arm but her mother hung on to Caroline's hand.

"He says you've agreed to marry him," her mother blurted. "Before I give my blessing, I need to know it's what you want. I won't have you pushed into anything for any reason."

Caroline swallowed, distracted by the intensity of Javan's eyes. "Yes, it's what I want..." Suspicion, realization, began to dawn and her eyes widened. "Now?" she squeaked.

"Why not?" Javan countered. "Archie there has the same rights as the Gretna blacksmith to marry us under Scots law."

She stared at him, the enormity of this step crushing her. Although she wanted it with all her heart, she hadn't imagined it would be quite so soon.

"I thought it might be more comfortable returning to Blackhaven already married, than putting you through *another* engagement which is bound to set tongues wagging."

"*Another* engagement?" her mother repeated, startled. "Who were you engaged to before?"

"Richard," Javan said impatiently.

Caroline regarded him with fascination. "And you imagine my leaving Blackhaven engaged to one cousin and returning there married to the other will *not* cause comment?"

A quick grin passed over Javan's face and vanished. "Richard believes he can just tell everyone they were mistaken and that you were always engaged to me. Personally, I don't see that it's anyone's business but ours. We can be married here, now, or we can go home and ask Grant to marry us whenever you like."

She glanced from him to her mother and the rest of the company and realized that of course this was right. Her mother and Eliza and Peter were here. She was happy. Everyone was happy.

Slowly, she took her hand from her mother's arm and laid it on Javan's. She smiled up at him. "Here and now is perfect," she said huskily, and the wave of joy in his face seemed to be all she could ever need.

EVEN IN HER wildest, most romantic, youthful dreams, Caroline had never imagined being married by an innkeeper in his coffee room. The morning passed in a blissful daze. Her hand was placed in Javan's, they made promises, and before the law and God, she was his. Mrs. Javan Benedict.

Rosa was silently delirious and kept hugging both of them. Mrs. Archie provided a wonderful spread, more luncheon than wedding breakfast, and Archie rooted out a few bottles of champagne that he'd never had cause to use before. Caroline felt she would burst with happiness.

And yet, it was a relief to escape for a little and just walk with Javan in the woods beyond the inn. His company both soothed and energized her, and it was unbearably sweet to pause in the shade of a tree and exchange kisses in the sharp, autumn-scented air, while the birds sang above them and the human voices were all distant.

"I do love you," she whispered.

"I hope you always will." It was light and gentle, and yet behind it, she recognized a genuine fear. If his first wife had ever loved him, it hadn't been for long.

But she would not bring that specter to her marriage. She merely kissed him and resolved to banish this shadow along with all the others.

His body grew harder, more urgent, pinning her to the tree as he ravished her mouth and throat with kisses, his hands on her hips to hold her where he wanted her.

"Do you know, my wife," he said unsteadily, "that Richard told me he would stay away from our chamber until well after midnight?"

The heat of her arousal seemed to flame. Words stuck in her throat. Having lived so long in the country, she was aware of the mechanics of procreation and linked it with some astonishment to the thrilling if unspecific desires she felt in Javan's arms. The thought of spending time in his bed, of pleasing him in this way both excited and scared her. But there was no way she would ever refuse him, and it had little to do with "duty".

"Do you want to go there, now?" she whispered.

"Oh yes," he said fervently, bringing his open mouth down on hers, caressing her tongue with his.

He seemed to wrench his mouth free and rested his forehead on hers, easing his body apart from hers until there was a sliver of air between them. "But I won't take you until you're well enough, until we have time and space to enjoy each other. For you, there should be more than a hurried fumble, at least the first time."

She swallowed, wondering if there was relief among the flood of disappointment. "It is a long time until midnight," she pointed out.

"And I feel very well. My arm barely hurts at all."

He smiled and kissed her at the same time. "You are a liar, and I love you for it. But I will be good for just a little longer."

Perhaps, if it hadn't been for the obvious betrayal of his body, and his devastating kisses, she might have been hurt. As it was, she couldn't quite understand how it was possible to be so enchanted and so frustrated at the same time.

And so, she spent her wedding night with her new stepdaughter and sister-in-law. And in the morning, she bade farewell to her mother and sister and little Peter, who were invited to Haven Hall for Christmas, and began the journey home to Blackhaven.

Chapter Nineteen

W HILE AWAITING THE return of Killer Miller to claim the other half of his fee, Marcus Swayle enjoyed himself spreading the word about Caroline Grey's disappearance. Not that he gave any impression of watching Haven Hall or its occupants. He preferred to ask people if they had seen Miss Grey, then exclaim with worry when they hadn't. He would then enquire, with obvious suspicion, about Colonel Javan Benedict.

Many people in Blackhaven did not seem to be aware of Benedict's former rank. Clearly, the blackguard was trying hard not to be connected to the Colonel Benedict of the late scandal. Swayle was happy to enlighten them as to that connection and reiterate the colonel's brutality to himself and to his wife.

"We truly thought he was dead," he said frequently. "And I have to say my poor, innocent Louisa had cause to wish he was. When we married, we believed we had a right to happiness. But he defeated both of us by returning. That I could not save her will haunt me forever... But I cannot bear that others might suffer as we did. It is my belief that poor Miss Grey is in terrible danger. And as for the child, whom I love as my own..."

He was slightly miffed that more people didn't react with sympathy and shock. The devil was in it that Lord and Lady Tamar and the vicar, damn them, seemed to have taken Benedict up. And the dullards in Blackhaven obviously took their cues from them. But they would see, they would all see, when Caroline Grey was found dead and Javan Benedict the clear culprit. With luck, this would turn even Richard against him before he hanged.

By the third day after Miller's departure, Swale began to get res-
tive. The task must have been proving harder than they had assumed,
but Swayle had faith in the villain to earn his fee in the end. He just
hoped it wouldn't take too much longer. He didn't want to think the
matter was getting out of his control, which was a suspicion when he
spoke to Mrs. Winslow in the pump room, on the day of the assembly
room ball.

"I suppose you have not seen Miss Grey from the hall?" he began,
as usual.

"I believe they are all away," Mrs. Winslow replied unexpectedly.

"All?" he repeated, startled.

"Indeed. Dear Lady Tamar tells me that there are only servants at
the hall right now."

"Then…little Rosa is not there? Or Miss Benedict?"

"None of them," Mrs. Winslow averred.

"My God," Swayle said uneasily. "Has he fled?"

Mrs. Winslow laughed. "What an odd word! I believe the servants
expect them all back soon."

"I pray you may be right," Swayle said sorrowfully and took his
leave.

This was annoying. He had hoped to have the whole matter done
and dusted by this time, so that he could soak up all the town's horror
and disgust at Benedict during the assembly ball. He'd planned to bask
in the glow of people's appreciation of his knowledge and perspicacity.
And perhaps even, in the moment of his fame, encounter an heiress.
Or a wealthy widow. He was not fussy.

Still, the subscription ball was a great place to intensify the rumors,
and if news of the death could only get there tonight, why that would
be even better. But he scarcely allowed himself to hope for such a
splendid outcome.

Instead, he made the most of what he did have and arrived at the
assembly rooms impeccably dressed as always. And although he took
his walking cane, he did not lean on it as heavily. Which meant he

could dance with the charming and the wealthy women he had already picked out.

He was just returning a very young lady to her guardians when a stir at the ballroom door attracted his attention. And not just his. The way everyone turned and stared at Javan Benedict spoke volumes for the success of Swayle's whispering campaign. Unfortunately, after one breathless moment of triumph, Swayle recognized his female companion as Miss Grey.

Oh, she wore a rather beautiful new gown of rose silk, and some-one had given her pearls to wind around her throat, but it was undoubtedly Caroline Grey.

"Colonel and Mrs. Benedict," the major-domo announced, and Swayle had to close his teeth on his furious oath. Still smiling, he made civil conversation with his partner's family and moved about the ballroom, desperate to find out what this meant for his plans. But damn it, he couldn't even say she had been forced into it, for happiness shone from her like a beacon.

Gone was the severe frump of a governess. In her place, had come a beautiful, fashionable, and confident young matron, more than fit to be shown off on any man's arm. Any man except Benedict, that is. As the couple moved into the room, Lady Tamar went forward to embrace her family's old governess. From all over the room came well-wishers and congratulatory back-slappers.

Rage began to surge within Swayle, for it was as if all his hard work, all his rumor mongering and all the seeds of suspicion he'd sown, had been for nothing. Not only had Javan so obviously not killed her, he'd married her. No one seemed to care either that she'd left engaged to a different Benedict, and that included Richard himself, who sauntered in behind the couple, as proud as if he'd made the match himself. Which he might have, Swayle supposed. Only, where the devil was Miller? What on earth had he been doing for the last five days?

"What a distinguished couple they make," said a female voice fondly beside him. Mrs. Grant, who gave herself such airs as though she were some great lady instead of a country vicar's wife. "It seems your fears were quite unfounded, Mr. Swayle."

"I'm glad if that is so," he said at once. "But I'll be happier when I discover what has happened to my little Rosa."

"Oh, she's very well and very excited to have a new mother. And of course, she got to meet some new family in Scotland."

"Family in Scotland?" Swayle repeated, trying not to stare at her. She was so beautiful in her dark, languid way, that in any other circumstances, he would have enjoyed her company. Right now, he had the horrid feeling she was torturing him.

"Of course. They all went north to meet Caroline's—Mrs. Benedict's—family. And married while they were there. Isn't it delightful?"

"Charming," Swayle said, sickened. "I shall be happiest if he treats her better than he did my Louisa."

Mrs. Grant smiled directly into his eyes. "Well, he will no longer be fighting abroad, so there will certainly be no opportunity for some scoundrel to move into his house, take his wife, and abuse his daughter." And without waiting for a reply, she turned on her heel and walked away.

Stunned by this rumor-reversal, it took him a moment to leap after her and actually seize her arm. "Mrs. Grant, I cannot allow you to repeat such thorough calumny. If this is what Benedict is saying…"

"Not Benedict," said Benedict himself, materializing at his side. "Rosa."

The blood sang in his ears. Benedict had always affected him this way, even before he'd kicked him literally out of his house. There was something harsh and inflexible about him, something that simply made Swayle feel small and less of a man. But right now, there was more at stake than Swayle's manliness. After all this time, Rosa had accused him.

In many ways, it would have been a blessed relief to faint and give himself time to think, to find a way out of this. But Benedict's hard, violent eyes seemed to hold him upright. He couldn't even pretend. Instead, he blurted, "Rosa has spoken?"

Benedict smiled. It wasn't pleasant. "We can't stop the flow of words from her now."

Swayle felt sick to his stomach. He could deny whatever the child said, but he could not denounce her, make out she was lying from hatred since he'd just spent weeks convincing everyone he and Rosa loved each other like father and daughter.

"You made her," he managed to choke out.

"Made her what, Swayle?" Benedict pressed. "And I really think you should remove your hand from Mrs. Grant's arm, for she does not care for it. And if Grant does not knock you down, I will."

"More violence, sir?" Swayle snapped, clutching at straws. However, he released Mrs. Grant, whom he'd forgotten in the sudden confrontation with Benedict. He needed to get away from here and either regroup or move on. Perhaps he should go back to London…

With what dignity he could muster he stalked past Benedict, ignoring the vicar and Richard Benedict who were approaching rapidly. He swiped up his cane from the corner he'd left it in and leaned on it a little more than before as he made his way out of the ballroom to the blessed coolness of the foyer.

Here he could at least draw breath and think. He could not ignominiously turn tail and run, for that would surely confirm his guilt. He would refresh himself in the gentlemen's cloakroom and pray for inspiration.

Forcing himself to smile and bow to the few late arrivals in the foyer, he walked past them and abruptly stopped, staring at the individual leaning beside the doorman as though having a pleasant chat.

"Miller!" he blurted.

Miller grinned and tipped his disreputable hat. "Mr. Swayle."

What the doorman was thinking of, allowing such an individual into these hallowed halls on the night of a gentry ball, was beyond Swayle. Presumably Miller had, finally, come to report his abject failure. Too late, for the evidence was flaunting herself inside.

"Get out," Swayle snarled. "I'll deal with you later."

"This the man?" the doorman said. And Swayle, peering closer, saw that it was a different doorman from the last time he'd been here.

"Aye, that's him," said Miller, and the doorman straightened so suddenly that Swayle knew without doubt that he'd made a deadly mistake.

"Name's Bolton," the "doorman" said conversationally. "I'm from Bow Street, and you, Mr. Swayle, are under arrest."

There was nothing else for it. Swayle leapt back and lashed upward with his cane.

"Watch out," came Benedict's warning cry from behind. "It's a sword-stick!"

He remembered, damn him, he remembered everything. But it was too late. Swayle had already drawn the sword free and thrust hard, not at the runner but at Miller.

CAROLINE HAD OBSERVED the moment Swayle began to make his way out of the ballroom. Although naturally outraged by his part in trying to kill her—for no better reason than to make Javan suffer—it was his cruelty to Rosa that made her really want to witness his downfall.

She excused herself from the group of people Serena had introduced her to and followed him. She wasn't surprised to meet her husband in the doorway. She even took his arm and felt the hint of tension in him. For he had planned this with military precision, including the unsettling of Swayle by their presence and by the accusations that had come from Kate Grant. They had been supposed to come from her husband the vicar, but it seemed Kate had got there first. Either way, the encounter had its desired effect. Swayle had left the ballroom, where the Bow Street Runner and Killer Miller awaited him.

There were only a few people in the foyer, and voices carried. Caroline heard Miller's identification quite clearly, and then the runner's somewhat arrogant introduction.

"Damn it," Javan muttered, detaching his arm from her hold. "Bolton's supposed to secure him *before* her reveals–"

He was already running across the entrance hall and shouting his warning when Swayle jumped out of easy reach and dragged the sword from his cane. His intention was clear—silence the man whom he'd paid to commit murder. And Miller was both bound and hemmed in by the door and the wall.

Terrified for Javan, Caroline stumbled after him. Two ladies emerging from the cloakroom screamed. A gentleman shouted a furious demand that the fight be taken outside.

Then Javan slammed into Swayle's back, his arm streaking around his enemy's throat and locking hard as he dragged him back. The sword missed Miller's heart by a fraction of an inch.

Swayle jerked, trying to shake him off, to make use of the weapon in his right hand. But the sword could not reach Javan, and Swayle could not dislodge him with his constricted elbows or his feet. Javan seized his right wrist in a grip so hard that Swayle cried out in his effort to hold on to his weapon.

"You, stay where you are," the runner instructed Miller and advanced menacingly upon Swayle.

The sword clattered to the floor, and Bolton, the runner, scooped it up. Javan's arm squeezed tighter until Swayle made a horrible choking noise. Caroline, her heart in her mouth, was suddenly terrified that Javan would kill him. She ran the last few paces, seizing his free arm.

"Javan, don't," she pleaded.

"Give him up to me now, sir," the runner said authoritatively.

Javan gave a last squeeze and almost hurled Swayle into Bolton's grip. "Of course."

Only then, with Swayle safe and choking in his hold, did the runner turn to Miller. "You still here?"

Miller shrugged. "I could have legged it while you wrestled with him. Didn't seem right when the colonel there saved my life. I take it kindly, sir."

"Don't," Javan said. "I need you to send this dog to prison, if not to the hangman."

"Happy to oblige."

"We got it written down and witnessed," the runner said carelessly. "Magistrate don't care if he's there or not."

"Then I'd no need to hurry," Javan said flippantly.

"Very glad you did," Miller admitted, jerking his head at the runner, "for *he* was no help, blabbing before he was meant to. Just cause a man looks like a cowardly weasel don't mean he'll come quietly."

Bolton had the grace to look sheepish, muttering that no harm had been done.

"No," Javan agreed, his fist clenching once more. "It gave me the chance to hurt him, to feel the breath leaving his body."

"I never laid a finger on Rosa," Swayle gasped. "She's lying if she says I did."

Sparks flew from Javan's eyes. Caroline couldn't prevent him stepping closer. "No, you didn't need to," he uttered with searing contempt. "You just threatened her, frightened her into never revealing your pathetic plan to kill me when I came home. She overheard you and Louisa discussing it, and you scared her, a child of eight, who didn't even understand most of what you'd planned, with vile threats I will not repeat here. You told her she'd never see either of her parents again if she ever opened her mouth. Children can be literal. She never did open her mouth. If she never said anything, she'd never say the thing you'd kill us for. Louisa dying only reinforced your threats in her mind."

Javan's fingers curled reassuringly around Caroline's pleading hand. He took a breath and even smiled, though it wasn't a pleasant smile. "But here's the thing, Swayle. She beat you without speaking. She wrote it all down."

She had. On their return to Blackhaven this afternoon, they'd called first on Dr. Lampton to get him to look at Caroline' wound. Afterward, he'd shown them his notebook where Rosa had written her answers to his questions on their last meeting. And where she'd drawn a picture of what had frightened her.

"I didn't think anything of it at first," Lampton had told them. "I thought it was just her doodling, a way of avoiding what I'd asked her to think about. For the answers she wrote down were evasive and uninformative in the extreme. But it was a good drawing for a child of her age, and I began to think I'd actually seen this fellow. Have I? Have you?"

And Rosa had come and taken the book from them, and without urging, had sat at Dr. Lampton's desk and written down a long, terrible stream of words. By the end, tears were dropping onto the paper, blotting the ink, and she'd clung to her father, trembling and weeping silently into his coat.

If Caroline had not already loved him to distraction, she would have fallen for him just for the way he comforted Rosa, a mixture of gentle explanations and praise and a secure, constant embrace. Caroline's throat constricted all over again at the memory, at the thought of the child's pain. And Javan's fury, so tightly controlled that his hand trembled as soon as it stopped stroking Rosa's hair.

Bolton opened the door to haul his prisoner out.

"And *him?*" Swayle asked, as though he couldn't help it. "How did you get a runner here so fast?"

"Actually, it took some time," Javan said. "I wrote to Bow Street as soon as I saw you at Braithwaite Castle. It wasn't my first discussion with the runners about you, but a year ago I had no proof. This time, because they thought you'd followed me, they were more interested." He swung away, dragging Caroline's hand through his arm. "For Rosa and for Caroline, I hope they hang you. Take him away, Bolton, before I kill him myself."

Inevitably, perhaps, it was Serena who lightened the moment. At the head of the throng that had spilled out of the ballroom to see the "fight", she gave a pleased little clap at Javan's parting line. And the applause was taken up by several people and then by everyone in the vicinity.

Javan looked startled, then amused in a slightly embarrassed way.

He bowed dramatically before the company, like a stage actor, which delighted them further. Then he led Caroline through the throng and back into the ballroom.

"You'd better dance with me now to let the noise die down," he muttered.

"It won't die down if you dance with your own wife," she warned humorously. "You'll be shunned."

"Oh well," he said, taking her into his arms, for it was a waltz which had struck up. He held her carefully, allowing her injured arm to lie across her breast. "They might as well know that the wicked governess who set her cap at an earl and a baronet before me, has finally caught her lesser man."

"There is nothing lesser about you, Javan," she said warmly. "There never was."

"And were you never a wicked governess?" he teased.

"No," she said with dignity. She let her thumb caress his hand. "Or at least, only in my thoughts."

Chapter Twenty

CAROLINE HAD NOTICED Colonel Fredericks almost as soon as they'd arrived at the ball, but with the matter of Swayle looming largest in her mind, she didn't truly consider his possible importance to Javan until she saw him again after the waltz.

Leaving Javan to explain the recent events in the foyer to Lord Tamar, she slipped away to speak to Fredericks, who was then sitting beside Miss Muir and her young sister-in-law. Caroline greeted the ladies, who were friends of Serena's, and turned to the colonel.

"I don't suppose you remember me, sir—"

"Of course I do, Mrs. Benedict," he said at once. "And I'm very glad you've led the colonel out of cover."

"I wonder if I might have a word, sir?"

Fredericks sprang to his feet with unexpected energy. "Of course. Excuse me ladies, must stretch these old legs of mine! Let us take a turn about the room, Mrs. Benedict, while you tell me what I can do for you."

"I believe," Caroline began delicately, "that you are most knowledgeable about the war on the Peninsula and privy to information that passes the rest of us by."

"Certainly I am curious—not to say nosey!—by nature."

"Do you know of the fort at San Pedro?"

"I know the place you mean."

"The British took it in the spring of 1812, and then I believe the French took it back in the summer."

"Fortunes of war," the colonel said with a shrug.

"How did the French take it?" she asked bluntly.

"Head on, I believe. We evacuated."

Caroline took a deep breath. "Were the British betrayed? Was that why they were so overwhelmed at San Pedro?"

Fredericks blinked and cast a glance that might have been involuntary, at Javan, who was then walking into the card room with Tamar and a couple of the marquis's cronies.

"Actually, it was a tactical withdrawal," he said. "We wanted a large number of French shut up in the fort so that a large contingent of troops could get through to Badajoz. And in fact, San Pedro was back in British hands within a month."

"Then it was already back in British hands by the time Javan escaped?"

"I believe so," Fredericks said, looking mystified. "Why do you ask?"

She took a deep breath and lowered her voice. "The French told my husband he'd babbled in his fever—no doubt torture-induced—and betrayed the way in to San Pedro."

She needed to know, for Javan's sake. For her own, she did not care what a man said when he had no control of his words. She would love Javan whatever he had said or done and nothing could change that now. But she so wanted to set his mind at rest. To stop the nightmares if she could.

"Spite," Fredericks said with a shrug. "Probably because he'd told them nothing. The French would always have got into San Pedro, because that was where we wanted them for those few days at least."

She frowned. "Did Javan not know that?"

"Of course not. His task was not connected to San Pedro when he was taken. His troops achieved their own objective before they were overwhelmed getting back to the main army. Some of them were captured. That I cannot discuss with you at the moment, so I hope it is not relevant to your...inquiry."

"I don't believe it is," she said warmly. "Colonel, might I ask you another favor? Would you speak to my husband? You see, I think he believes his honor is lost. That is why he sold his commission."

"And spoke to no one but Wellington before he did," Fredericks said thoughtfully. His gaze refocused on Caroline and he patted her arm, before presenting her with a glass of champagne and sauntering off to the card room.

Five minutes later, Caroline couldn't help glancing in. Her husband sat some distance from the card tables, his elbows on his knees, his eyes on his crossed hands as Fredericks talked beside him. His scar was livid from the rigid set of his jaw. Then, slowly, Javan raised his gaze to Fredericks's face. He did not blink.

Fredericks stood and briefly gripped his shoulder before walking away to the tables. Surreptitiously, like a boy ashamed to reveal grief, Javan dashed his sleeve quickly over his face, then sprang to his feet and strode away to the opposite door that led to the foyer rather than the ballroom.

Caroline smiled rather shakily, praying she'd done the right thing. But when she walked into the foyer, it was in time to see Javan's unmistakable figure leaving the building. Without thought, she hastened to the cloakroom to change into her outdoor shoes and retrieve her new evening cloak. They'd come home via Carlisle, and Javan had insisted on making a few purchases, including the ball gown and pearls and the engraved gold ring that she wore tonight.

Despite her hurry, he'd vanished from the street by the time she got there.

"May I send for your carriage, ma'am?" asked the doorman—the genuine doorman, this time.

"No, I thank you…my husband is waiting for me. Goodnight."

She thought she knew where he'd gone, and it wasn't far. She turned right up the road toward the harbor.

He leaned against the harbor wall, gazing out to sea over the bobbing fishing boats and the small pleasure yacht which had tied up since Caroline had been there last. She went and stood beside him.

For a moment he didn't say anything, but he knew she was there, for his fingers found hers and threaded through them.

"I was coming back," he assured her.

"I know. But I thought it was time to go home. Rosa may not sleep until you're back."

"I think she will. I think what she wrote eased her in some way. And she understands Swayle cannot hurt me or anyone else she loves."

"He could spill venom at his trial," Caroline warned.

"That will hurt him, not me or Rosa. I've protected her from the wrong things."

"No, you've just protected her."

He looked at her at last. "As you're now protecting me? You set Fredericks on me, didn't you?"

"I asked him about San Pedro. He seemed shocked that you believed what you did."

He shrugged. "I didn't believe it precisely. I was just *afraid* it was true and even more afraid to enquire in case I found out it was." His lip curled. "I never thought of myself as a coward before."

"It's not cowardice, it's confusion. You had too much tragedy in your life at one time to think clearly about everything. Your capture, torture, escape, leaving the army, returning home to…what you did."

"Perhaps," he allowed. His thumb stroked her hand. "You light my way, Caroline Grey."

"As you light mine."

"Do I?" he whispered, caressing her cheek.

"I, too, have been lost, in my own way."

He kissed her lips, a soft brief kiss that sparked deep inside her. "Then let us go home and find each other."

As JAVAN HANDED her out of the carriage in front of Haven Hall, a hulking figure loomed out the shadows.

"Oy!" Williams called indignantly. "What do you think you're doing here?"

"Miller?" Javan said incredulously, pausing in his act of thrusting

Caroline behind himself for protection. "Aren't you supposed to be with Bolton?"

"He let me go," Miller said cheerfully as Javan shone the lantern on him. Then he sighed. "Well, sort of. I nipped off while he was more interested in the gentry cove—Swayle. I don't think he'll mind, especially if you was to take me on."

"Take you on?" Javan repeated incredulously.

"I can look to your horses, drive 'em, be your bodyguard, whatever you want."

"You want to work for us?" Caroline said carefully.

"No one ever saved my life before. Never thought enough of me, I suppose. I never gave 'em cause to. Give you my word, sir, I'd never do no wrong to you or yours again—whether you take me on or not. But I'd like to pay it back. For shooting your missus. Because I'll be honest, I never wanted to shoot her, but I did it anyway, for money. Never meant to kill her either, but if it had happened—and it easily could have—I wouldn't have lost any sleep over it."

"And all this has changed because I stopped Swayle sticking you?" Javan asked dubiously.

"Na, it was changing before. Being with your family and Williams there made me think, made me see things...different. I was going to run off and be a soldier like him, and you, do some good with my shooting. Then I thought I'd rather work for you."

Javan and Caroline both looked at Williams who stood by the horses' heads.

Williams shrugged. "I could use help in the stables. And in the house, but that's a discussion for another day. You and me, sir, we've knocked worse men than Miller into shape before now."

"Trial for a month," Javan said, walking away to the front steps and drawing Caroline with him. "You obey Williams implicitly and show respect to the other servants or you're out."

"Understood, sir," said Miller blissfully.

ROSA SLEPT PEACEFULLY in her bed. Caroline and Javan stood for a few moments looking down at her. Javan touched her hair for an instant, and then they tiptoed from Rosa's chamber to Caroline's and quietly closed the door.

Javan gazed around it. "I drove myself mad thinking of you in here, wondering what you were doing, if you were sleeping. If you were thinking of me."

"I usually was," she confessed. "I listened to your footsteps every night, as you left Rosa, and imagined them coming to my door."

His lips quirked. "What would you have done? Would you have invited me in? Or cowered in the corner and left first thing in the morning?"

Embarrassed suddenly, she made light of it. "Oh, I wouldn't have left. I had nowhere to go!"

"That's why I never came," he said ruefully. "I never found my position of authority, of power, so damnable. And yet, feeling helpless is worse. I couldn't have borne to be allowed into your bed from fear of destitution or worse."

"I don't think that would ever have been the case," she admitted. "You always...affected me."

He lifted one hand and cupped her cheek. "Do I affect you now?"

For answer, she leaned her cheek into his palm, then took his hand and placed it over her galloping heart. His breath hitched. He stood very still, gazing down at her, By the dim glow of the single candle, his face was dark and shadowed and unutterably thrilling. She craved his embrace, his kiss, so intensely it felt like pain.

But when she released his hand to reach up and hold him, he turned away from her. It felt like a blow. Under her bemused, desperate gaze, he picked up her old hairbrush and sponge from the washing stand and dropped them into her carpet bag that lay open on the bed. Then he went to the dresser and wardrobe, pulling out the few meagre garments he found there–a thin under gown, a pair of darned stockings, and Serena's altered peach evening dress. They too went in the bag before he walked to the desk and swept up her pens and letters and laid them on top. He reached over and lifted the book from her bedside table, adding it before he picked up the bag.

"You have so little," he said, "and yet, you give so much. What did I pay you?"

"I'm not sure we ever discussed that. A pair of boots, certainly."

She heard his breath of laughter as he lifted the flickering candle. "Come."

Her throat constricted as she followed him out into the passage. He turned left, in the direction she'd never been, toward his bedchamber. She swallowed convulsively. He was moving her to his own chamber. Because he was making the point that she was no longer merely the governess? To whom? To her or to the servants?

Or was this, at last, her wedding night?

A lamp and several candles bathed his bedchamber in a warm, friendly glow. The fire in the grate added to the atmosphere of welcome. Old but still heavy velvet curtains hung over the windows in two walls, for his was the corner room. Faded carpets broke up the polished wood floor. There was a grand wardrobe and chest of drawers, an escritoire under one window, and bookcases around most of the available wall space. An open door led to a small dressing room with a truckle bed and wash stand.

Her gaze came back to the main room, finally settling on the large, curtained bed that dominated the chamber.

"Could you be comfortable here?" he asked softly. "We can redecorate it to suit you, of course, change—"

"It's perfect," she interrupted. "At this point, there is nothing I would change."

He dropped her bag on the floor, pushing it aside with his foot as he blew out the candle in his hand, and set it down on top of the nearest bookcase. "I have a question."

"I hope I have the answer."

He glanced at her over his shoulder, half of his face in shadow. His lips parted to speak, then closed again. His brow furrowed. And then he said abruptly, "Shall I sleep in there?" His head jerked toward the dressing room and the truckle bed.

Her instant reaction was pain that he did not wish to be with her. Only then she registered his erratic breathing, the difficulty with which he asked. He was considering her injury, her tiredness, her inevitable virginal fears. He was sparing her.

"I do not wish to be *spared*," she whispered, all but running to him. "Javan, I *love* you."

He caught her in one arm, still being careful of her wound, and cupped the back of her head. "Then, my sweet," he said hoarsely. "May I take you to bed?"

She raised her face to his, searching for his lips, which came down on hers so suddenly that she gasped. His hands in her hair, drew out the pins until it tumbled loose about her shoulders, and he drew back to look.

He smiled. "That is how I long for you."

Slowly, deliberately, he unfastened her ball gown and let it slip to the floor around her feet. Under gown and stays quickly followed, until she stood before him in nothing but her chemise. Taking her hand, he led her to the bed, and sat, drawing her down beside him while he kicked off his shoes and unbuttoned the skin-tight legs of his pantaloons.

Daringly, she slid one hand up under his shirt, caressing the warm, velvet skin of his back, finding other ridges, other scars that were part of his past and the man he had become. As he straightened, she drew the shirt up and over his head, and he gently pushed her back until she lay flat on the bed with him looming over her.

He lowered his head, kissing her until she was lost in his mouth and her own fire. Only then did he drag the chemise up her body and over her head. His already erratic breath caught. His Adam's apple jerked as he swallowed.

In sudden shyness, she moved her arms inward, to cover herself, but he caught them, pressing them into the mattress above her head while his gaze devoured her. And somehow, she was no longer embarrassed but triumphant, powerful, and even more desperate for what was to come. He shifted, lowering his head once more to kiss her breasts, and she thought she would die of this new bliss.

Her eyes closed and she held him to her in wonder. He shifted, letting her feel his full, glorious weight for an instant. His pantaloons and undergarments were gone, for it was hot skin which caressed hers, the hard length of his erection stroking between her thighs.

"This will be a first for both of us," he said shakily. "For I have never done this before with so much love. With true love."

She touched his scarred cheek, kissing his lips with longing. His fingers roamed over her body, stroking and caressing in her most intimate places until her shock turned to wonder and pleasure.

"Tell me to slow down, or tell me to stop," he got out. "I will. It may kill me, but I will…"

The fierce, male passion in his face should have frightened her, and perhaps it did, somewhere, but it seemed she trusted him more, for even the short pain, the strange stretching of her body was part of the wonder and somehow added to her blind desire. For the caresses of his hands and mouth, the movements of his body were all miraculously, deliciously tender. He was so gentle compared with the wild ferocity of his eyes, that she got lost in curious new delight. She held on to him, following him, until her body seemed to act on its own, undulating with him. She kissed him, bit his shoulder in this shock of need until waves of bliss began to grow out of it and consume her, building and flooding within her until there was only joy.

And in the midst of that, the sound of Javan's ecstatic release powered through her and made her weep with love.

At some point after he collapsed upon her and they lay in a tangle of tingling limbs and soft, linen sheets, his lips found the wetness on her cheeks.

"Oh, my darling," he whispered, stricken, "what have I done?"

She clung to him. "Made me the happiest woman who ever lived. I never dreamed you would be so gentle… Will it always be like this?"

His relief turned quickly into something much more sensual and predatory. "Never exactly like this. I have much to show you, and much I hope you will show me."

"Oh my," she said weakly.

He moved, laying his head on her breasts. She stroked his hair languidly, lost in sheer feeling.

"Javan?"

"Mmm." He nuzzled her softly.

"Do you know," she said, a trifle breathless all over again, "I think we have made this a *happy* house."

"I hope so."

"I think we can make it happier yet," she said confidently.

And they did.

Mary Lancaster's Newsletter

If you enjoyed *The Wicked Governess*, and would like to keep up with Mary's new releases and other book news, please sign up to Mary's mailing list to receive her occasional Newsletter.

http://eepurl.com/b4Xoif

Other Books by Mary Lancaster

VIENNA WALTZ (The Imperial Season, Book 1)
VIENNA WOODS (The Imperial Season, Book 2)
VIENNA DAWN (The Imperial Season, Book 3)
THE WICKED BARON (Blackhaven Brides, Book 1)
THE WICKED LADY (Blackhaven Brides, Book 2)
THE WICKED REBEL (Blackhaven Brides, Book 3)
THE WICKED HUSBAND (Blackhaven Brides, Book 4)
THE WICKED MARQUIS (Blackhaven Brides, Book 5)
REBEL OF ROSS
A PRINCE TO BE FEARED: the love story of Vlad Dracula
AN ENDLESS EXILE
A WORLD TO WIN

About Mary Lancaster

Mary Lancaster's first love was historical fiction. Her other passions include coffee, chocolate, red wine and black and white films – simultaneously where possible. She hates housework.

As a direct consequence of the first love, she studied history at St. Andrews University. She now writes full time at her seaside home in Scotland, which she shares with her husband, three children and a small, crazy dog.

Connect with Mary on-line:

Email Mary:
Mary@MaryLancaster.com

Website:
www.MaryLancaster.com

Newsletter sign-up:
http://eepurl.com/b4Xoif

Facebook Author Page:
facebook.com/MaryLancasterNovelist

Facebook Timeline:
facebook.com/mary.lancaster.1656